THE CRICKETS DANCE

A Novel By

Deborah Robillard

Deborah Robillard

DEDICATION

For Rachel and Zachary
and

*In loving memory of Dorothy Hardy
and Dr. Jeff Jarrett*

ACKNOWLEDGMENTS

To my Scottie, I would never have been able to write about love in any capacity or fashion if you had not shown me what it really was. You have made a reality of the hope I have always had to be loved unconditionally and supported infinitely. The dream of having you in my life is where the motion in these pages comes from. You make these words real for me. I am so blessed to be able to live that love every day with you. I love you, my sweet boy, with all my heart.

For the strong women in my life who I love and have remained faithful to me as sisters, friends, and mentors—Mom, Joanie, Ann, Brenda, Roni, Bonnie, Shirley, Missy my sister, Susan my sister, and Susan my friend. Without your love and support throughout my life I would never have known how strong women can be, especially when we lean on each other. I am so blessed to have so much wisdom and encouragement from you all.

Grandpa and Grandma, I love and miss you both so much. Thank you for a lifetime of memories that never fail to make me smile.

Thank you, Carol Zimmerman, the best agent, editor, and friend, who believed in me when I didn't believe in myself.

Thank you to the Meeks family for loving and being a part of The Crickets Dance.

The Crickets Dance

Thank you McGraw family for putting your hearts into this project and becoming such a special part of the journey.

Chapter 1
"Miss Claudia"

I could write volumes about her character and still never capture her spirit for it abides in her forest, these fields, and within these walls. If someone who'd never been to Georgia asked me to show them a picture that would explain everything they'd need to know about the South, I wouldn't choose the peach orchards in bloom, the kudzu, or an unpaved road covered in red clay. I'd show them an old black-and-white photo mounted in a silver frame that was kept on the mantelpiece of Miss Claudia Wainwright. If her memory served her correctly, it was taken in 1925 when she was about ten years old. She is standing next to a tall white column on the veranda and there is an old magnolia and a few dogwood trees in the background.

The photograph was taken just after her father purchased the house, which had been rebuilt after its untimely destruction in the early 1900s. It's located on the same site upon which it was originally built. According to the stories passed down through the generations of townspeople, the house was reconstructed in all of its antebellum glory. It's said to be an exact replica of the first rendition. Miss Claudia's father was an architect and a history buff, so he knew he had to have that house the moment he first laid eyes on it. It literally sung the old hymns of the South. She used to say, "If I stood real quiet in the woods around the back, I could hear every word." She grew up, lived, and died in that old house. Like her house, she personified the South.

Miss Claudia fit every stereotype of a Southern woman. She was full of stories of the good old days. She planted a vegetable garden in her back yard and azalea bushes in the front. She was fiercely independent, never married, and could be seen on any given day, right up until she died, wearing a floppy hat and gardening gloves, and working in her yard, that is, unless it was Sunday. On the Lord's Day, she could be found sitting in the third pew from the front on the left side of the church she had attended all of her life. It was her spot and had been since she was a child. You might say that like that old house, she was a big piece of history in a town where everybody knew everybody and there were no secrets—or so we thought.

I delivered Miss Claudia's medicine to her twice a month when I was working at the pharmacy while I attended high school during the late '80s and I thought she was old then. I would always wait until the pharmacy closed before I went to her house. She lived on the outskirts of our little town, Fort Valley, right smack in the middle of Peach County, Georgia. Everybody knew the house—it was the big blue and white landmark on the back road. It became known as the "place where you turn right to take the short way to Macon." I was sixteen, had just gotten my driver's license, and loved making the trip.

Every time I left the store to bring Miss Claudia her blood pressure medicine, vitamins, and a few candy bars, Mr. Kent would always remind me to go slow around the curve just before her driveway. "There are deer out at night," he'd always call out behind me as I swung open the glass door to leave.

Being the expert driver that I thought I was, I would just wave at him and head out. I never realized until later that he really did worry about me driving in the dark, even though it was only about a ten-mile round trip. I often wonder why it seems people aren't like that anymore, taking time to care about the little things—a fading tradition of the Old South that Miss Claudia taught me well.

The Crickets Dance

Mr. Kent and Miss Bonnie were the last of a dying breed. They owned a small Mom-and-Pop drugstore and had been in Fort Valley for at least twenty years before I started working for them after school and on Saturdays. No matter what, their store was closed on Sundays. They still made deliveries to some of their elderly customers who were either used to the old ways or unable to get out and run errands for themselves. They never minded me making Miss Claudia my last stop because they knew how much I enjoyed her company.

I never left her house without a belly full of freshly squeezed lemonade and at least three jars of one canned vegetable or another. My friends never could figure out why I loved going there so much. To them she was just the odd old lady who had never married and lived all alone. She was much more than that to me. She was my friend.

Miss Claudia had no family except a niece, Hannah, who worked on Wall Street and blew into town twice a year. She would squeeze in one visit on Easter and the other on Thanksgiving. She tried to cover up her accent and act as if she had always been a big city girl, not really from "Nowheresville." That's what she called Fort Valley every time I happened to be visiting Miss Claudia when Hannah was in town. I think it made Miss Claudia a little sad that her only kin was ashamed to call this place home. For every aging Southern belle like my friend, the South is not just about the location of the land, it's about a set of values and pride that she wanted to pass on to Hannah. On the other hand, Hannah had been dreaming of leaving this place since she was old enough to know it was only one of many from which to choose. She had been hacking away at her Georgia roots since she was a child. At age eighteen, she applied to and was accepted at NYU.

It just so happened that I was a transplanted Georgia peach. My father had been in the military. Although Georgia was the only place I had ever lived in the States, because I was born overseas I was mistakenly labeled a "Yankee". My grandparents lived in the little town of Massena, located in upstate New York, which also gave me Yankee blood, or at least everyone thought it did.

One summer between my sophomore and junior years of high school, my grandparents came to visit and I took them to meet Miss Claudia. I think it was the only time that Hannah visited other than her scheduled holidays. She explained to me that something had come up and she had missed her Easter pilgrimage home. She went on and on about how she was stuck wasting her summer vacation in the last place on earth she cared to spend it. It was as if growing up here had been a burden to her, while to so many others it was a privilege. So many people who are born and raised here, regardless of their lineage, carry a deep sense of pride for what their ancestors fought for, believed in, and overcame. The spirit of both the Southern people and the land reflect darkness and light, pride and sorrow. I too find it a shame that Hannah chooses to distance herself from a heritage of which so many are extremely proud.

After I graduated from Peach County High School, I went to college at Mercer University, a reputable school about an hour's drive away. I had always wanted to study law and they had a good program there. I commuted each day while continuing to live at home and work at the pharmacy. Miss Claudia was very proud of me when I graduated and even more so when I took a job with the county as a public defender. Maybe some considered me a transplant, but I was rooted nonetheless.

I easily could have gone to Atlanta and gotten a much higher paying and exciting job, but as Miss Claudia always said, "Most people spend their whole lives looking around for a place to call home, but never realize they've found it until they finally look down at the dirt they're standing on." I was lucky to learn that lesson early. I guess traveling in the military with my dad when I was a kid taught me a lot about how much some people spend their whole lives breaking ties that could mean everything to someone who got theirs late in life. By the time we moved to Peach County, I was in the sixth grade and had seen most of the world from Europe to Asia and back again. Miss Claudia once told me that I got my roots and wings backwards. I guess that made me appreciate the roots more.

It went on that way for many years, my grandparents making their summertime visits until two summers ago when my grandma passed away. I miss the days when we would all get together and sit on Miss Claudia's front porch. She and Grandma would swap stories for hours, while Grandpa would fix one thing or another around the house. My grandmother and Miss Claudia discovered early in their friendship that despite very different geographical upbringings, they'd been raised with the same principles. Grandpa never commented much about his childhood, growing up in the north, mostly he just kept busy while the "womenfolk" chatted. It wasn't until years later that I learned why he didn't join in their reminiscing about the past. The ladies clung tightly to the lessons of their youth. They told me in unison, "That's why we grew up in the *good* old days." They always followed that bragging with a giggle much too young for their actual ages.

"You see," Grandma said one day after our visit to Miss Claudia, "North or South, if you grew up in my generation, you learned respect and Christian values. Times change so fast, people forget about the little things these days...saying *please* and *thank you*, lending your neighbor a hand...the small gestures that go a long way." She wanted to pass proper manners on to me, even if the rest of the world seemed to have forgotten them. I listened, but the seventeen year-old rebel in me only half nodded in understanding. Everyday when I look at her picture, I wish I could have that conversation with my grandmother one more time. I want her to know that I really did hear every word she said. There were a few years of growing pains before I took them to heart, but they are nonetheless in me forever.

Fall always came all too soon and my grandparents would have one last visit with Miss Claudia before returning to New York, anxious to be on the road before winter came. The last meal of the season was always the same: fried chicken, garden vegetables, and peach cobbler. Hannah had married and her trips dwindled from twice a year to once every other summer. I think she will never fully appreciate what she missed. I never learned as much in any classroom—high school or college, as I did sitting under the shade of that old magnolia, listening to the history and wisdom that came from the mouths of those three. I think knowing I was there keeping Miss Claudia company let Hannah off the hook. She knew as long as I was around her aunt would never be lonely or in need of anything.

* * *

The sad news that Miss Claudia died came to me early one Saturday morning as I was walking out to my mailbox. The fastest way to get news in this town is to be plugged into the grapevine. No newspaper or television station has ever figured out a way to break a story faster than the small town express.

"Morning, Mr. Baxter." I was waiting for him to drive the last five feet to the end of my driveway and hand me my mail.

"I thought I'd save you the trouble of opening the box this morning and get a little exercise for Keno and me at the same time." I gestured toward my overweight border collie. The exercise excuse also explained the tattered sweats, worn tennis shoes, and old faded T-shirt. He had seen me dressed for court in my best suit before, but I still felt the need to explain before he could drive to the next house and tell my neighbor I was looking a little "homeless" today.

"Morning," he smiled in return, appreciative of my effort to spare his "tennis elbow" from having to reach into the box and the fact that he had someone with whom to share his fresh news. It was so new that it was not yet even in the morning newspaper he'd noticed me collecting from the paperboy's misguided toss into my bushes.

"Did you hear about poor Miss Claudia?" he asked, knowing that I probably hadn't since I obviously hadn't made it past the end of my driveway and most likely hadn't talked to anyone else. He loved to be the first to pass on the latest gossip, but sharing tragedy and the misfortune of others seemed to be his specialty.

My heart skipped a beat before I answered. I knew this day was coming, but never really allowed myself to think of it—after all, she was eighty-five this year. "No," I answered with a heavy heart and a sigh, hoping he would tell me something other than what I knew was coming.

"Poor soul passed away in her sleep last night, but I suppose if the good Lord wants you to come on home, then she went the best way," he was putting his truck in park while waiting for my reaction. Ready to delay his route in case I was about to have a breakdown he could describe in detail at the next house. He knew, as did the rest of the folks in town, that Miss Claudia and I had been friends for quite a few years. When my grandma died, it felt like a piece of my life that had become comfortable and familiar had been stolen from me. I'd also unexpectedly experienced that feeling as a child and was discovering that it didn't get any easier with age.

"Well," I paused, searching for something meaningful to say. "She was healthy and independent until the end." I was immediately disappointed with my response. It sounded so trite and unfeeling, but it was all I could come up with in that moment. I knew that anything more personal would cause me to cry in his presence and I didn't want to do that. I just wanted to take my mail, my newspaper and my dog, and go back up the driveway. I guess I've always been the sort of person who likes to settle my own feelings before I discuss them with anyone else. He cocked his blond head to the side, I think I read disappointment in his deep blue eyes that spread all over his face. He wanted me to create a scene and give him a story to tell. He'd be disappointed today, but that didn't stop him from fishing.

"From what I gather, it just happened a few hours ago," he was leaning forward, hoping to see the tears shed I am sure he could see in my expression. He was blatantly too eager to get more of a reaction out of me. He wasn't exactly being intrusive or intentionally cruel, just a busybody.

Wanting some information of my own, I choked back my pain and prolonged our conversation a moment longer.

"Has anyone called Hannah?"

"Not as I know of," he answered casually, shifting back into drive as he saw that I was turning away in the middle of his answer. I suppose he knew I'd be the one to make that call. I'm sure he drew some comfort from the fact he could tell everyone he was the first to break the news to me. Maybe my lack of reaction in his presence would be his story. He seemed satisfied as I heard him whistling over the quiet purr of his new mail truck engine.

Not being one to put things off, I collected my thoughts on the way back up to my house. Having lost all motivation to jog, I took advantage of Keno's slow pace to mull over what I wanted to say to Hannah. Since we had nothing in common and nothing to say in person, I imagined the awkwardness might make the sadness a little bit worse.

I knew Hannah was most likely still asleep, but I also knew if I didn't catch her before her day started, I might not reach her at all. The phone rang about four times before I heard a very groggy "Hello?" I sat in silence for a moment, forgetting my thoughts and nearly losing my nerve. The second "Hello?" was a little less sleepy and a lot more annoyed.

"Hannah?" I asked. This was the awkward part. I said her name as if I wasn't sure it was her, even though we both knew better.

"Yes, this is she," she answered in her best New York accent. She must have realized just by the way I drawled her name that she was talking to someone from home.

"Hannah, it's Angie." I tried to stop it, but my voice dropped on the last part of my name, as if I felt bad to be the one calling.

"I have some bad news." I heard her take a deep breath. Here came the sad part. Just as I had at the mailbox, I think she knew before I said it what was coming.

"Hannah, your aunt Claudia passed away in her sleep last night." There was a long pause filled with the most uncomfortable silence I have ever had the misfortune to be a part of, even worse than the lull in a conversation on a blind date. *Great...more awkward.*

"I see," she finally responded after having recovered her usual business-like tone. "Hold on just a minute, please." She covered the mouthpiece of the receiver, but I could still hear that she was telling her husband and making plans to fly home to make funeral arrangements.

* * *

Hannah arrived late that evening, without her husband. He too was a business tycoon type and was unable to make the trip due to "more pressing matters"—I believe that's the way she put it. We sat in my den drinking some sweet tea, probably the only Southern tradition she had not been able to leave behind.

"I suppose you knew her better than just about anyone." She was looking over at me, wanting to get my opinion and settle all of the arrangements immediately.

As usual, she was wearing one of her many designer suits. This one was gray with black pinstripes and had a short skirt instead of pants. I'd seen her wear one similar to it before and thought to myself how they were all the same, some just cut a little differently than others. *I'm sure she has one in every color.* I wagered with myself that she'd be wearing one in solid black on Tuesday. Since the last time I'd seen her, she'd started streaking her long brown hair with blonde highlights. She was also sporting long, red acrylic nails and bright red lipstick. She had completely transformed herself over the past few years and I suppose achieved the look she most desired. She would not have fit in anywhere I could think of in this small town, certainly not at any social gathering Miss Claudia would have attended. Hannah considered herself superior to everyone in Fort Valley. She fancied herself more dignified and refined than us simple country folk...whatever.

I smiled a little on the inside knowing what her aunt would have said at the sight of her. "Pretty wrapping paper looks just as good on a pound of manure as it does on a sack of diamonds." It was Miss Claudia's favorite saying and she used it often where she thought shallow people were concerned. She would have hated to say it about her own niece, but I have a feeling she would have done it anyway. Hannah kept talking at the speed of light about her ideas for the funeral, not even stopping to breathe. She was flitting around the room like a bird in a cage as if her discomfort with the situation and her desire to do anything that would cut this experience short were the most important issues on the table. She made her decisions quickly and with very little insight into her aunt's character. Caught up in my own memories and growing tired of the sound of her fake accent, my mind wandered and I lost track of what she was saying.

"Well, what do you think?" she asked, leaning toward me after she'd finally taken a seat and a breath.

10

Her question snapped me back to attention. It was another one of our awkward moments. I'd been daydreaming about Miss Claudia and I knew I had to come up with an answer so that she wouldn't suspect I'd been ignoring her.

I took a stab at it. "I think that would be fine." It proved to be a decision I'd regret for Miss Claudia's sake at the funeral on Tuesday.

* * *

I felt weird sitting alone in church on Sunday, looking over at Miss Claudia's empty place. She always covered her legs with a yellow lap blanket that she'd knitted herself. She made it with huge knitting needles, so it had big holes between each knot. She'd completed it during the sermons over the course of many Sundays while sitting in that very spot. She was always cold in church, so she left it hanging over the back of the pew from week to week. It was still there, almost as if it was waiting for her to come and use it again. When I was a teenager, sitting in the back, watching her knit during the sermon, I always thought it was a rude thing to be doing while the minister was talking. I mean, those big fat needles weren't exactly quiet when she clinked them together. She told me later, "If the preacher doesn't want me knitting in church, then he should turn the heat up every once in a while." She knew that older people could get away with anything and frequently used it to her advantage.

* * *

On Tuesday morning at 10:00 a.m. I was back in church, sitting next to my grandfather. I knew as soon as I called him that he would want to come. We were listening to Hannah read from her 3 x 5 index cards about what a fine woman her aunt was. *It's a pity that she's the only one in the room who didn't really know how true her standard issue funeral words were.* I sat there looking around at the flowers she'd ordered, the style and color of the casket, even the outfit she'd chosen for her aunt, it was all wrong.

I could almost hear Miss Claudia sarcastically thanking me for not paying attention while the plans for her funeral were being made and allowing Hannah to ruin her last big hurrah. Her shoulder-length silver hair was curled and flowing around her face. She never wore it that way. She was dressed in a frilly, cream-colored lace dress that most likely had been hanging in the back of her closet because it was a gift from Hannah, but she'd never worn it. Now her body at least would get to spend eternity in it. To top it off, she had on a ton of makeup. Miss Claudia hated makeup. The most she ever wore was a little peach blush and neutral lipstick for church on Sundays. She was naturally tan from working outside and despite her age, her skin had held up rather well. I silently apologized, hoping she would forgive me and not find some way to make me feel guilty about it for the rest of my life.

* * *

Hannah came up to Grandpa and me after the graveside service. "Thank you for coming. I know it was a long trip for you," she said, reaching out in her quiet, yet condescending and patronizing way to take my grandfather's hand.

"About the same as it was for you," he replied, trying not to take offense at her ageist comment. My grandpa was the same age as Miss Claudia and every bit as feisty. He had all of his marbles and likely a few that belonged to someone else. He was mentally sharp and determined not to allow anyone to treat him like an old person. What he lacked in speed these days, he made up for with his quick wit; however, I still felt a bit sorry for him. He had lost my grandma and one friend after another over the past few years. Not only had recent years been unkind, the ones from decades ago had been downright cruel to us both.

The scars were bone deep, numbed by denial and neglected in their jagged healing.

We walked by the headstone one last time before we left the cemetery. At least Hannah had gotten that right. There was an image of the old plantation house etched in the shiny black granite. The inscription read, "....and I will dwell in the house of the Lord forever." The one thing Hannah remembered Miss Claudia saying is that she hoped her mansion in heaven looked just like her beloved plantation home.

"I hope so, my friend...I hope so," I whispered softly, as Grandpa and I walked arm-in-arm away from the large pile of red dirt that would soon cover Miss Claudia and the dress she would have buried long ago in her back yard if it would not have hurt Hannah's feelings.

"Miss Lawrence! Miss Lawrence!" I heard someone calling me as I was putting the key in the door lock of my old Chevy truck.

"Yes?" I answered, unsure who was speaking to me until I managed to get my high-heeled shoe out of the mud and turn around. It was Paul Hammond, Miss Claudia's lawyer. He was a tall, thin man with wispy, receding blond hair and round glasses. I remembered seeing his tenth grade yearbook picture years ago when I was still in high school. It remains on display in the trophy case to commemorate his win on the debate team in 1972. He hadn't changed a bit.

"I didn't know you still had your daddy's old truck," he reached over patting the side of it. "And you're wearing your mother's beautiful brooch," he went on, tactlessly bringing up other painful losses my grandfather and I had endured. I'm sure he remembered the pin because we'd laid my mother to rest in this same cemetery just fourteen months ago. He had settled nearly every estate in town. He knew exactly 'who got what from whom' for the past several years.

"I don't use it every day," I clarified, referring to the truck and hoping to change the subject. "It sits higher than my car and is easier for Grandpa to climb in and out."

He smiled in hasty understanding, eager to move on to the reason he'd detained me.

"I have Miss Claudia's Will in my office and I would appreciate it if maybe you could come for the reading around 3:00 this afternoon." He paused, realizing this was an awkward place to make such a request.

"I know my timing is poor," he apologized, "but I'm going out of town early tomorrow morning. I was hoping to get this settled. Hannah has to leave before I get back and I need both of you present to carry out the final wishes."

I was more than a little surprised. I knew Miss Claudia cared for me, but I just assumed she had left everything to Hannah. Maybe that's why she did it; she knew I never wanted anything but some lemonade and her friendship.

"Sure," I agreed and nodded slowly, mentally checking my schedule for the rest of the afternoon. "I'll be there at 3:00."

He thanked me, shook my hand, and walked back across the paved walkway, shuffling his feet to wipe the mud off his loafers as he went.

* * *

Paul Hammond, Attorney at Law, had hung his shingle on the only main street in Fort Valley. His office was in a small brick building that shared common walls with a pizza place on the left and a dry cleaners on the right. The main street was a one-way tour of all the businesses in town, easily seen in less than five minutes. If you missed the one you wanted, you had to circle around and make the loop again. It was a huge pain, especially when it came to parking, but that's the way it was built and the street was too narrow to make any changes now.

Wisely, I drove my much smaller two-door, canary yellow, vintage MG convertible. It was my gift to myself when I graduated from law school. I was barely able to squeeze it in next to Hannah's rented Lincoln Towncar parked in front of the small office. I could see her through the picture window, sitting in one of the waiting room chairs.

When I walked in, she shot me a split-second dirty look. I took this to mean she had no idea her aunt had included me in the Will. She was still wearing her black suit when she stood to greet me and threw on her fake smile. Her once-crooked teeth were now straight and polished to a shine that would have rivaled her aunt's new headstone. Once again, I caught myself looking at her suddenly much larger chest, hard to avoid since this suit was low cut...okay plunging at the neckline. *I wonder if those things are fake or if she has found a magical illusion bra.* Having known her for years, I knew it had to be one of the two.

Once seated across from Paul, he could see that we were both feeling uncomfortable and graciously expedited the process. "Let's see," he smiled almost nervously, pulling out the lengthy document. He mumbled to himself as he skipped the "of sound mind and body" part and all of the *wheretos* and *heretofores*. "Here we are," he said after flipping through several pages to get to the heart of the matter. As a fellow lawyer, I could tell this had to be his favorite part. He looked as if reading the words kind of made him feel like Santa Claus.

"Hannah," he said, looking up and smiling at her, "your aunt left you all of the contents of her home and the twenty thousand dollar savings bond she purchased last year."

"The contents of her home?" Hannah repeated, leaning forward and putting her hands on the corner of his desk while trying to read the document upside down. "What do you mean the contents?" It was kind of funny because when Hannah was mad her Southern accent came right back.

Paul could see and hear she was upset and quickly hurried to explain. "Angie, she left you the house itself."

Unlike Hannah, who was leaning forward, the news came as such a surprise that I was propelled back against the burgundy leather of the winged-back chair in which I was sitting.

"Why would she do such a thing?" I asked, hoping she had explained herself to him.

"She went on and on about how she knew you would appreciate its history and that you had no intention of leaving the area." He cleared his throat nervously, as if to find the courage to go on. "She hoped you would live in it and keep it from falling into ruin," he said, looking up at the ceiling as if he could see into his memory better that way. He tried to quote his client exactly, word for word, though his recollection of that conversation seemed to elude him, possibly due to the disdainful gaze emitting from Hannah's blazing brown eyes, aimed directly at him.

"And what am I supposed to do with all that junk so she can live in the house?" Hannah asked. Her easily detachable mask of gentility was quite obviously removed. "I'd planned to lock the place up and tend to it during my vacation next summer. Now you're telling me I have to figure out what to do with seventy years of rusty, dusty junk?" The ignorant statement showed how little Hannah actually knew about her aunt. Nothing Miss Claudia owned was rusty or dusty and she was no pack rat, so there was very little junk.

"Now wait, let's just think about this before we get upset," I tried to interject and bring a voice of reason to the conversation before it spun out of control.

"*We* get upset?" Hannah said, handing my words back to me, dripping with sarcasm. "This *WE* is the one who's going to have to figure out what to do with all that stuff.

"Now I'm going to have to call my office and extend my time off. This is wasting my vacation days and quite possibly some of my sick time."

There it is again, I thought to myself, *that pretty paper around that big old sack of manure*. Before I had a chance to offer a solution, like staying in my own home until we could work out a schedule that was convenient for both of us, Hannah was up and out the door. Paul and I stood there watching her through the waiting room window as she pounded her expensive black Italian leather, high-heeled shoes across the street to the newspaper office.

The next morning over breakfast, Grandpa and I read the huge ad for which Hannah had likely paid quite a bit of her Wall Street cash. It was at least a third of the front page and read:

Estate Sale
Everything must go
309 Pleasant Tree Road
Saturday 8 a.m.
Until the walls are bare!

"Well, at least she's taking it graciously," Grandpa said with a smile. I ignored his untimely sense of humor and tried to think of a solution.

"The least we can do is to offer to help. Maybe she won't be quite so mad if we lend her a hand." I was really trying to be gracious and take the high road, even though I thought it was stupid of her to sell all of her family's heirlooms without even the slightest deliberation.

"Aren't you being just a little selfish?" he asked with a straight-as-an-arrow face.

"How do you figure offering to help is selfish?" I answered, pretending to be offended. Once again, I was missing that dry humor of his.

"If we go offering our services, won't that get her on a plane back to New York that much faster?"

I saw his point and decided to find the humor in it anyway. Like I say, what he lacks in speed, he makes up for in wit.

Chapter 2
"Grandpa's Passion"

I remember with vivid clarity the few precious times our military lifestyle afforded us to visit my grandparents when I was a child. I loved pulling up to that little red house on King Street. There were always at least two or three cats in the yard and their big white Samoyed lying on the yellow linoleum in the kitchen. My grandfather was usually sitting at the table eating one of those miniature, powdered sugar donuts and drinking a ginger ale.

If we visited in the wintertime, my cousin and I would take my grandma sledding down old Hatchet Hill. We rode that toboggan until we couldn't drag it back up the hill one more time. If we visited in the spring or summer, we'd go down to the locks on the river and watch the big ships coming in from all over the world. No matter the season, there were always my two favorite activities: playing rummy with Grandma and watching Grandpa fiddle around with his stamp collection.

Wherever we went, Grandpa was always looking around flea markets and garage sales for old stamps. When he would find a stamp he wanted, most of the time it was still attached to the envelope. He would explain how each one had been cancelled, where it had been sent from and where it had gone. I was just barely able to see the high flip-down shelf of the desk where he sat to pursue his passion. He'd soak the stamp and then carefully remove it from the envelope using tweezers and a magnifying glass. Sometimes he'd put cigarette lighter fluid on the back and show me the watermarks. He had huge volumes filled with history, each stamp telling a story.

Now and then, if he got lucky, letters would still be inside the envelopes. It always struck me as funny the way he would put the letter aside and concentrate solely on the stamp. I was always excited to see what some person who lived a hundred years ago thought was important enough to write in a letter. It has become a lost art form with our modern e-mail, telephones, and text messaging. Every inch of paper was precious and the author would fill it from the very top to the very bottom on both sides. The ink was often faded, so you'd be left wondering what ailment Aunt So-and-So was stricken with or what the preacher had to say on Sunday after Cousin So-and So was baptized. I loved it. I soaked in every word as if I knew the people and by the time I'd finished reading the letter, sometimes I felt like I did. Every time we went to visit, I would beg Grandpa to take out his stamps and tell me the stories again—the tales of how he found or traded for some of them were often just as exciting to me as the actual stamp itself.

It was these memories that kept me from being surprised when Grandpa emerged from the basement of Miss Claudia's house, now my new home. He was carrying a dusty, rickety old crate held together by rusty nails. I was sure that Hannah would be thrilled to see it and remind me that I'd assured her we wouldn't find much junk.

"How much you want for this?" he asked, interrupting our price tagging.

Hannah stopped appraising the mantle clock in her hands and turned to look at him. "What is it?" she was really, wanting to be sure not to lose a nickel.

Once again showing the colors of his age, Grandpa replied, "Looks like an old crate to me." I turned back to my Hummel figurine to keep from laughing.

"I can see that." Hannah was almost rude she was so annoyed with his attempt at humor as she walked over to him, but some small trace of her southern roots made her bite her tongue and respect her elder. "What's in it?" she asked, taking it from his hands.

"Looks like some old books and papers and stuff," he answered casually.

"He collects things like old stamps and letters," I said, looking at him as if I was a parent and he was a child trying to pull a fast one.

Hannah haphazardly flipped through the contents of the crate and then looked back up at Grandpa. "Ten bucks," she offered firmly. She couldn't hand it back to him fast enough, wiping the dust off her hands and onto her designer overalls. Weird to see her wearing clothes regular people wore or something close to it. There was also a smug look of satisfaction on her face that she'd been right and I'd been wrong.

"Sold," he almost shouted like an auctioneer, reaching into his pants pocket for his wallet.

"Are you sure there's nothing of value in there you want to keep?" I wanted to give Hannah a chance to back out of the deal just in case she was cheating herself. It was Grandpa's turn to give me the look that I'd shot at him a moment before.

"What do I want with a bunch of cobweb-covered books and papers?" She looked down her nose at me like either of us would be thrilled to have any old piece of garbage she wanted to throw out.

"Well, the basement is older than the rest of the house, so there might be something of value in there." I wanted to clarify that we weren't just two dumpster divers wanting her trash. I looked at Grandpa and could tell that he was about to burst. I knew he wanted the crate and he knew I was going to be honest about its possibilities.

"It's not as valuable as this," Hannah stated flatly, slipping the ten-dollar bill into her pocket. Grandpa breathed a sigh of relief. He would never say, but I'm sure his conscience also felt pretty good about keeping the deal honest, just in case he did find something. Hannah had had every chance to keep it. Now whatever it was would really be his.

All our hard work paid off. The days we spent going over and tagging every item made the sale a huge success. Hannah's sentimental side eventually got the best of her. She ended up shipping two boxes of family pictures and memorabilia back to New York. She even gave me the old black and white photo in the silver frame.

"You should have something personal of hers too," she said, almost sincerely enough for me to believe she meant it. My opinion is that she ran out of room in the box she was packing for herself, but still trying to give her the benefit of the doubt and be the bigger person, I graciously accepted. In that moment, I could never have known how much more that picture would come to mean to me.

Everyone knew Miss Claudia had impeccable taste and the whole town showed up for the sale. Everything was gone by lunchtime. Including the twenty thousand dollar savings bond and the proceeds from the sale, Hannah left town with forty-five thousand dollars in her bank account. I think that more than made up for the bruise on her ego when Miss Claudia left the house to me. She even commented before she took off for the Atlanta airport what a burden it was off her shoulders not to have to worry about restoring the "old place." Reading between the lines, I guess that meant she thought I had inherited a piece of junk and she'd gotten all the cash. I hoped the person she sat next to in first class on the plane didn't try to peel away some of that pretty paper and have a conversation with her. It would be a shame to open a bag of manure in such a small space.

I wanted to walk around the house with my memories of Miss Claudia. Grandpa could tell I wanted to do it alone and kindly gave me an excuse. "I'm pooped," he admitted, taking the crate he had purchased and placing it in the bed of my old truck. I think it hurt him a little to see that old blue bomb. It brought back memories of his son, my father, who said the day he bought it in 1970 that he was going to drive it until the wheels fell off. They almost had a few times, but I kept it up and running in his memory. Grandpa had gone with him to pick it out, just before my dad left for the Air Force. It had spent a lot of time stored in Grandpa's garage while we traveled the world.

"Peanut," he sighed, using his pet name for me, "it sure is hard to say goodbye to someone you love isn't it?" He ran his weathered hand over the old fender of the truck. Maybe it felt like he was hugging my dad.

I knew he was remembering the day he and Grandma received word that my father had been killed on the autobahn in Germany and that we were coming home without him. I think it was just as hard for him to watch my mother take me, his son's only remaining child, back to her home in Georgia with her. My six-month-old baby sister was also in the car when it crashed, but we have never talked about that, it was part of the jagged scar and just hurt too much.

"Sure is, Grandpa, sure is." I put my arm around him knowing the time we had left together was more precious than ever.

"Well, at least your daddy got to come home one more time that last Christmas and drive his old truck."

It never struck me until now how devastating it must be for a parent to lose a child. As hard as it was for me to lose my dad, and Sissy, it must have been a nightmare for my mother and my grandparents. With the three of them all losing a child in one short moment, they might have been some comfort to one another, if they had ever been able to talk about it. I remember Grandpa saying to some of his friends after the funeral that it was against nature for a father to outlive his own son. Now here he was, having survived longer than nearly every friend and family member he had. After we lost Grandma and then suddenly my mother, my grandfather and I were the only two left. It seemed like the look on his face was something more...regret maybe...or maybe we were both tired—tired of saying goodbye and tired of the hurt that never went away.

I accepted his unspoken offer to be alone while he went back to my house for a nap. "I'm not quite done here," I handed him the keys to the truck and promised to be home later.

"Well, it's a good thing we drove separate vehicles then," he assured me with a weak, forced smile. "I don't have one ounce of work left in me and I don't envy you the task of cleaning up after our little sale here." He was alluding to the fact that Hannah had left for Atlanta the second she had changed clothes and collected the last dollar, leaving me to clean up all the empty boxes and discarded price tags, not to mention the dirt from the shoes of every shopper who had set foot on the hardwood floors.

"I'll be home in a few hours," I promised and then headed back up the driveway to clean up the last little bit of Miss Claudia's life. I heard the loud motor of the truck turn over as I closed the half-wood, half-stained glass door behind me. I felt overwhelmed when I surveyed the hours of work still ahead of me. I thought how odd it seemed that eighty-five years of living could be gone, boxed up, or sold in one afternoon.

After I had gathered up all the boxes, the old newspapers used for wrapping glassware, picked up all the price tags, and taken down **"ESTATE SALE HERE"** posters alongside the driveway, I went to Miss Claudia's shed to get a broom. It would be hard to stop thinking of everything left here as mine and not hers.

I had paid Hannah one thousand dollars for the contents of the shed. The only things I couldn't stand to part with were her gardening tools and clothes. A pair of worn, patched blue-jean overalls, a pair of gardening gloves, and that old floppy blue hat still hung on a new brass hook in the corner. Whenever I thought of Miss Claudia, in my mind's eye I would always see her wearing them. She had more tools than a hardware store hanging on a pegboard on the far wall. I knew I'd also need her old John Deere mower to cut the front yard grass. It was an entire acre from the porch to the road and took at least a couple of hours to cut during the spring and summer. Unfortunately, the mower was as rusty as the nails in Grandpa's crate.

Hannah had taken one look inside the shed and had no problem selling all of the items together as one. She sold them all to me without a second thought. She couldn't close her eyes and see her aunt in here the way I could, smiling and adjusting her hat. It's true, the tractor was old, the green paint was chipped and faded by the sun and weather, but it ran like a champ. I know because for the past three years, Miss Claudia had finally decided it was time to give up cutting the grass herself in the hot, humid Georgia summer heat. I was happy to hear it until I realized she was passing the loud, green, rusty torch to me. It wasn't pretty to look at, but it got the job done.

I stood on the veranda for a few minutes looking out over the front lawn, imagining all the times I'd cut it and wondering how many more miles were in that old John Deere's future. I would rumble along, occasionally glancing over at Miss Claudia trimming the bushes or tending her flowers. I remembered how she would point to a spot on the freshly manicured grass and say, "I bet there was a slave hanging wash out right over there," or "I suppose horses used to come up that dirt drive instead of cars when the original house stood here." I could almost see it clearly as she described it down to the smallest detail.

For a few minutes, I wanted to be sixteen again. I wanted to be sitting in one of the rockers or on the porch swing next to my friend. I loved drinking in both the lemonade she had made and the stories that came partly from her imagination and partly from the Southern history she had learned from her father. I was never really sure where the line was drawn. I looked over at the shed. It was at least thirty years old, but was still the newest thing on the property. It was built years ago by Mr. Wainwright, his architecture skills standing the test of time made it look rustic, but not broken down. He built it out of oak in the side yard on the perimeter of the woods to mark the edge of his land. The orchards and cotton fields had gradually disappeared over the years as the once sizeable plantation was sold off piece by piece. The county had bought some of it to build roads on opposite ends of the original boundaries, some had been sold to farmers, and the rest used as grazing land by my neighbors, most of whom own at least one horse. All that remains of the original land is the five-acre parcel on which my house and Ms. Claudia's memory stand.

When Miss Claudia was a child, she helped her father plant trees on the four acres that lay behind the house, mostly pines with an occasional pecan or magnolia mixed in along the outside periphery. She'd also planted the dogwoods that now flourish at both corners of the front of the house. All these years later, the backfield had grown into thick, deep woods. Kudzu blanketed the tree trunks, branches, and most of the forest floor. She told me her father loved to look out the tall window of the bedroom he shared with her mother on the second story. He relished seeing all those green trees and listening to the birds. The thicker the woods became, the better he liked it. He would take evening strolls to enjoy the fresh air and the wildlife. She told me tale after tale of seeing deer, raccoons, and squirrels for the first time whenever she walked with him. Even in her old age, I think the sight of them reminded her of her father and instantly took her back to another time and place. I don't know how long I'd been standing there daydreaming, but my hands were getting sore from my tight grip on the broomstick and I realized that I had a lot of sweeping to do inside.

The swishing of the broom's rough bristles echoed against the high ceilings and bare walls. The house looked even bigger now that it was empty. It had extra-wide doorways, creaky, honey-colored hardwood floors with matching steps guarded by an ornate banister. The foyer was large and echoed every time the screen door slammed against the doorframe, even in the slightest breeze. The parlor had a huge brick fireplace, while the opposite wall was composed almost entirely of glass—large windows overlooking the front lawn. All of the rooms were open and spacious, each leading to the next through tall, square archways with Doric columns on either side. Those columns matched the ones supporting the second story balcony that wrapped itself around the outside of the house and hung over the veranda.

The kitchen was large and luxurious, thanks to Hannah. It was newer looking than the rest of the house. About three years ago, she had insisted on coming down and helping Miss Claudia pick out new appliances. She referred to the place as a firetrap and the rest of the house as kindling. Now there was a brushed silver refrigerator, stove, and built-in double ovens. I have to admit, Hannah does have good taste in some things. The silver metal appliances look great against the grey stone fireplace and black granite countertops, but the floor and cabinets are still that same honey-colored wood. Miss Claudia would not budge on that. Anything that could be stripped, cleaned, or refurbished stayed as it was.

The old stairs creaked with age in a few spots as I climbed them to look at the bedrooms. I had already decided to sleep in the one on the front side of the house with its large glass doors that open to the second story balcony. I thought I'd be able to see farther down the driveway from there, so that I could decide whether or not to pretend that I wasn't home if any uninvited guests approached. It also had its own connected bathroom with a huge tub, always a plus.

There were four spacious bedrooms. Each one had its own special history. Miss Claudia always liked sleeping in the one that had once belonged to her parents. She would stand at the floor-to-ceiling windows where her father stood years ago. She loved to look out into her forest, remembering her childhood and imagining those of the children who had played in that field long before she had ever planted trees on it. As I stood in their spot, I suddenly realized that the sun had gone down. I pulled myself from my memories and noticed the stars were out and my watch read quarter past eleven.

I decided to make a quick stop in the bathroom downstairs before I locked up and went home. While looking in the mirror at my smeared eye makeup and the reflection of the white claw-foot tub behind me, I could almost see Miss Claudia standing there too.

"Blonde hair, blue eyes, five seven, and about 128 pounds, and such a pretty face." she would say, making an hourglass-shaped gesture with her hands. "Why you don't have a boyfriend is beyond me."

"Me too," I answered her, as if she were really standing there. For a moment, I felt like a teenager, wondering where the years had gone.

Grandpa warned me about the fleeting passage of time when I was about fifteen. "Enjoy your youth," he'd say, shaking his finger at me as if I had done something wrong. "It doesn't come back again." As I suppose all teenagers do, I paid little attention.

His words were coming back to haunt me now as I wondered what in the world I was going to do with all this space for only myself and Keno. While I don't think thirty-three is necessarily old, I just can't help thinking about the fact that I'm still single. Despite the efforts of every friend and co-worker I know who have been setting me up on dates since I was at least eighteen, I think total hopelessness and abandonment of the idea of marriage is just a birthday or two away. I have tried to adopt the "all the good ones are taken" theory and accept the single life, which is easier than answering the question "What's going wrong here?" I spend a lot of my time working, but now that I have a home meant for a family it sure does make me want one of my own and brings back memories of the one I lost. Sometimes I think I can hear my ovaries crying—a crazy thought, I know.

"Someday, Angie," I said aloud, looking at my reflection, trying to reassure myself in as convincing a tone as possible. "Someday."

Chapter 3
"The Crate"

It was midnight before I made it back across town to my other house. It felt weird thinking about that. Normally, when I think of people who own two houses, I think of celebrities or rich people. Being a public defender in a little town the size of a dot on the map made me neither. Grandpa was sitting at the dining room table when I came in. He always was a night owl. I guess I get that from him.

"Not one stamp," he grumbled a little, stacking the last bundle of paper back into the wooden box.

"Sorry," I said trying to sympathize with him, but still feeling a little too blue over my lack of a husband and 2.2 kids to really work up any other emotion. It was all I'd been able to think about on the way home.

"Why do I hear sad notes coming from your instrument?" he asked, pointing to my throat and alluding to the singing he says I never do for him anymore.

"Just tired, I guess." By the look on his face, I knew he knew it was more, but after we had been through this weekend, he let it slide.

"Well, you'd better get to bed if you expect to get those lazy bones up for church in the morning."

"I don't think I'm going tomorrow," I answered and then decided I needed to give him an excuse. "I just want to rest up for next week. You never know, we could have a crime wave and I might be really busy."

Grandpa laughed. "You have a case of the mulligrubs, young lady, but I suppose everyone is entitled to pull the covers over their head and hide every once in a while."

I smiled, remembering the first time my grandpa explained to me in great detail what the mulligrubs were. "It's those times when you're sad, but not crying, and blue, but not exactly depressed. You're not sick or especially tired, but your energy level is way below the "E" on your gas gauge."

Yes, I would definitely say Grandpa was right on the money—I was sure I had a good case of the 24-hour mulligrubs.

* * *

I woke up the next morning around 11:00 to the sounds and smells of brunch. Grandpa was cooking again. He loved it, but all I ever got was spaghetti and a ginger ale. I laid there for a few minutes watching a hummingbird buzzing around the feeder outside my window. I remembered the day Miss Claudia just showed up and announced that the first thing I should see in the morning was one of God's creatures.

"In the middle of a stressful day, you should always remember the Creator and something He made. It'll start your day off right and help you through the rough spots," she told me. She pulled her 78 year-old bones up the ladder to screw the hook into the eaves, despite my offering to do it for her. Maybe she did it because she too had seen me during a time when I had a case of the mulligrubs. *Probably after yet another disastrous blind date*, I thought to myself as the little bird moved on. She was right. I had gotten out of bed many a Monday morning with a smile after having seen one of those tiny, colorful birds on my sill. She was wearing her overalls when she came over and hung the feeder up and I could see her standing there smiling at me clear as day. I missed her.

Sunday was usually the day Miss Claudia and I ate lunch together. I was trying to remember the last one we missed, but not one came to mind. Our little white church was right across the street from the Dairy Queen and every Sunday, as soon as we had shaken the preacher's hand, we would walk across the street and order cheeseburgers and split a basket of onion rings. Miss Claudia would always say that since it was "Sundae" it would be wrong not to celebrate by sharing one of those too.

Grandpa was pulling warm garlic bread from the oven as I walked into the kitchen wearing my fuzzy pink bathrobe with my hair pulled up into a floppy ponytail on the top of my head. I smiled to myself, comforted by the familiarity of the situation.

"You never fail me, Grandpa...spaghetti and ginger ale." He grinned knowing I was right about his limited menu.

"When you grow up poor like I did, you learn to fix one meal well and hopefully it's a cheap one. Even after I got married, spaghetti never failed your grandma and me." He winked at me reminding us both how she'd loved it. The vivid happy memory made us feel like she was at the table. He slid a full plate in front of me and said grace before he reminded me of something I had forgotten. It set me back at least two hours on my 24-hour mulligrub clock. "We should be getting on the road soon. My plane leaves at six tonight and the ticket agent told me I need to be there at least two hours early."

It had either slipped my mind or I'd blocked out the fact that he was leaving today. I wasn't looking forward to the trip to Atlanta, the two-hour drive home by myself, or saying goodbye. Not wanting him to worry about my sullen state, I tried to say something positive. "At least it's Sunday and the traffic should be bearable." I even managed to give him a smile as I slurped up another bite of noodles, just like he told me not to do when I was a kid. Smiling, he shook his finger at me like I was ten and doing something naughty.

I watched him pack, trying not to let my feelings show. I watched his slow, precise movements and wondered to myself how much longer I would have him in my life. How many more times would he be able to make the trip down to see me or me up to see him? I promised myself it would not be long before our next visit. He was wearing his same old tan pants, white shirt, red suspenders, and golf cap. My grandma had always picked out his clothes and as I assessed his outfit, the familiar one I had seen a million times, I wondered if he wore the same clothes she'd given him in order to remember her or simply because it had been more than fifty years since he'd picked out anything himself.

* * *

In spite of my mood, I smiled when I heard him whistling as he walked toward the ticket counter to get his boarding pass. He had his crossword puzzle book in one hand and his pencil in the other. "I love you, Grandpa!" I called after him just before he rounded the corner and out of my sight.

"I love you too, Peanut," he said, turning to wave as he was about to step through the security gate. I wish I'd had a camera, so I wouldn't forget even the smallest detail, knowing that in the years to come, it would be my favorite picture.

* * *

It was still early when I arrived home. I'd made the trip back from Atlanta in record time. There was no traffic at all and I'd sailed all the way, except through Forsyth—the home of the state trooper training center. Speeding isn't tolerated in Forsyth—a lesson that a few clients of mine and I had learned the hard way.

I tossed my keys on the small table in my foyer and was about to make my way upstairs to take a hot bath when I passed through the kitchen and noticed Grandpa's crate on the table. He must have put it there when he hurried back inside saying he'd forgotten something. It never dawned on me that he'd come back out to the car empty-handed. I was worried that he'd be late to catch his plane and I just didn't think about it.

There was a note taped to the side of the splintered wood. "Dear Peanut, I thought you might enjoy this. I know how you love old letters and darn my luck, not one stamp." I smiled, almost hearing him speak the words as I read them.

It was always funny to me when he'd leave a yard sale, an antique store, or a flea market and curse his terrible luck at not having found anything. He would always tell me stories of a fellow stamp collector friend of his who would just be walking along, not even looking, and practically trip over some unlikely find of great value. I suppose that over the years the hunt had become just as much fun as the hobby for Grandpa.

His poor luck had evolved into a family joke started by my grandmother. She always said, "The last lucky find he ever had was me." Each of his stamps was a hard-won treasure, another reason I cherished the story behind each one. Grandma teased him and took some of the credit for any stamps of worth, she used to say she was there every time he found something good. She was his lucky charm and he was smart enough to know it. It reminded me of how cheated I feel that I don't have what they had.

I put the note aside and decided I'd look through the crate later. I had about twelve hours until my Monday workday would begin and I was determined to get myself into a better mood or else it would be a long week. I was going to have to build my spirits up to deal with all the "I'm so sorry for your losses" and the town gossips asking how Hannah felt about my getting her aunt's house. I put my hair back up in that same floppy ponytail and soaked my cares away for at least an hour under a sea of bubbles and the soft glow of candlelight. When my hands looked wrinkled as a prune, I let out the warm water and a little bit of my mood seemed to go down the drain with it.

Chapter 4
"Past and Future"

My office was upstairs in the courthouse that sat in the center of the town square. It was located across the street from a rather stately looking library built by our local college. Next to that was our small, but new, police department building.

"Morning, Janice," I walked in, waving at her with my free hand, the other gripping the handle of my briefcase, orange juice, and a donut.

If our little town's grapevine had a root, it was definitely Janice. She was the receptionist and every person, prisoner, warrant, speeding ticket, divorce decree, and death certificate went across her desk before making it to the appropriate office or judge. She had worked in the courthouse since two years after she graduated from high school. If ever we needed an exact measurement of her backside, there was one easily accessible on her office chair. It had to be at least ten years old. I suppose the county sprung for her to have a new one every ten years or so as she had been sitting behind that desk for at least forty years. At that rate, she'd be in the process of making imprint number four. Instead of coming inside the building and handling their own affairs, police officers, city officials, and anyone else in a hurry just handed whatever needed to be filed or delivered to Janice and she saw to it. She once told me she couldn't help it if she accidentally happened to read a few of the documents when they crossed her desk.

Her short brown hair matched her stature. She had her chair jacked up to its highest position and sometimes even padded her imprint with a round pillow she had made herself and brought from home. She alleged it was for comfort, but I think it was because it gave her a few more inches. The gold link chain swung from the sides of her bifocals as she pulled them down to look at me. The desk was higher than normal, like the ones in the bank where you can stand and write comfortably, only this one was stately and official-looking. It was circular with an opening to enter from the back. When Janice eased down off her chair, all you could see was her head floating behind the mahogany countertop. On occasion she happened to be leaning down getting something from a drawer and popped up showing only her head and scared a few unsuspecting people half to death. She nearly gave one of our new naive police officers a heart attack.

I was about five feet from her and before I'd even had a chance to comment on the outcome, I knew by the smell that she'd spent the weekend giving herself another home perm. The other thing she'd had since the day she'd taken this job was a passion for home beauty makeovers. Luckily, I'd been "busy" every time she offered to give me one. Everyone joked that Janice had been standing behind that desk since the day the last brick of the building's foundation was laid. She'd become invaluable to our small town system and I couldn't imagine not seeing her every week. She was sick only once, when she had to have her gallbladder removed. Janice always told everyone the place would fall apart without her and she was right, it nearly did.

"You have a client over in the jail," she said, knowing she was always the first to inform me about anything to do with my job. I knew she would know all about it, so before I wasted my morning tracking down Phillip Welling, our District Attorney, I asked her to fill me in.

"What's the charge?" I asked with an obvious lack of enthusiasm, which showed in both my posture and my inflection. I could tell she was curious as to why, but kindly refrained from asking. She was a busybody, but one of the rare kind who knew that waiting for the scoop sometimes filled your cup even fuller. "A juvenile shoplifter, second time offender," she didn't usually consolidate her report she must have noticed my stride slowed, but I didn't stop. "He's an old friend or yours," she called after me with a playful warning sound in her tone.

"Great, a regular customer. He must keep breaking the law just because of the service with a smile around here." I walked on, not really caring who it was but mentally flipping through the rolodex of petty juvenile criminals I had defended. After a while, they all look the same. Generic wannabe gangster kids from a small town, same clothes, same attitude, same trivial crimes.

I passed Phillip in the stairwell and before he could tell me about my client, I decided to save us both some time. "How about one year probation and some community service?" I asked. He just shook his head. "Not sure about that this time. Willie Jones is eighteen now and obviously a slow learner." He handed me the folder we had on him and it was about two inches thick. Come on, Phil, this is just mischievous kid's stuff." I took the folder and quickly flipped through the pages. "Vandalizing a dumpster and taking a few candy bars hardly warrants the state pen." He smirked at me, not wanting to agree.

"Yes, well this time it was electronics from Radio Shack."

I read the police report more carefully. "A pair of headphones? C'mon, that doesn't really qualify as electronics and there wasn't even a weapon or anything. I know...I know..." I conceded. "I'm sick of seeing him too, but maybe he's learned something. I'll go over to the jail and scare him a little about this going on his adult record."

Phil hesitated for a long minute, debating Willie's character or giving me my way, I wasn't sure which. "This is the last time. Anything else and I'm gonna get tough on him. I just got a feeling here, Ang." He took back his folder and continued down the steps.

"You're doing the right thing," I assured him with a smile in my voice that hinted at my victory.

"Remind me of that next time he wastes my time and the taxpayers' money." He let the heavy stairwell door slam behind him, but opened it again before I had a chance to get up two steps. "I want a provision of his probation to be if he gets in trouble at all or misses any of his community service he's going to jail. Make him understand that." "I know the judge will back me on it, he is no stranger to Willie or his gang."

"I'll dare him to give me a reason," I promised with a tone that held no real threat.

"Deal then," he conceded, reaching out to shake my hand and make it official. "Go see him and have the paperwork on my desk by noon."

He knew that translated to 'I'd do it, but give it to Janice to make the necessary copies and he'd have them by about two o'clock.'

"On it," I assured him as we both turned to go. I love a good trial, but the great Radio Shack caper was not exactly front page news. The paperwork alone for a stupid pair of $20 dollar headphones would have been ridiculous. *Dodged that bullet*," I thought and continued up the stairs.

* * *

Phillip was from Charlotte, North Carolina. He'd given up city life and the suburbs because his wife Kathy was from here. They had three kids and she wanted to be near her mother. Family would be about the only reason I could see him living in a small town. He didn't exactly approve of the way we did things. He was a very "by-the-book" kind of guy and thought that having a receptionist as the heart of legal communications was unprofessional, but he'd been here for six years and seen how difficult it was to change the old ways. To save his sanity, he had given up long ago and stopped fighting the system.

If he were a comedian, he would have definitely been the straight man. We settled many cases in the stairwell because, after all, nothing exciting ever happened here. The last big case we had was fifteen years ago when Mr. Kent and Miss Bonnie were robbed at gunpoint in their own pharmacy. I always hated having missed that, but it happened about three years before I started working for them. I think knowing something so bad could happen to such good people solidified my decision to pursue a law degree, not to mention it was the last exciting thing to ever happen around here and I certainly didn't want to miss the next one.

* * *

By phone from my office, I managed to get the house into shape so that I could move in by the weekend. I had painters repaint the veranda, the railing around the upper balcony, and the shutters white, then redo the rest of the house in the same bright blue. When they'd finished, it looked almost brand new. I had one of our local carpenters and a few of his crew strip and polish the floors, then fix a few rickety places in the banister and kitchen cabinets.

The old place was shining like a new penny on Saturday morning when I enlisted every friend I had who owned a pickup truck to help me move. I quickly realized that I didn't have even one-tenth of the furniture I needed to fill the house. After I'd finished putting all of my belongings away, the rooms still seemed empty. I thanked everyone profusely who had volunteered, then fell into bed. It was late and I knew I'd better get some sleep so I could make it to church in the morning. If you miss two Sundays in a row, the women in the Sunday School class assume you're sick and they bring casseroles to your house.

* * *

I came in from church, pulling off my heels as I entered. I was hopping around trying to get the left one off when I tripped over the crate Grandpa had left behind. I'd told one of the guys to leave it in the foyer since I still had no idea what was in it. I took a deep breath and sighed. I was not in the mood to read any of Miss Claudia's old letters. I just didn't have the heart to see her handwriting and start missing her all over again. It was bad enough she was the only topic people seemed to want to talk to me about these days. It was more than idle chitchat for me. It was painful. I think people knew that but sometimes their curiosity beat out their tact. I also knew there was no harm intended. I mean, how could a group of little old ladies at church not focus on their friend? I'm guessing they might be wondering who was next. I was polite and smiled, but I was glad when the preacher said his last 'amen,' I ducked out quick and skipped the Dairy Queen. I ate lunch at home, threw on some jeans, and took Keno for a walk around his new yard. I wanted him to get used to living here and not just thinking we were here for a visit.

When we came back inside, I sat in the quiet, wishing I had remembered to call the cable guy when my attention once again fell on the old crate. My curiosity got the better of me, so I sat down on my freshly polished foyer floor and began to pull out its contents. I was surprised that I didn't recognize any of the handwriting to be that of Miss Claudia. It was the day Grandpa's passion for history and my dreams for my future collided. I didn't know it at the time, but I was literally opening up a completely new life for myself. I had no idea the events that would be the answer to my prayers and the absolution of my pain had occurred over a hundred years ago.

Chapter 5
"Annabeth"

There was an old hardback book at the bottom of the crate that caught my attention. It was smudged with soot on both sides, but I could tell that it used to be light pink. There were two frayed pink ribbons attached to the covers—one to the front and one to the back so that they could be tied together as if the words inside were meant to be private. It looked like a diary. I wiped away some of the grime and found the name "Annabeth" embossed in gold in the bottom right hand corner of the front cover.

I sat and thought for a moment, trying to remember if I had ever heard Miss Claudia mention that name. Coming up blank, I untied the ribbon and opened the book. The binding had held together remarkably well and much to my surprise, none of the pages fell out. The beautiful handwriting and smudged ink reminded me of some of my grandfather's old letters and then my curiosity turned into excitement. In my mind, I saw a picture of myself as a young girl, sitting at my grandparents' table, reading letter after letter. Now it seemed I had stumbled upon a whole book of them. I carefully flipped back to the first page and started reading.

February 11, 1863

My sweet angel, I felt your precious wings flutter deep inside me today. It is late and I am writing this with the lamp very dim in the hopes my father will not see that I am still awake. I know in my heart that you, my child, will be a boy. If so, I have already decided your name will be Andrew. Please do not misunderstand because both your father and I would be just as pleased with a daughter as we would a son. Our love knows no boundary when it comes to acceptance. I feel that in order for you to understand why you are different, I should start at the beginning of my story, which is also yours.

We live in a very uncertain time where you will likely face obstacles I could never even dream of. Just remember that you were made of love, a love so deep that you should never be ashamed of who you are or how you came to be. I am writing this down so that even if I am gone when you are grown, you will always know how very much you were loved and wanted even before you took your first breath.

My name is Annabeth and I am your mother, but in order for you to know exactly where you came from, I need to tell you about my mother. Before she married, her name was Emmaline Lagoy. Her family is French-Canadian and she is the second generation in her lineage to be born on American soil. She is also one-quarter Mohawk Indian, a fact that does not show in the characteristics of her face, but one that would most certainly have kept my father from marrying her. When she was a small child, her father moved her, her mother, and her two sisters from the snows of the North to the cotton fields and orchards of the South. They settled not far from here and her father began to work the land.

My mother was the youngest girl, eight years behind her nearest sibling. Both of her sisters were married before her father had built up his cotton plantation enough to start acquiring slaves. First, he purchased some field hands, as he had no sons to help him in his labors.

Soon afterward, he produced the largest crop he had ever known and was able to purchase some female slaves for the house. The family became wealthy nearly overnight and my mother's upbringing changed drastically from that known by her sisters.

My mother was born April 25, 1828 and had reached the age of ten when her mother, my grandmother Lagoy, decided that she needed to have her own personal maid. The young slave girl chosen was purchased from a man by the name of Levi McGrath. Like my mother's father, Levi had three children, only his were sons, one of whom was my mother's age. Although they were only *children, as the families grew closer, it was expected that my mother and Jackson McGrath would marry someday.*

On my mother's tenth birthday, Mr. McGrath brought his family and a young slave girl around the age of fourteen over to my parents' house to celebrate the occasion. The girl had been sold away from her family, knew no one, and spoke very little English. She was shy and very introverted, no doubt from the deep-seated fear she had acquired of anyone with white skin. She had been raped and tortured on the slave ship that sailed from Africa to this country and then separated from the only family she had ever known. Mr. McGrath had originally bought her for his own wife, but then thought she would be more suitable to my mother's needs. Knowing how badly my grandmother Lagoy wanted her precious little Emmaline to have a maid, Mr. McGrath made quite a tidy profit on the sale of her to my grandfather Lagoy.

My grandmother explained to my mother that the girl was to be her personal servant. My mother had seen the slaves working in the house and fields, but it had never occurred to her ten-year-old mind that she could have one of her own. My grandmother Lagoy allowed her daughter to name the new slave and waited in great anticipation, wondering what name her little girl would choose. Young Emmaline thought for a few minutes, twisting her ringlet curls around her finger, while

Grandmother Lagoy straightened the bows on her daughter's party dress. My mother had always been fond of her grandparents and debated which one of her grandmothers' names she would choose. In honor of the one she remembered them burying most recently, Emmaline settled on the name of her father's mother. Grandmother Lagoy was a bit disappointed that Emmaline had not chosen to use the name of her mother, but did not protest her daughter's decision. From that day forward, the scared, lonely slave girl was known as Ophelia Lagoy.

Emmaline was not truly in need of a servant, but she quickly became a status symbol for my grandmother. They had become so wealthy that even their child owned a slave.

From that day forward, at the tender age of ten, my mother was put in charge of her new servant, Ophelia. It took some time, but eventually they learned to communicate and Ophelia began to speak English as best she could without any formal training, other than what she heard around the house. My mother was instructed that even though Ophelia was only a few years older than she was, she was not allowed to go to school and nobody, including my mother, was to teach any slave to read or write.

It never struck me how bizarre the whole situation was until I just re-read what I have written on this paper in black and white. My *mother was given a human being for her tenth birthday and allowed to name her as if she were a puppy or a pony. My beloved unborn, Ophelia is your grandmother. I hope that I can make the story of your heritage clear to you in these pages. I hope that you will understand that love, true love, is a slave to no one. On the other hand, we can very easily fall servant to it.*

I will continue to write to you until all has been said. You have the right to know. I want you to have the facts of your beginning laid before you so they can lead you down the path of your life, a life I hope will be filled with as much wonder, hope, and precious things as your anticipated arrival has given me. Father is walking up the hall, so I must say goodnight for now and sweet dreams, little one, until I see your face.

* * *

I noticed as my eyes began to droop that my feet had begun to tingle because I'd been sitting cross-legged on the foyer floor reading for longer than I had intended. The story of Annabeth intrigued me and I wanted to read more, but after the busy weekend and exhausting move, I decided to turn in early and pick up where I left off later.

I went to bed that night dreaming of a young slave girl named Ophelia following the commands and every whim of ten year-old Emmaline Lagoy. The journal said that they lived not far from here. I imagined that the house or any trace of it was long gone. Maybe that's why Miss Claudia and her father spent so many hours looking out that window into the forest. Maybe they had both dreamed of what the South used to be and had shared a sense of what really happened here. Maybe that's why Miss Claudia's father had gotten his 10-year old daughter to help him plant all of those trees. Maybe he was trying to turn the sins of the past into something he thought was beautiful.

I wished more than ever that Miss Claudia was here and could lend me her thoughts on the matter. Right now, though, I was too tired to think about it and decided to put it off until I'd gotten some rest. As I lay there, just before my mind finally shut off for the night, I wondered why Miss Claudia and I had not found this crate years ago. *The trouble with death is that all the sharing stops. All the memories have been made and no matter how much you want to make just one more, the opportunity is gone.*

Luckily, I fell asleep before I allowed myself to imagine all the future memories that Miss Claudia and I would never share.

* * *

No one had the heart to fold up Miss Claudia's lap blanket, so it remained hanging on the back of the pew where she'd left it. I tried to look straight ahead at the preacher and not focus on it, but I couldn't seem to stop catching a glimpse of it out of the corner of my eye. I was thinking about it again on Monday morning while sitting in my office chair, swiveling back and forth, when I heard Janice knock at my door.

"I noticed you didn't come in with your OJ and donut this morning," she was kindly, bringing me a fresh sample of each.

"I got a late start. I spent the afternoon and early evening reading and hit the snooze button too many times. I'm thinking I should have gotten more rest after the move."

I gratefully accepted the juice and took a swig.

"Must have been really interesting if it kept your eyes open after all you've been through this past week." She knew she didn't need an invitation, so she sat down, making herself at home across from me in the chair facing my desk. I don't know what it is about people who were born a few generations before me, but I always feel more at ease around older people. I would put Janice at about sixty.

"Just some old papers my grandfather found in the basement of my new house." I paused for a moment, thinking about how the words sounded. "I can't really get used to saying that. I think people will always call it the Wainwright house."

Her interest was piqued. "You know, that basement is the original foundation of that house. It dates back to before the Civil War. It's the only thing that survived the fire."

"Oh yeah, I guess I had heard something about that years ago." I always wondered about the basement knowing the rest of the house had been rebuilt.

"Was it burned in the War? I have heard partial embellishments from Miss Claudia, I guess I'm more curious now that I live there, I should have just asked you." She smiled at my subtle admission that she knew everything and everybody and every rumor connected to this town.

Janice rolled her eyes but the secrets behind her expression confirmed I was right. She knew I knew she was omniscient when it came to Fort Valley and she had the scoop on everything that happened—past, present, and sometimes future.

"No, nothing quite so dramatic. My mother was twenty-one in 1920 when it happened. She must've told me the story a hundred times. When I was a kid, every time we'd drive by there, she'd tell me about the night the original house caught fire. In her grandiose Southern way, she'd describe how the flames shot up into the sky. The only thing left was the basement and the fireplace that's in the kitchen now.

"Well, that tells me something I didn't know," I was smiling as if I knew a secret of my own. She stared at me, narrowing her eyes as if that would help her see my thought. She couldn't stand it, only took her two seconds to ask.

As always, her curiosity got the better of her. "What's that?"

"Now I know where you get your grandiose Southern way!"

Janice sat back in her chair with a look of chagrin on her face. She knew I was right. I decided to stop teasing and let her off the hook. After all, she'd told me what I wanted to know.

"Well, that explains why the stones match," In my mind, I was picturing and comparing the large grey rock in the basement wall and the fireplace.

"The story was that a candle's flame flickered in the wind next to an open window and caught the curtain on fire.

Some distant relative who was kin to the original owners had it rebuilt in 1925." She thought for a moment and then added, "Seems to me like Momma told me his last name was McGrath."

I sat up, recognizing the name as the one from the diary I had read last night. I wondered how Annabeth's journal found its way to the bottom of that crate. The fire story did explain the soot on the cover of the book.

"Anyway," Janice went on, "he died only three years after it was completed. It sat empty for another two years until the Wainwrights bought it."

I flashed to the picture of the old black and white photo of Miss Claudia I kept on the mantle. Picturing her face made me wonder why she had never shared the whole truth about the home she loved so much. I couldn't stop thinking about it for the rest of the day. Knowing a little more about the history of the house made me want to go home and finish reading the journal. I wanted to know Annabeth, what happened to her baby, why she expected it to be so different, and how that crate ended up in my basement.

Chapter 6

"Emmaline"

I rushed home after work and threw some dinner together. Thank goodness for microwaves and Spaghetti-O's. I wanted to get right to the journal, but then after walking Keno in the humidity, I decided I'd enjoy it more if I took a shower first. Clean and wearing my favorite Mercer University T-shirt and shorts, I climbed the two steps up to my high four-poster, king-size bed and reached for the faded pink book laying on my nightstand.

February 12, 1863

This is our special time together, my angel. It is once again dark and the lantern dim. I wanted to finish telling you the story of my mother and Ophelia. Despite having been warned by Grandfather Lagoy, my mother, Emmaline, treated Ophelia more like a friend than a servant. They developed a deep friendship and respect for one another. They grew up together and were rarely apart. Emmaline made sure that no matter where she went, Ophelia was also allowed to go. They pretended it was because Mother needed a servant, but they both knew it was because they had become best friends. As they grew older and wiser to the world, they had to become better at hiding their friendship. The Lagoy family remained close to the McGraths. They would often get together for picnics and parties, sometimes recalling the day Ophelia was purchased for Emmaline. Mr. McGrath frequently joked about how he thought he had gotten the better end of the deal until he saw just how well and how quickly Emmaline had become used to being "a little master." The girls would hear the story and exchange knowing looks with one another about just how wrong everyone was regarding the true nature of their relationship. Ophelia was allowed to experience the social settings and events to which any white girl was privy and she lived them throughout my mother's childhood.

When Mother turned seventeen and Ophelia was twenty-one, the patriarchs of the Lagoy and McGrath families decided it was time for my mother to marry my father. They had been expecting it all of their lives, but despite the fact that Mother had definite reservations, she had no say in the matter. On November 21, 1845, Emmaline Lagoy became Emmaline McGrath. Ophelia kept the last name Lagoy, since it had been assigned to her when she was fourteen years old. Ophelia was part of my mother's dowry. She went with her and once again became a possession of the McGrath family. Emmaline's new husband would someday become my father, your grandfather. His name is Jackson McGrath. Although the journey between their houses took only a little over a day on horseback, Mother felt *like she was moving a million miles away. She thanked God that she was taking with her the only person on earth she truly loved – Ophelia. The prospect of living in the McGrath family home with both her new husband and her new in-laws was unsettling for Mother. She was comforted by the fact that Ophelia would be living in the strange house as well, but she would soon learn that she was wrong.*

"Well," I mused, "that explains why the book is here. Emmaline lived in the original house." The answers only brought more questions. "If Annabeth was trying to hide the journal by writing in it at night, why would she store it in the basement where her father would have surely found it? She would have had to sneak downstairs and get it every night, then hide it again in the morning. Stop talking to yourself, Angie," I said, feeling a bit silly sitting up in my bedroom having a one-sided conversation. Keno was never much of a chatterbox, but I found myself talking to his brown eyes more than I would care to admit. It was then I looked over at my alarm clock and realized that I had once again kept myself up way too late.

Janice and I had our usual Philosophical discussion the next morning. Today we decided to shake things up a bit and have chocolate milk and powdered donuts instead of the usual. The powdered donut reminded me of Grandpa. *If only I had a ginger ale, it would be as if he were actually here.* I forced myself to push the feelings of how much I missed him from my thoughts and asked Janice the question that had been running through my mind on the way to work.

"Did you feel like you knew your children before they were born?" I asked as casually as possible, washing down my last bite of donut with a swallow of Nestle's Quick. She looked at me funny, as if she were taking in the full spectrum of the question while at the same time wondering why I would ask her such a thing.

"Well, I suppose before I ever met my husband or got pregnant, I dreamt of what my children would be like, picked out their names, and planned their futures. Sometimes I even tried to picture my grandkids. I suppose every female does that at one time or another in life." She paused and then leaned closer to me in case I was about to whisper. "You got something on your mind?" she asked, giving me an ever-so-slight smirk. She sat back, waiting for me to tell her that I was pregnant or something, but there was to be no such news today.

"No," I shook my head, trying to make myself clear. "When you were pregnant, did you feel like you knew Sloan and Ashley before they were even born? Could you see their faces, sense if they were a boy or a girl?"

Janice looked a little disappointed that I was really asking a question and not preparing to lay some juicy bombshell on her. I can't imagine who she would think the father was—perhaps the guy with B.O. who loved sleeveless shirts—the one that the file room girls set me up with a few weeks ago. Maybe she thinks it's the guy with absolutely no sense of humor and really bad breath that I went out with last month. I picked him myself when we ran into each other with our shopping carts at the Piggly Wiggly. It's a shame it wasn't in the mouthwash aisle. She cleared her throat, realizing I wasn't paying attention. I'm just glad she couldn't read my mind because the thought had occurred to me to wear baggy clothes and mess with her for a couple of days. I decided to give her a break since she really was trying to be helpful and give me some answers. Her desire to reminisce about her kids got the better of her curiosity as to why I was asking. Must be a gene that kicks in after motherhood—not that I would know.

"With Sloan, I'd have to say yes," she answered thoughtfully. "With Ashley, I was so absorbed with my toddler that the little things I noticed the first time seemed to go by so quickly that I missed them. I was so busy trying to take care of a two-year old that all I wanted was for the second one to hurry up and be born. It's hard to chase around an active child with swollen feet and your butt and belly getting bigger by the day, not to mention the inability to tie your own shoes."

Remembering those days with a smile on her face, she seemed to recall something she hadn't thought about in quite a few years.

"During my second pregnancy, the unborn baby was usually the focus of my attention at night, just before I went to sleep. That's when I had a chance to slow down and really pay attention to her every movement and every change in my own body...and that's when I dreamed of what she would be and what she would look like."

"She?" I asked, knowing it was not common to know the sex of an unborn baby back in Janice's day.

"I just knew," was the only explanation she could give me. She looked at her watch and realized she had left her desk, jokingly referred to as "Grand Central," unmanned for twenty minutes. "I've got to get back."

When she got up to leave, I could tell the suspense was killing her. She couldn't resist. "Are you sure there isn't something you want to tell me?"

Knowing she was the root of our grapevine and having experienced a dry spell, I could tell she was thirsty for an answer.

"No," I answered with a cryptic smile.

Janice's experiences and thoughts did give me some insight into how Annabeth must have been feeling. I had no doubt that she was as in tune with her unborn child as the moon is with the tide. The question was, if she loved it so much and was excited about the birth, why was she being so careful to hide it? Only the journal could answer that question and I was determined to know the explanation for myself.

I can't really explain it, I just felt connected to her. She had lived so many years ago, in the same house where I live today. She had probably walked on cotton fields where trees are now. Quite likely she knew the basement well that lay just beneath my feet. I needed to know her. I decided there and then that I would use whatever clues the journal provided to research her family as much as possible. I would let Janice hang on the vine for a while. I knew when the time was right, she'd likely be the best source of history, but if not, she'd know where to find the answers I'd needed to find. For now, though, I wanted to keep Annabeth and her child a secret just for me. It's odd, but it almost felt like telling too soon would be betraying a friend.

Chapter 7
"Ophelia"

February 16, 1863

My angel, it has been several days since I have been able to continue the story of your unique and wonderful heritage. Your grandfather and grandmother McGrath have been hosting my mother's family for a weekend visit. It has been difficult for me to slip away to share my thoughts with you. When I am in the room with them, I feel that I have a secret that only you and I share. I have only felt your tiny presence in my womb for a short while, yet I am already concerned about how I will continue to keep you a secret for as long as possible. If only your father was here. I long to talk to him, to hold him, and for him to put his arms around both of us. He has been gone for nearly a month and I miss him terribly, but I have gotten ahead of myself. My time may be short.

Occasionally, I stop writing and listen quietly for footsteps coming down the hall, but the story of Ophelia on the McGrath plantation is one that requires some time to tell. I want you to fully understand and appreciate how much she has contributed to your safety and well-being, but once again, I am ahead of myself.

When my mother arrived at her new home, she was shown inside the stately plantation house, but Ophelia was taken directly to the slaves' quarters. The accommodations did not tip the scales evenly and Emmaline was upset by the situation. As a child, she had been able to protest and insist that Ophelia be allowed to live in the room that adjoined hers, once occupied by her older sisters. Now that she was grown and expected to conduct herself as a proper Southern woman and heir to a great fortune through her husband, she began to find herself doing something to which she was unaccustomed. As a wife, she was expected to be submissive and practice mindless obedience to my father.

As a child, Mother had been spoiled by her parents' newfound wealth and with this new sense of entitlement, she began to exhibit a stubborn, strong will and independent nature. She was now given no other alternative but to put her childish will aside and follow her husband's every command. She had no idea that becoming a woman and losing her childhood would steal her voice and opinions, thereby rendering her speechless and powerless.

Despite Mother's request for her "maid" to be near her, Ophelia was taken away to the slaves quarters which were little better than the barns where the animals were kept. My grandfather McGrath, my mother's new father-in-law, was a wealthy man and owned many slaves. He had no problem forcing them to stay in what would best be described as very cramped conditions. There was one small bunkhouse for the women and one for the men. They were expected to bathe in the creek that ran behind their quarters without any respect or regard for their privacy. The white foreman would often "guard" the female slaves while they bathed themselves. The living conditions for Ophelia went from that of private house servant who shared in the daily life of my mother to sleeping on a small cot in the corner of what was often a cold, rat-infested hovel. Mother would sneak her extra food whenever possible and the two did their best to maintain and conceal their secret friendship. Mother also confided to Ophelia about her deep unhappiness regarding her marriage to my father. She would say that Jackson McGrath was cold and cruel to her in private, but doting and attentive in public. They were both slaves on very different levels.

Being a young, attractive woman, it was not long before Ophelia started receiving the attention of one of the other slaves. His name was Ruben McGrath and he is your grandfather. Those who are bought and sold on this soil are forced to take on the last names of those who purchased them. Ruben was quiet and soft-spoken—a good, kind man. He immediately fell in love with Ophelia and would often bring her gifts.

On the McGrath plantation it was forbidden for the male slaves to visit the female quarters after they were confined to their respective places at the end of the workday; however, Ruben would always figure out a way to spend some time with the woman who was soon to become his beloved. Father and Grandfather McGrath wanted to ensure the women would be occupied only by the work given them and not making babies. Grandfather would often playfully chastise his friends and fellow plantation owners for allowing their slaves to procreate. He made it perfectly clear that he did not intend to feed any extra mouths that were unable to work in his fields or in his home. A slave's baby would have been just that— an extra mouth. Once, at a social gathering, I heard Grandfather say that wasting the slave's time raising babies was pointless when there was a fresh "crop" of able bodies just waiting to be bought.

Ruben was an excellent craftsman and using a homemade knife and scraps of wood, he carved Ophelia a beautiful bead necklace. Anyone else would have thought the discarded pieces of wood to be useless and simply thrown them in the fire, but Ruben could always see what was inside the wood, not just its exterior. Although Ophelia was initially a bit shy around him, I believe he saw inside her just the same. He strung the beads on apiece of twine and gave the necklace to her shortly after they met. Mother told me that she never saw Ophelia without it from that day forward.

Within a few months, their courtship had blossomed into a deep, albeit secret love. It was nothing short of miraculous and romantic the way they managed to communicate across forbidden boundaries with unspoken words. It was nearly midnight under a full moon where without the guests, flowers, and pretentious circumstances under which my mother had wed my father, Ruben and Ophelia spoke their vows of love to one another under a clear, bright sky. There was no minister, only God's ears hearing their pledges. Their only witnesses were a million stars and a brilliant white moon.

Mother was so excited when Ophelia whispered in her ear about her new union. The beautiful, young slave girl was certain that she had indeed found her true love and bound herself to the man whose soul she considered to be half of her own. Mother knew she had to extend her hand in some sentimental gesture. She wanted to show her friend that not only would she guard her undisclosed truth, but also that she was genuinely pleased to see that Ophelia was finally happy and making the best of her downgraded living accommodations on the McGrath plantation. Mother went to her room and found the silver band that had belonged to her grandmother after *whom Ophelia was named. Its design was that of beautiful flowers strung together, creating a perfect circle, each petal and leaf polished to perfection. It was part of her dowry, but my father was unaware of its existence. Mother never wore it for fear of losing the precious family heirloom, but she knew that it was meant for a purpose other than to adorn her own hand.*

Ophelia protested, but finally accepted the band at my mother's insistence. It came to represent her marriage to Ruben, as well as many childhood secrets and the friendship the two young women shared. Although she was not able to wear the gift for fear her dear confidante might be punished in some way, she would often take it out from beneath her mattress and hold it in her hands, dreaming of her beloved husband and the childhood memories that only she and my mother would ever know.

I laid the book down, unable to read another word. I wanted to relish every sentiment and let it fully sink into me before I went on. Annabeth had something I didn't. She seemed to face things with the heart of a young child, without fear, only pure and honest emotion. I wondered why I couldn't be like that. I discovered in college when "real life" situations came my way, I usually tried to cover up my emotions with sarcasm or humor. Reading these words was making me realize that I could use a little of Annabeth's spirit and Ophelia's courage.

"Maybe true love is possible," I laid the precious volume aside. I couldn't help but think that after everything they went through, if Ophelia and Ruben could hang onto love, then maybe someday I can too. Maybe someday I'll meet the man who will love me the way Ruben loved her. Despite the potential risk, Ruben pursued his true passion. I hadn't had true passion about anything since I graduated from law school. I wanted to find the Ruben in me. Maybe someday, someone will see the Ophelia in me, but how can they if I can't see it in myself? Maybe all I can be is jaded. Maybe instead of knowing how to love, all I can do is dream about it. *Why me?* I wondered. *What's wrong with me...or maybe there's nothing wrong with me.*

I put the pillow over my head and tried to sleep. Self-analysis was exhausting. At least my dreams took me places where my heart couldn't go during the daytime. I was really looking forward to the nap and the escape, but no such luck. I was too absorbed with thoughts about my own flaws to sleep. I went downstairs and sat in my easy chair pondering the uncharacteristic spark of emotion the journal had ignited in me, I began to wonder how Miss Claudia would be feeling about my new revelation. She always used to say that I had a sappy side, but was very out of touch with it. "I think my sap is starting to come to the surface," I, looked up, hoping she could hear me.

I still wanted to know when the story of Annabeth began with regard to Emmaline and Ophelia, but I also wanted to savor every word and make it last. It was kind of like a good bowl of Rocky Road, so I decided to wait and start again tomorrow. Keno was in complete agreement as he sat nudging me to take him for a walk. "Okay buddy, let's go." Sometimes I think he speaks better English than some people I know. He promptly got up, headed to the door, and then sat down, waiting for me to catch up with him and open it.

Before I could get there, the doorbell began playing the beautiful chimes Miss Claudia loved so much. I would always ring it instead of knocking whenever I came to visit. Being the astute watchdog he is, Keno just sat there looking at me as if to say, "Are you going to get that?" Until I adopted this one, I'd never met a dog whose vocal cords weren't directly attached to the doorbell, but to him, it was just another sound. In his ears, it was almost like the telephone ringing or the teakettle whistling.

I opened the door only to discover that I'd completely forgotten I had a blind date, another "fix up." It was rare that I agreed to go out in the middle of the work week, but there was a comedian appearing at The Comedy Club in Macon that I really wanted to see. The "gift" standing on my front porch was one of our local police officers, given to me by Kathy Welling, Phillip's wife. I kind of owed Phil for the whole Willie deal so when Kathy had been at the office the other day, she overheard me talking about going to The Comedy Club and remembered her cousin was looking for someone to go with. I'd seen him in uniform and he seemed likable enough. Besides, we had at least one thing in common—a sense of humor, so I'd decided to take a chance, only to be disappointed the moment I opened the door. His ensemble immediately overshadowed the only point of interest we had in common. Instantly, I lost not only my ability to laugh, but my dinner too—well, almost. Then, when I took a second look, my ability to laugh came back to me in spades and I had to choke it back so as not to hurt his feelings.

I tried to act as if I hadn't forgotten our date and was simply running a few minutes late. He was wearing sandals, a mortal fashion sin for most men as far as I'm concerned. He also had on black socks that unfortunately didn't match even one of the many colors in his shirt, a bright, flowered Hawaiian print which hung about an inch above the waistband of his faded blue jean shorts. Needless to say, he looked much different in uniform. He had brownish strawberry-colored hair, so naturally everybody called him "Rusty." He was also younger than I thought he was. Maybe that's why some women love a guy in a uniform—it makes men look more distinguished and well...taller. I invited him in and asked him to have a seat while I "finished getting ready.

I ran upstairs and found a cute little sundress. I knew I'd be overdressed compared to him, but maybe there would be some other guy out there who would see me and think Rusty was my brother or something. I stopped and looked at myself in the full-length mirror before going back downstairs.

"Now that's just wrong," I berated myself. Keno looked at me and cocked his head wondering if I was scolding him about something. I explained it to him in a more normal tone. "I might be lonely at times, but I am certainly not *that* needy. Going out on a date with one guy while searching for another goes beyond looking and crosses into desperate." His response was to circle once on his pillow and lay down with a grunt of agreement—or maybe I had just bored him. I changed into an outfit that was more in tune with Rusty's, only the flowers and sandals looked much better on me, if I do say so myself. I put on a smile and decided to try to have a good time, even if it killed me.

The comedian was funny, but I couldn't enjoy the show because Rusty was what I like to call a "clapper laugher." Every time he laughed, he'd clap his hands and stomp his sandal-clad feet under our table. I wasn't sure if everybody else was laughing at the performer or us.

The car ride home was painfully silent and I knew the sappy side of me that had emerged so easily while reading about Ruben and Ophelia had completely run dry in Rusty's company. He wanted to walk me to the door, but I used my usual "the porch light is broken so would you mind sitting here and shining your headlights on the door so I can see to get in" routine. Naturally, wanting to be a gentleman, most men usually oblige without argument. It has always been my standard practice never to put a bulb in the front porch light.

Chapter 8
"Revelations"

I had forgotten to leave a light on in the living room. I dropped my purse in the dark foyer and fumbled for the switch.

"Don't..." was all I heard and it took my heart about half a beat to start racing double time. Just one word, but it was sharp like a dagger, cold like ice, and cutting like a razor, straight through to my soul. I looked up and nearly fainted. I wanted to run or scream...something other than just stand there, but I was frozen. My legs felt like blocks of concrete. He was standing as still as a statue in the far left corner of the entryway. I felt like a deer staring down the barrel of a hunter's gun. The whites of his eyes shone against his dark skin and the shadow of the charcoal grey hooded sweatshirt he wore, while the black pupils burned with rage. We both stood motionless, waiting for the other to move. Though the hood of his sweatshirt was drawn tightly around his face, I could see enough of the shape of it and recognized him by the one word he'd spoken. Willie.

I ran over every scenario in my head in a second. I'd locked the deadbolt with a key, so I knew I couldn't open the door before he got to me. There was no way I was a physical match for him. Somewhere in the back of my mind I realized I could still hear Rusty's engine. I had to signal him. It felt like we had been standing there staring at each other for an eternity, but I knew it had only been a few seconds. I also knew there were only a few seconds left before Rusty would be out of sight.

I reached up for the foyer light switch and started flashing it frantically before he was on me.

"Willie, you don't want to do this!" I screamed.

"You gonna be all high and mighty and threaten me with doin' time in front of my boys, then I might as well make it worth it." Somewhere it registered in the back of my mind that the day I had gone to the jail to meet with him there were two other men in the cell. I had threatened him. He must have been humiliated. I berated him like a child in front of his gang. Whimsically, I dared him to cross me again, treating him like the fourteen-year-old boy I once knew him to be. Revenge.

He grabbed my hair and dragged me away from the windows and into the kitchen. I was kicking my feet the whole way, trying to stand up so I could run. "You want a reason to put me away, lawyer lady, I'll give you a reason, I got your reason tonight." "You think you know me, You think your better than me? I got something for you. You gonna know me real good too...White trash, stupid lawyer whore think you can disrespect me in front of my boys. I got you now, don't I? Right here is your reason, he started ripping at my clothes and unzipping his pants. You're not better than me...and you sure ain't better than my boys."

"Willie...stop! Please...stop! Stop!" It was too late. I didn't even see his fist coming until I heard the smack as he punched me hard on the right side of my face. He used the handful of my hair to flip me off my back and onto my knees to get a better angle and then the blows came...again and again...pummeling my face, every time yelling, swearing at me, "You got a reason now, don't you?"

I remember hitting the cool hardwood floor when he let go of my hair. The last thing I saw was his steel-toed boot coming at my face. Instinctively, I covered myself with my hands so the blows were diverted to my ribs. The obscenities were flying, but I couldn't really hear them clearly anymore. Everything seemed to slow down and blur in and out of focus.

Then next thing I heard that made any sense was Rusty's voice. "You move again and I'll gut you like a fish." The kitchen light bounced off the blade of the biggest butcher knife I had in my kitchen. The words sounded so calm and deadly serious. He hadn't even raised his voice, but there was no need. There was no doubt he would have done it without hesitation. I was still lying on the floor, but I managed to turn my head and see Willie at my eye level about three feet away. Rusty was standing over him, with a sandaled foot in the middle of his back and his head wrenched back with the butcher knife mere inches from his throat. His peripheral vision must have enabled him to see me move, but he didn't take his eyes off Willie.

"An ambulance is on the way. Stay still."

"No problem," I groaned. I tried to focus on the ceiling, but I could tell my eyes were nearly swollen shut. The pain in my ribs felt like a dagger stabbing me when I took a deep breath and I could taste blood in my mouth.

* * *

The doctor was stitching my lip when Phil walked in.

"How is she?"

I didn't bother to turn my head to look at him it would just hurt to try and open my eyes anyway. It wasn't like I could talk to him with a needle going in and out of my lip, but Dr. Sullivan glanced up from his work.

"She'll live. We x-rayed her from head to toe just to be sure. Two broken ribs on her right side, sprained left wrist, her face is gonna be black and blue for a while, and a laceration here at the corner of her mouth. All in all, I'd say she's very lucky."

"Was she...umm...umm...you know?" Phil couldn't even say the words, but both Dr. Sullivan and I got his meaning. I pulled against the tugging of my lip and turned my head.

"Rusty, was in time...he didn't rape me," I whispered, embarrassed and terrified to even say the words.

Phil breathed a sigh of relief and I went back to staring at the bright white light over my face through my barley open lids.

"He's going away, Ang." There was audible disdain in the declaration.

I closed my eyes and nodded, remembering how cavalier I had been when I promised Phil I'd threaten Willie. I was regretting everything I had said now. A regret that was slowly turning to bitter fear.

The next voice I heard was Janice. If I could have rolled my eyes, I would have. I knew Phil had found out through the police department, but Rusty must have called Janice.

"Are you keeping her overnight?" she asked.

I answered for Dr. Sullivan. "No, they are not."

The doctor smiled at me as he tied off the stitches. "I guess not, he conceded, but not to look defeated he clarified.

She should be okay at home. Like I was telling Phil, she's lucky."

Janice opened her purse to answer her cell phone.

"Oh hey! Yes, she's fine." She paused. "Yes, I'm looking at her right now. She's a sight, but the doctor says she's lucky." She paused again, listening. "The guy's over at the jail...still booking him in, I guess. Yes, I'll thank Rusty for you." She stopped talking and handed me the phone. It's your grandfather."

I glared at her through the swollen slits of my eyes. She could read them clearly even through the narrowed space. She knew exactly what I was thinking, and how many daggers I was throwing at her. "Hey, us grandparents stick together," she said with no apology at all.

"Hey Grandpa, I'm so sorry they called you." My lips were sore and swollen and it was hard to sound like myself, but I knew he needed me to sound normal, to act normal and be okay.

"Yes, I'm fine...Yes, I promise...Yes, I'll call you tomorrow.

I love you too." I flipped the phone shut and gave Janice a dirty look when I handed it back to her.

Dr. Sullivan had stepped out, promising to be right back when he picked up on the wordless disagreement she and I were having. We waited in tense silence until he returned.

"Here you go, some pain pills for tonight and a prescription for some more that you can get filled tomorrow. Be sure not to drive and go right to bed after you take them."

"I promise."

"And I'll make sure of it," Janice volunteered.

I wanted to object, but I could tell I had no say in the matter. She would insist on spending the night on my couch. It was hard to stay mad at her when I knew deep down how much she really cared.

I dozed off in the car and by the time we got to my house, I was feeling woozy from the drugs.

"What happened to my door?" I asked, seeing for the first time that the glass was broken out and scattered all over the porch.

"Rusty had to break it in." I think from the look on my battered swollen face she could tell that I didn't want to talk about it anymore tonight.

When I finally got in bed, the pain medication and my dreams took me to scary places. I spent most of the night running from Willie and faceless slaves through thick white cotton fields in the back of my house. I was running for home, but never quite made it to the door. My eyes popped open many times, as wide as they were able. Sweat was pouring off me and my heart pounded as I recalled the sheer terror I'd felt. I realized that even with my eyes open, I could still see Willie's face staring at me as still as a stone surrounded by the darkness.

I woke mid-morning to find Janice gone and a note next to a bottle of pain pills in the kitchen. She hadn't wanted to wake me, so she left the pills and quietly slipped out to work. I could tell by the label on the bottle that she'd taken my prescription to the pharmacy where I used to work, so I figured I was probably the talk of the town by now. Not wanting to think about it, I took two of the pills and went back to bed.

I woke at seven-thirty that evening. Instead of feeling the pain in my ribs, what I noticed first was a bitterness and anger welling up inside me. Before I had a chance to explore it and give it a voice, the phone rang. In the time it took me to reach over and answer it, my brain processed what was wrong and I was stuck in the same old place. Most of the time I could cover it up, lie to myself and push the feelings away, but not today...maybe not ever again.

"Peanut, you gave me quite a scare! That's not a smart move given my age." He tried to laugh and make the conversation easy, but he sounded too nervous to achieve the desired effect.

"Hi Grandpa, I'm fine," I lied.

"No, you're not and I'm not talking about the bruises that Janice told me about. He waited in silence. *Dang it! Why did he have to pick up on every little thing?*

"I'm fine, Grandpa. I promise." It sounded a little too annoyed to be true.

"I'm going to sit here quietly until you're ready to talk about it. Ang, you know I'm not going anywhere until I know you're okay. I know you better than you think. I know how you think and you know that's true, so you might as well just say it. We never have and maybe today we should. Maybe today I'm going to keep calling until we do."

"Fine," I snapped at him. "You want to know, I'll tell you! If I was married and carrying my baby inside that house behind my husband, this never would have happened." The bitterness and anger I woke up with now had a voice.

"Single white woman attacked in her own home by a young black man is not something people would be saying about me all over town today if the word '*single*' was not a factor."

He was silent and I wondered if he was still there until he sighed. "You're obsessed, Peanut. You're so focused on this you can't see anything else."

We both got quiet because he didn't understand and I didn't want to yell at him. How could he know what I was going through? He was married to the love of his life for so many years. I had no idea he was seeing me from an entirely different angle. *No*, I thought bitterly, *maybe he does know me well enough to how I'm feeling, but he certainly doesn't know how it feels.*

"You can't bring him back, Angie. You can marry twenty men and your dad will still have died when you were a kid. You can have twenty babies and your baby sister will still be gone. You've been trying to make a family to replace yours for so long that I think you don't even know that you're doing it...and now you've gotten to the point where you can't see anything but what you don't have. I'll tell you what you have — you have a job that requires you to not be everybody's friend. You have a job that sometimes makes people mad. Let's say you did have a husband who went in the door first and you were carrying a baby...well, they might have been victims too and gotten worse than you got. This isn't about you not having a husband, Ang, it's about you letting go of what has been gone a long time now.

I started to cry. He waited in silence. We never say it. We never talk about it out loud. *Why is he making me face this today?*

It was like a brick wall had been knocked down in my heart, like a light coming through a window that had been opaque. At that moment, all I wanted were my bricks back up. I knew he saw right through me.

"Okay, even if you're right, even if I am trying to subconsciously...*replace* what was lost, what's wrong with that?

What's wrong with me wanting a husband to protect me and a baby to love?"

It took him a minute to form his answer. "Because, Ang, nobody can love you like your dad did and no baby will ever be your Sissy. I remember your mom saying from the day Sissy was born that you were a little mother to her, but that's wrong, Ang. You were *not* her mother and her dying is not your responsibility.

"I knew it," he said. "Every time something tragic or happy or important happens in your life, you look for them to share it or take the pain of it or rejoice in it with you. They're gone, Ang, and no amount of anger or tragedy or joy is going to bring them back."

"Stop, Grandpa! Please, just stop! I can't think about this anymore...not today."

I was suddenly calmer now, the anger turned into a quiet resentment and I did what I always do....shut down. My tears were starting to dry and I wasn't going to try to make him understand. How could he, how could anyone?

"You don't know anything about the hollow ache of being lonely. You had Grandma forever. You never had to face any of your life alone, so I just can't explain it to you, okay?"

His tone was somewhere between hurt and deeply sad, but he let it drop. "We can leave it alone for now." There was a long silence, but in the quiet there might as well have been a million words. I knew I needed his help, but I was too ashamed to tell him about it.

Again, he knew there was more and again he waited patiently, quietly. There was something else on my mind and I just wanted to get it all out, I fought the shame and said it anyway. At least it was a change of subject, not a good one, but very different from my typical recurring, shut down kind of pain, this was new. The tears started again, but I wasn't sure if they were because of sadness or humiliation.

"I had dreams last night about black men chasing me...always black men." My tone was angry and I think some of it was that I was angry with myself. I'd never faced these feelings before either. I was still sobbing a little, but my words were clear enough. His patience was endless as he sat listening.

"A few days ago when Janice told me I had a client over in jail, before I saw Phil I had already pictured him as being a black man. Why did I assume my shoplifting, repeat offender criminal was black? Why were the men in my dream last night all black? Why do I feel anger and resentment towards every black man I have ever defended? Right now even the innocent ones seem guilty."

He sighed again, this time like there was heavy weight in the words to follow. "So much anger in you right now, Peanut. Don't go down that road. If you want to be angry that your dad and your sister are gone, go ahead...but don't want a husband for that reason. Don't have a baby that you're not ready to have for that reason. If you want to be mad that you were attacked by a man, then be mad, but not this way...not against anyone but him...*only* him.

"I want to tell you something I've never told you before. All these years nobody has ever known. My brother was a troubled man, held grudges, became bitter, couldn't see beyond his own anger. He died in prison in Alabama, where I was born and raised. I left and came up here when I was nineteen years old just to get away from it. He was a Klan member. He was full of hate and it killed him, just like you're dying inside now because you're jealous of your friend's husbands and children, resentful of the black man who would have taken your life. He was not a *black* man, Ang, he was a *BAD* man—a bad man who will be punished."

I cut him off. A million thoughts, questions, emotions, and accusations went spinning through me. What was he saying, my mind couldn't make it make sense, I just couldn't wrap myself around it, but with the questions came memories and then in an instant a bit of clarity. I knew it was true.

"So that's why you never talked to Miss Claudia about being raised in Messina? That's why you never talked about your side of the family? You lied?" I didn't give him a chance to answer.

"What are you saying...that racism is born in me? That it's in my DNA? Is that why I picture my clients as black in my subconscious mind before I meet them? Am I a closet racist hypocrite?" I was sarcastic and yelling at him, which was totally out of character for our relationship. "How could you hide this from me all these years?"

"I'm telling you now, Angie, because you need to know. If you keep harboring the hurt over your dad and the anger over what happened last night, you'll never have any peace. Stop trying to change the past. Believe me, I've tried. Your great uncle died in misery because of his hate. He couldn't let things go either, Ang, and he died in prison because of it. You have tangled every feeling you have together...related or not...and you have to start unraveling how you really feel or you're going live in it forever. You have to let go, Angie. For your own sanity, let it go...all of it."

"I have to go," was all I could say. The conversation had been too much. I hurt inside and out. "I love you, Grandpa, but I can't talk about this anymore."

"I love you too, Peanut."

Chapter 9

"Ruben"

Three days later when I walked in the entrance hall of the courthouse, Janice was looking at me funny. I forced myself out of bed and back to work so I would stop thinking about my conversation with my grandfather. I'd spent three days either awake thinking about my dad, my imagined husband, and whether or not I was a racist or asleep having nightmares. I didn't even touch the journal for fear the images in it would bleed over into my dreams. Despite my situation, I was still hoping for a happy ending—for Annabeth and for me. An hour after my alarm went off this morning and plastering on way too much make-up, I left home, driving against the doctor's orders.

"I can't stay home forever. I have to face it sometime," She looked doubtful as I, passed by her desk at a turtle's pace. My guess was that she was likely wondering if I was just a glutton for punishment. She'd called me "hard-headed" during many a flu season when I came in sick, but she didn't know this time I was hurting in more ways than she could see in the bruises on my face. What she did know is that I had a date with Rusty the other night. I was sure that as soon as things got back to normal, she'd be asking me about it. I was also sure she cared too much about me to think of mentioning it now. *Grandpa's right*, I sighed. *No man will ever measure up to my dad.* The last thing my sore jaw felt like talking about was another bad date.

Mercifully, she looked at my shuffled gait and less-than-stellar appearance and said, "Lunch?"

It was her welcome back and her gift to me to let me pass with no questions or protest about my coming back to work when we both knew it was too soon.

"Sure," I answered as normally as I could through my still swollen lips. "How 'bout we order in from that new chicken sandwich place?" Just before the stairwell door swung shut, I could see the mix of emotion on her face. She was relieved that I was up and about amongst the living and worried that her intuition told her something else might be going on.

* * *

I love the law and being a public defender is often rewarding. Helping people who would otherwise not be able to afford counsel is a good feeling; however, today I spent a fourteen-hour day tied up with a woman accused of neglecting her child due to her drug and alcohol problems. I chastised myself all day for noticing she was black and before I could stop myself, instantly feeling disdain towards her. I knew in my heart that her color had nothing to do with the fact she was a deadbeat mother. I'd seen that kind in every color. The one plus was that the long day was a distraction from my physical wounds.

I wondered if I was ever going to make a dent in life's injustices...including my own. I sat at my desk, thinking about what my grandfather had said and began to resent it more and more. Deep down I knew he was right about everything. It's just harder some days when all around you is a sea of paired-off people who take one another for granted. Women and men who make babies and take no responsibility for their care are the worst kind of paired-off people. I knew that because it was my client's first offense —that we knew of anyway—and because she was willing to go to rehab, she probably wouldn't serve any time in jail. I also knew that most likely she'd lose her child to Social Services and foster parents. Tough not to think about that when you're the one who has to do all the paperwork to clean up the mess of someone else's life.

Grandpa was also right about my thoughts and feelings about everything in my life being too connected. The client being black and throwing her kid away and the anger I felt over both didn't really line up until the incident with Willie...until Grandpa explained it to me. Why couldn't I see this in myself before? Like it or not, I could see it now, like a neon sign. It's my job, it shouldn't be personal. As far as I knew, it never had been. Now I would work hard to make it not be.

I decided not to focus on the work thing and focus on the single thing. Maybe I could make some progress there. I was trying not to question God and ask 'Why others are allowed to have "perfect relationships" and children, yet here I am driving home alone again with a container of Chinese take-out on my passenger seat?' That makes it a little harder not to ask, 'Why not me?' or better yet, 'Why me? Why am I alone?'

Was I really looking for my dad? I thought about that for a minute. I do remember him as sort of perfect. When you're single and don't want to be, waking up every morning alone is like a little mini-death. I feel such a void and so alone, like someone very important is missing from my life, but it escapes me who it is. Now I wonder if it isn't my dad and my Sissy, but I just don't know if that's right because I still feel lonely when I look over and see the other pillow still perfectly fluffed, not slept on or the single plate and cup from last night's dinner left unwashed in the sink.

Just as I rounded the corner leading to the last stretch of dark road to my driveway, it occurred to me that I resented my client for throwing away what I wished I had. It's stupid, I guess, but sometimes even my sarcasm and humor can't mask everything, and Grandpa had seen right through me—apparently for years. My feelings seem to get bigger and more profoundly evident when my personal struggle with solitude collides with my work, especially when the thoughts of Willie, who I am trying to see as only a *bad* man and not a *black* man, come screaming back into my mind. *Dang! I almost made it home without tying up my life and my work again.* Life was so much simpler when I had no idea about my own head. I love my grandpa, but I really hate it that he knows me better than I know myself right now. I owe him an apology and probably a thank you.

My loneliness brought my thoughts to the journal and the love between Annabeth and her unborn child, and Ruben and Ophelia. They would keep me company tonight. Annabeth's words brought me comfort, not only because they were true, but also because if love can happen to them in another time and place, it could happen to me today. *If love that strong has always existed, then maybe it exists somewhere for me.*

I turned off the car's engine and switched off my headlights. I tried not to focus on the plywood covering the broken window on the door. As I looked towards the front window of my living room, I saw Keno's eyes shining and his tail wagging. I grabbed my take-out and went inside. "At least somebody loves me," I rubbed his ears almost thanking him for being there, trying to pull myself out of my bitter, self-imposed misery. We bonded over some sweet and sour chicken and by the end of my meal and a warm bath that took some of the ache out of my ribs, I was feeling a little better and ready to see what Annabeth had to say next.

February 17, 1863

It's early in the morning, my precious. I have risen before the sun to write to you. Last evening I was forced to sit up late playing the piano for my mother's parents, your great-grandparents, the Lagoys. Thankfully, they will be leaving at sun up. Whenever they are here, I feel like I am required to perform like a well-trained dog, displaying only my best manners, talents, and intellect. It was difficult this time because of our circumstances. I am afraid that my body is beginning to show signs of fatigue. You are still so tiny that my midsection remains unchanged, but I am beginning to feel your presence in the very core of my being. I will have to tell someone soon and I believe that someone will be your grandmother, Ophelia, but before I tell her my secret, I must tell you how she told my mother of hers.

Ophelia and Ruben had been sneaking out and secretly meeting one another for months after their exchange of vows. He loved her more than his own life and she felt the same for him. I could never imagine hiding a love as deep and passionate as theirs— that is, until I felt it for your father.

My father did very little in the way of overseeing the plantation. He was more of a businessman and spent a great deal of time either in his study going over his finances or away trying to make the best deals for the cotton his slaves worked themselves nearly to death to plant and harvest. Although he was the youngest boy in his family, my father would inherit the entire plantation and all the duties associated with it. Both of his brothers, my uncles, had bitterly disappointed my grandfather. They left for the rapidly growing industry of the North to seek their *fortune. Grandfather McGrath was aging quickly and preferred to spend his days in leisurely fashion. He gradually gave up control of the plantation and allowed my father to run it in his place. This did not however stop his interfering entirely, much to Father's dismay. He gave his opinion on matters that pertained to how Father managed both the plantation and his personal affairs. Most of the time, he and Grandmother simply became the hosts of our home. They were known for their social activities and gave many fine parties.*

Running the affairs of such a large estate alone became a burdensome task, so Father hired a foreman to assist him. They were kindred spirits, my father and his foreman. Both strict taskmasters who didn't believe in wasting one moment of moneymaking daylight. The foreman's name is David Kincaid. The slaves know him only as "Master David." He was hired to take over the fields and slaves, while Father handled the business and finances.

David Kincaid carried a whip that hung from the waistband of his trousers and dangled down his right leg. It made a swishing noise as he walked. He wanted the male slaves to fear him and the women to submit to him. It was not long before Master David began to take advantage of his position as far as the female slaves were concerned. He was often seen crouched in the bushes that ran along the water's edge behind the slave quarters, watching the women bathe. He immediately took a particular interest in one…Ophelia.

One evening it was nearly dusk when Ruben was returning from the fields. Master David saw him walking and seeing he was the only one of the McGrath's possessions not otherwise occupied, accused him of being lazy and insubordinate.

Ruben tried to explain that he was going to the barn to replace the shovel that he had been using. He had worked so hard that day clearing a new field that his shovel had become quite dull from striking against the roots and rocks that lay just beneath the hard Georgia clay. Clearing new land was back-breaking work and usually given to only the strongest men, while the others planted the already broken earth. Ruben was one of the best field hands my father had ever purchased and one of the strongest.

Master David was determined that if he could break him, the others would fall in line. He ignored Ruben's reasoning and dragged him to the whipping post beside the barn. Ruben allowed his hands to be tied, even though he could have easily defended himself. Ophelia later explained to me that he was afraid resistance might make things worse for the others. Master David stopped all work on the plantation and even sent one of the field hands inside to gather the house servants. They all congregated and were horrified to see

Ruben standing there, shackled to the pole. He was charged with the crime of laziness. Master David and his whip were his judge and jury. He untied the whip from his waistband while silent tears fell down Ophelia's face. Just before the first lash ripped open the skin on his back, Ruben looked over at her and shook his head, his expression begging her to keep quiet and safe.

Ophelia sneaked across the path between the slaves' quarters under the cover of a moonless night. Until dawn, she cleaned and dressed her love's torn, bleeding skin. The tears rolled down her cheeks, falling into his wounds. She tried to sob quietly so that her presence would go unnoticed. The slaves knew that life on the plantation had changed. Mr. Jackson, as they called my father, was strict, but usually harmless as long as the work was done.

Master David not only wanted the work done, but dominion over every breath the slaves took.

Two days later, while Ophelia was bathing herself, she noticed Master David in his usual spot crouched behind the bushes. As always, she pretended not to notice him, but simply turned her back to his prying eyes. It was a dark night, lit only by the stars. Ruben knew she would be in the water and quietly crept from his bed to join her. He nearly tripped over Master David in the bushes. Ruben, who was normally calm and gentle, lost control of himself. He punched Master David in the face several times leaving him bleeding and nearly unconscious. He was ashamed of losing control that way and worried Ophelia would be angry with him for putting himself in danger. He crept back to his cot and waited for the consequences the morning would bring. The price would prove to be far too high.

The next morning at sunup, Master David stood outside with his bruised, swollen face, and ego. He had just awakened in the bushes and the memories of Ruben beating him came back. Knowing it was too early for work to begin, all of the slaves came out wondering why someone was clanging the dinner bell at such an odd hour. This time my mother and father were also in attendance. Once again, Ruben was singled out of the crowd and bound to the pole. Master David informed my father that the beating he had received came from Ruben's hands. Despite his battered face, you could easily see the rage as Master David walked over and ripped off Ruben's shirt. Once again, he pulled out his whip. Upon seeing the raw, open wounds on Ruben's back, my father asked Master David if he insisted on punishing him in the same manner as before. The irate foreman stopped and looked around at the horrified faces. He agreed that whipping Ruben again might cause the loss of a day's work, so he decided that if one of the others was willing, they could take the well-deserved *thrashing. Ruben yelled for them to all hold their tongues and be still, but Ophelia was already in motion. She removed a piece of clothing with every step. She stood naked from the waist up and was unashamed, of either her nudity in front of the others or her Rubens actions. She knew whatever the reason for the beating he had received Master David was more than deserving. She also knew Master David would likely have beaten her beloved Ruben to death, but would perhaps have mercy on a woman.*

Ruben yelled at her to get back as she defiantly stood between him and the end of Master David's whip, her naked back exposed. My mother screamed and ran to cover Ophelia, begging my father for mercy. My father grabbed her arm and practically threw her to the ground, saying this was not her business — it was for the men to decide. My father asked Kincaid if he would feel vindicated if this woman took the lashings. Seeing Ruben's love for Ophelia, Master David agreed. He knew he could have beaten Ruben to death and not hurt him as badly as whipping Ophelia would.

She screamed when the whip ripped her flesh. Ruben fought the men who were holding him back. They all knew that if he broke free, he would kill Master David, but then he'd be hanged later. It was almost as if revenge took over reason and David, the cruel "Master," lost control of himself. His arm flailed the whip across Ophelia's back again and again until she went limp and fell to her knees. My mother sobbed and begged my father to make him stop. When Ophelia was no longer able to hold her head up, the relentless beating finally ceased.

Ruben was sold two days later. Master David convinced my father that Ruben was a troublemaker and keeping him would only serve to incite the others. My father conferred with his father and after seeing the bruises on the foreman's face, my grandfather agreed. The three of them seemed to forget about the broken, beaten skin on both Ruben and Ophelia. They also agreed the other slaves would learn the lesson that disobedience would not be tolerated. Ruben's fate set an example of how things would be from that day forward.

Despite my father's warning that she was not to interfere, my mother secretly nursed Ophelia for two days while he was away from the plantation. She hid Ophelia in the basement, fed her, brought her fresh water, and washed her wounds. It was nearing harvest season and like all the wealthy plantation owners, Jackson McGrath would soon need fresh hands to tend his cotton. He went in search of a new field hand to replace Ruben. It was during this time of recuperation that Ophelia confided to her best friend, Emmaline that she was with child. That child was your father.

I am sorry that I am unable to tell you more about your grandfather Ruben. For Ophelia's sake, my mother did her best to discover his whereabouts, but my father dismissed her, saying it was the business of men to determine the fate of slaves. About a month later, Father received a letter from an address my mother did not recognize, postmarked from somewhere in South Carolina. Fearful of enraging Father if she got caught, she took a chance and decided to open it. The letter was from a man who was obviously a foreman at a large cotton plantation. He had written to inform my father that the big, strapping slave he had promised would be an asset to his harvest had escaped and they never found him. It was assumed he had made his way north. The tone of the letter was irate, as if the man felt that Jackson McGrath had purposely cheated him. Mother smiled, tucked the letter inside the sleeve of her dress and then gave it to Ophelia as soon as she was able. Ophelia read it over and over, imagining Ruben a free man.

My eyes were heavy from lack of sleep and full of tears from the words I had just read. I imagined the bruises on my own face and wondered if they were any more severe than Ruben had given to David, but I couldn't see Ruben as the same monster I pictured when I thought of Willie. Their actions of aggression were nearly the same, but the reasons could not have been more different. For the first time since I was attacked, I imagined a dark angry face, but without fear in my heart. It was what I imagined Ruben would have looked like defending his Ophelia.

He wasn't a black man hitting a white man, in my imagination he was a good man punishing a bad one. When I closed my eyes and tried to picture Willie, I still felt the fear of his dark angry face, but I could also find compassion for Ruben...maybe that was because I had taken the first tiny step toward healing...and not just my face. I called my grandpa.

"I'm thinking about things a little differently now." I really didn't know which things, just sorting out tangled feelings that I didn't really have words for just yet. I don't think he cared, so long as there was progress. He didn't pry and I was glad.

"I'm proud of you, Peanut," was all he needed to say for now. There really wasn't any need to beat this horse between us anymore. We both knew the problem, but not the solution.

I wished him "goodnight" after our atypically short conversation.

"Love you, Ang. Rest well."

I felt lonely when I heard the dial tone again, but I still had some thinking to do.

I was happy that there was even the remotest possibility that Ruben had escaped and sad that Ophelia was separated from him. I had to close the journal and leave both the words on the page and the stories of the people inside for a while.

I looked over at my clock and realized it was 1:00 a.m. I turned off my bedside lamp, but knew after what my imagination had just seen that very little sleep would come to me. My mind wandered to the thoughts I'd been having about love, a husband, and a family. When I let myself think about it, I knew my grandfather was right. I realized for the first time that I'd been idealizing those things for so long that I'd forgotten that love comes with a price tag, just like the ones we placed on the items we sold that belonged to Miss Claudia. Maybe that price had been too high for my client today and maybe it had been too high for the man with whom she had created her child. Maybe my price was letting go of the past and allowing myself to love in the real world instead of just dream of its perfection in my fantasies. I finally drifted off with thoughts I had never had before.

Love is not always a fairytale, not perfect. Sometimes it's the hardest job there is. I had been blindly seeking it for so long, I had never stopped to open my eyes to see what it was I was striving for—true love, the kind that Ruben and Ophelia had, but having it doesn't mean you'll be able to hang onto it. In their case, love's survival was dependent on secrecy and circumstance. I realized the love that brought them such joy also had the potential to cause them tremendous heartache.

Once again, my dreams carried me back to the faces of the oppressed souls who had once lived on this land and some who walked in my basement. I dreamed of a cruel, power-crazed man, but this time in my dreams, David Kincaid had a black man's face.

It was odd, somewhere in my mind, in my dreams I wandered from the plantation to a bare empty room. My steps echoed across the floor against the empty windowless walls. There were two men sitting in the corner and without being told I knew instantly who they were. One was David Kincaid, once again a white man, but the other's face was just as pale, but blurry and not quite there. I stood frozen in the corner farthest from the two men and watched my grandfather reach out to both of them. Despite his efforts and begging, both men slowly shriveled like old tree branches that cracked and turned to dust. My grandfather only uttered a few words.

"The other man was my brother." He hung his head in sorrow as he watched what his brother had become.

"I know," I comforted him in a calm serene voice.

"But not us, never us."

Chapter 10
"Black and White"

I awoke early with memories of my dreams still fresh and swirling around in my head. I pressed my hand over my heart and felt the pounding slow to a normal pace, but there was no fear, just an odd sense of peace to be awake and in a familiar place. I looked over at the faded pink book on my nightstand as if it too was a dream.

"Thanks for the history, Grandpa," I said in my sleepy morning voice, not sure if I really meant it or not. Every word in that journal was changing the way I felt about my own life. It was making me think about my own goals for my future and unpleasant things in my past and now my family's, already tragically written histories that despite my wanting them to be different, could never be changed. I was asking myself hard questions in my sleep, like how I really felt about love, slavery, the South, the color of a man's skin and even about living in this house. All of these thoughts forcing their way to the surface of my mind were on some mental list that I had unconsciously decided long ago either to deal with later or not at all. Now, all I could do was think about the people who lived between the pages of that journal and wonder if I would have been the master or the servant. My subconscious was knocking at the door of my dreams and it made me wonder if I would have been like Emmaline. Would I have had the courage to defy my husband and my upbringing and care for Ophelia or would I have been too afraid and simply found myself conformed to a lifestyle to which I had been born and known all of my life?

The story was not new and had presented itself in many forms throughout the ages. For the first time in my life, I felt a part of it, like a player in the game instead of a spectator. The bruises on my face and ribs were proof I was right in the middle of the action. It seems the entire world's history has been about domination—who gets to dictate and who gets to fall in line or die. Only a rare few step out of that line and make real change. I had never wondered if I would have been one of them, but I was wondering now. How could I think of myself as blindly holding a balanced scale of justice if I could only see the color of skin and why had I not noticed this about myself before if it's always been there just under my hypocritical surface. Had Willie implanted these prejudices in me or simply awakened what was already there? My pillow-top mattress was so comfortably conformed to the shape of my body I knew getting up would be difficult. I had tossed and turned and finally found a position that didn't make my ribs ache. I hated waking up ten minutes before the alarm went off. It gave me time to dread getting out of bed and to analyze my dreams, the entire spectrum of my life, and the history of the world. *Quite a big bite to chew, before I'd even had breakfast*, I thought to myself.

"Okay, Angie, get up. It's Friday. You have to do it." It sounded like an inspirational cheer as much as a fact I had to face. Keno was lying on the bottom corner of my bed. He raised his head just long enough to look at me like I was crazy for talking out loud to myself again before he flopped down and went back to sleep.

* * *

Janice's perm was beginning to relax nicely and looked pretty good this morning. Like my face, it had lost some of its puffiness. She must have been able to tell by the bags under my eyes that my makeup couldn't hide that once again I'd had a sleepless night. She had broken some ribs as teenager and remembered how hard it was to deal with the pain. I wasn't ready to tell her that wasn't the only thing making me uncomfortable at night. I went upstairs to my office, closed the door, and was almost asleep when I heard her knocking.

"Come in," I answered, without raising my head. I smelled the coffee before I looked up and saw her walk in with it.

"I know you don't like this very much, but you sure do look like you could use it," she said, placing the steaming mug on my desk. I raised my head and looked up at her, squinting my eyes as the bright sunlight streamed in through the window. As usual, she made herself at home in the chair across from me and waited for my topic.

"Janice, do you think racism is a big problem here?" I made a face while taking my first sip of the bitter, hot coffee. I never could understand how people managed to choke down something that tasted like it was squeezed from bitter beans. I mean next to a *nice* steaming cup of prune juice, in my humble opinion, coffee had to be about the worst tasting beverage in the world. I took another tiny swallow and allowed my brain to hang onto that ridiculous train of thought for a few moments. I suppose my eyes must have been focused on Janice, yet I managed to look right through her.

After about a minute of being lost in thought, the intensity of her gaze made me realize that she had been staring at me the entire time. I must have been truly engrossed in my scholarly comparison of the coffee bean and the prune. I finally forced my weary brain to focus because despite my short attention span, I was actually very interested in her answer. My daydreaming had initially caused me to miss the half-confused, half-concerned look on her face. I was also unsure if she had answered my question. The only thing I was certain about was that I had to get a decent night's sleep soon.

"What's going on with you, Ang?" She was trying to sound mad, but I could also hear the worry. "You've been dragging in here every morning, not that anyone expects you to be here at all. A few days ago you were late for the first time ever. Now, all of a sudden you want to know all about pregnancy and racism and you can't even seem to remember to bring in your standard orange juice and donut." She sat back and studied me intensely. "You've been working here for years and I have never seen you forget breakfast. Come on now, what's up? Are you okay, I mean really okay? Anybody would be shook up after what happened to you. Are you sure you don't want to talk about it? Are you sure you shouldn't take some more time off?"

I decided to answer her questions with a question because that seemed to be all I had these past few days. "Doesn't it strike you as odd that we must have at least seven churches in this little town and everybody knows which ones are black and which ones are white?" I didn't give her a chance to answer as my brain was starting to wake up from the coffee and I wanted to finish before the caffeine wore off.

"You remember when I graduated from high school? Every year before 1990, we had a black prom and a white prom." I held my hands palm up, as if holding the weight of the concept on an imaginary scale. "Nobody ever questioned it or thought it was odd, it was just the way things were. I'll never forget the big hoopla because my senior class wanted to have ours together. I mean, you remember all the TV stations and reporters trying to stop our cars on the way to the gym to interview us?" I tried to tune out my taste buds as I took another sip of the coffee. "I remember going into that lunch room everyday and the black kids sitting on the right and the white kids sitting on the left. It's not like there were signs posted or anything, but everybody just knew where they were supposed to sit."

Janice had no idea what had brought all of this on, but I could tell by the look on her face she knew exactly what I was talking about. "I suppose some towns in the South are better than others in the way of progress," She took a weighted thoughtful breath and sighed. "Peach County isn't as bad as some, but it's not as good as others. I've seen the colors of this community interact a lot longer than you have," her conviction on the subject reminding me that she had lived here forever and a day.

"When I was in high school, I will never forget the day a tornado ripped through the middle of town. People, mostly business owners, lost everything. My junior class volunteered to help clean up the mess for at least a month of Saturdays and we worked side by side, black and white together. Some of the churches were destroyed, but it didn't matter if you were a member or not, everybody volunteered their time to help rebuild in anyway they could. I remember thinking that it wasn't a black town or a white town, it was just *our* town and we needed to come together to rebuild it."

She took another deep breath, without the weight, almost carefree and I could see she remembered the days of unity fondly, however fleeting they were. "It seems folks forget how much we really are alike and need each other until there's a reason to remember." I could tell by her tone that it was an issue to which she'd given more than a few hours of meaningful thought. After all, she had seen the South come through quite a few years of setbacks and progress. She was a witness to things I had only read about.

"Why all this talk anyway?" she asked, stepping out of her role as head of the grapevine and into the one of just being my friend. I was certain she was genuinely concerned and I hated to worry her, but I still had no answer. There was no way I could sum up everything I was feeling in just a few minutes. I could see her thought process deepened when I didn't respond. She was mulling something over, but I wasn't quite sure just what.

"You need to take the rest of the day off. You never did have time with all your moving and your grandfather being here to grieve properly for Miss Claudia and now this." She motioned to my bruised face. "You must be exhausted, that's all." She moved around my desk to where I was sitting. Even though she is much smaller than I am, without touching any part of me that hurt, she carefully pulled me out of my chair and ushered me to my office door. "There's nothing pressing on your schedule today. I'll tell Phillip you're not feeling well, like he doesn't already know it. You just go on home now and get some sleep. By the looks of those red, baggy eyes, you haven't had any for awhile."

"I didn't realize I looked *that* bad," I called up the stairwell behind me, trying to be good-natured, even though I knew I did look pretty awful.

Janice always wanted the scoop, but I knew in my heart, she was sincerely troubled by my new, odd behavior. I also had no doubt that she would keep trying until she got the whole story out of me. She loved to gossip, but Janice could also keep a secret when it counted most.

I must have been tired because as soon as my head hit my pillow, I was asleep. The next thing I knew it was 4:00 o'clock in the afternoon. I got up and went to the bathroom only to discover that I hadn't washed my face before going to bed and not one tiny bit of my makeup was where I'd put it that morning. It looked like my entire face had shifted about two inches south. Between that, the swelling, and the multi-colored bruises, I hardly recognized myself. I filled the tub with bubbles and filled the room with lavender-scented candles. I closed the drapes and sank down into the steamy water. When I lifted my head off my inflatable pillow, I was chilly and realized I had once again fallen asleep. I warmed up the water and washed my face and then decided I also needed to brush the stale coffee taste out of my mouth.

I was starving, but had no energy to fix dinner, so I ordered a pizza from our local pizzeria. They don't usually deliver, but the owner is a friend of mine and lives just down the street. If I call before they close at seven, he doesn't mind stopping just long enough to hand me a veggie lover's with extra cheese out the window of his car. We have a deal: I give him free legal advice and I get an occasional free pizza. He owes me a few more since his employee slipped and fell in his kitchen a few weeks ago. Since I hadn't seen him since Willie's visit, I was sure he'd also want to get a look at me. I knew he cared, but sometimes we all fall victim to that small town curiosity. Even if he was busy, I knew I'd get a pizza tonight.

I sat on the porch swing waiting on my dinner and thinking about the black and white situation in our town. It suddenly dawned on me that we could be any town. These were age-old problems and questions that could exist anywhere on the map—or the planet for that matter. People have always been fighting over a few shades of difference in their skin color. Why should Peach County be any different? It started over a hundred years ago and Annabeth's journal was proof of it. Maybe it just seems more real here because the blood and the roots run so deep into the clay. Maybe a hundred years isn't long enough for the human condition to recuperate from such a catastrophic illness. Maybe my own guilt over southern roots I didn't even know I had that left blood and tears and hate in Alabama were making me over-analyze everything. I jumped at the sound of a car horn and realized my pizza had arrived. One thing for sure, I may not have the answer to racism or be able to come to terms with my own genetic link, no matter how far removed, but it's clearly black and white that my mind wanders way too much. I decided that's why things other folks seem to be able to put away bother me so much. My subconscious always keeps meandering back to the shelf, not to mention wondering about how much I was personally affected by what I thought was an issue other people dealt with. I wish Grandpa had never told me about his brother—or maybe I wished his brother could have been the same kind of man as my grandpa.

Chapter 11
"The Plan"

I had eaten way too much pizza. My stomach reminded me that I
hadn't had anything except that nauseating coffee since early
this morning, but now I was stuffed and I was wide awake after
having slept all day. With my cable finally connected, I eased
down on my overstuffed couch and turned on the tube, hoping to
turn off my brain. I started watching TV, but as it always does,
my gray matter separated itself from my conscious thought. All I
could think about was the pink diary on my bedside table. I
stopped fighting it about 9:00 p.m. when I realized it was either
sports or a crime show. I hated sports and I got my fill of crime
watching at work, so I switched off the TV and went upstairs.

February 18, 1863

*I am unable to eat today. I fear that someone
is going to notice my poor appetite and frequent
need for an afternoon nap. I am hiding you, my
little one. I will protect you as long as I am able. I
miss your father today more than I can tell you.
We hear stories of the war from those lucky few
who have actually returned. I stand outside my
father's study while he talks to some of the men
who run other neighboring plantations. They often
discuss the negative impact of the fighting on their
finances. I wait, silently hoping for some word,
any word, of your father's troops. I want to make
sure that you understand exactly what your*

grandmother Ophelia did to ensure your father's safety when he was born. I only wish I felt he were as safe now.

When Ophelia disclosed to my mother that she was expecting, the two women devised a plan about how they would hide her condition. My father had been gone for two days and returned on the third with a new slave to take Ruben's place. During Father's absence, Mother and Ophelia concocted a scheme that they hoped would spare Ophelia's life and that of her unborn child. My father had seen his father put female slaves to death rather than support their convalescence during a pregnancy and after the birth. My grandfather believed that no matter how hard she worked, a pregnant woman was not able to do the same amount of work as one who was not. My father adopted his father's way of thinking and made that fact perfectly clear to his slaves. No babies. No mouth would be fed that did not work.

They decided that the only way to get Ophelia out of the fields and the slave quarters and back into the house near Emmaline was for her to allow herself to also become pregnant. They thought that if my mother was also expecting, my father would have to allow Ophelia to be by her side, in her service. He was often traveling or too busy running the affairs of the plantation to be bothered with a burdensome woman.

Their only real concern was my grandparents. They needed to figure out a way to remove the elder McGraths from the house. Their entire lives revolved around the plantation and the intimate details of the lives of everyone in it. My mother knew that Grandmother McGrath most certainly would have volunteered to care for her if she were indeed to find herself in the family way. Although my grandfather had long ago stepped aside to allow my father to run the McGrath fields and business, he still managed to keep himself involved, however indirectly it appeared.

My mother wrote to my uncle Clayton, my father's eldest brother who lived up North. She explained in some detail that Grandfather was working too hard on the plantation. Since he seemed to be aging so quickly, she suggested that it might be better for both he and Grandmother to stay with him for a while. Mother implied it would be sort of a forced rest and would be best not to mention her concerns to either Jackson or their parents. The letter was so eloquently written and spoke in such great detail of her concerns and the strain of life on the plantation that no son who cared for his parents could have refused her.

She received an answer within three weeks. Uncle Clayton swore to her he would never mention her true intent and after a great deal of convincing and conniving on her part, my grandparents went North to live and retire to a life *of leisure. Father needed less convincing than his parents. He simply looked at their leaving as an opportunity to have full control of the land, slaves, and business of the plantation without having to worry that his father might not approve of all of his decisions. He simply bid his parents farewell and immersed himself in his work.*

Unfortunately, it left Father even less time to spend in the fields with Master David and the slaves paid a heavy price for the foreman's increased autonomy. It was a detail my mother and Ophelia had overlooked in their plan. It was an unintentional hardship, but not one with which the other slaves were unfamiliar. They had each had the misfortune to experience all manner of cruelty due to the harsh lots they had all drawn in their lives. Over the years, Mother and Ophelia would secretly do all they could to ease the burden that being born with dark skin in the South cast upon those in its lineage.

Ophelia smiled to herself as she saw the carriage with my grandparents and their belongings leave the plantation. She would occasionally look up from the row of cotton she was harvesting to catch a glimpse of them getting farther and farther away. The thought that her friend Emmaline would do whatever was necessary for her safety and the safety of her child took her mind off her aching back and blistered fingers. She remembered all of the childhood secrets they had told one another and kept for so long and she knew this time would be no different. As she had heard my mother do many times, Ophelia prayed that the second half of their plan would also be successful and come to pass in short order as the child she and Ruben were expecting would not hide itself much longer.

When my father returned with the new slave he had purchased to replace Ruben, he noticed an odd change in my mother's behavior. She presented herself to him night after night, begging him for a child. He assumed it was because she was lonely and needed company while he was away.

Later, when my grandparents were gone and no longer provided her with a social outlet, it seemed logical to him that she would want a baby. His heart was not truly in favor of the idea, but my mother's seduction was more powerful than his will and his manhood would not allow him to turn her away. She did not realize she would tire of him so quickly.

Her nightly visits became more a labor of love for the child she hoped to produce than any display of affection towards her husband. She simply used her body as necessary and allowed her mind to wander elsewhere. Ophelia's prayers had been heard and my mother's efforts were promptly rewarded. God graciously provided for both of them. Within six weeks, my mother knew, just as

Ophelia had known, that she was with child. That child, my love, was me.

Years later, Emmaline McGrath was to become your other grandmother. They could never have known it at the time, but by conceiving their own children, Emmaline and Ophelia would someday also create a blood tie between them, stronger than any bond they had known before.

I put the book down after having read the entry. Like the facts of any case I studied, the facts of this case became quite clear. I was so obvious, duh. I put my palm to my forehead as I pieced it together. "Because Annabeth was pregnant by the son of Ophelia, she was forced not only to hide her condition, but to keep this record so that her baby would one day understand its complex and distinctive heritage. That's why she hid her condition and why she decided Ophelia would be the first to know. It's also why she felt the need to explain to her child why he or she would be different from others and face hardships in life—the baby would be half black and half white." I knew that some of the slave owners raped the slave women. I'd never heard of a young, white, wealthy plantation owner's daughter becoming pregnant by a slave. Just as the journal had done before, the answers only posed more questions. "Why wouldn't she tell her own mother first? What happened to the father of Annabeth's baby? If Jackson McGrath found out, surely he would have killed him." I felt a little crazy for saying all of this outloud to myself and the only one listening again was Keno, but hearing the words somehow made them more clear...more true. He also had eaten way too much pizza and was looking at me with those pleading brown eyes. I laid the journal aside and slid on my Birkenstocks. He knew that meant it was time for a walk. He doesn't move when the doorbell rings, but stand clear when he thinks he's going outside. He will throw all of his eighty-five pounds right on top of you to try to get to the door. I was in no condition to support his weight and mine.

It was around ten when Keno and I came in from our excursion around the yard. I could hear the phone ringing as I ambled up the front porch steps and quickly turned my slow stride into a painful trot. I kicked off my shoes in the foyer and was winded when I answered.

"Hello," I was almost too breathless to get the greeting out, holding my ribs I was hoping the person on the other end had not hung up.

"Hello, Peanut."

"Hey, Grandpa," I was happy to hear his voice as I stretched the cord of Miss Claudia's old rotary phone around the chair and slid onto the soft cushion. The old mustard-colored antique was something else Hannah had chosen to leave behind and I had many fond memories of talking to Miss Claudia on it, so I kept it within reach. I was now using it to make more memories with my grandfather. For a split second, remembering the empty feeling I got when both my grandmother and Miss Claudia died, I asked him the standard question I'm sure all people over eighty get sick of answering, "Are you alright? Have you been feeling okay?"

He laughed. "I think I should be asking you that, kiddo, but just to get it out of the way...I'm fine, my health is fine, the cat is fine, and I'm eating well and taking care of myself. Does that about cover the next portion of the quiz?" At least he was good-natured about my concern, even if his answer was a little condescending.

"That about does it," I answered sarcastically. "Okay, what's so important you want to skip our normal healthcare banter?" I asked, anxious to get to the real reason for his call. I knew it, I just wanted to hear him say it. No need to answer questions he didn't ask and worry him with my mental quest for the answer to worldwide racial harmony. He kindly skipped the hard parts about my dad and Sissy and the whole family bit and started on a topic he thought was lighter. Wrong. No matter how hard we tried, once we opened that box, I knew we would have to start sorting through the years of hurt we'd stored in it. He started light, but I knew it would evolve into a conversation we'd needed to have for years.

"I was just wondering if you've started going through the box yet? I read bits and pieces of it the afternoon I brought it home when you stayed behind to clean up. I've been waiting for you to call me and tell me all about it. But it seems like..." *ahem*, he cleared his throat... "stuff keeps getting in the way."

I took a deep breath, hardly knowing where to begin. "How much time have you got?" I asked, kind of joking and kind of hoping he'd say as long as I needed. Remembering he was a night owl like me, I hoped he would choose the latter.

"You just start talking, Peanut," he said, giving me the answer I wanted to hear. It was then I knew that the bits and pieces had piqued his curiosity. He wanted to know the ending just as much as I did. He told me where he had stopped reading and I told him where I was in the story. We were on the phone until 2:00 a.m. We not only discussed the facts, but analyzed them until my ear hurt from holding the phone to it. I promised to call him in a week or so when I had finished and tell him how it turned out. I was grateful my grandpa and I were kindred spirits. He was the only one who could have understood why the journal had affected me so. I knew once we had discussed Annabeth, the conversation was due for the turn I knew it was coming since I'd answered the call. Now that he had been honest about our own family history and the black and white lines drawn in the sands of time, he knew I'd be seeing the story and the people in the book from a much different perspective. I decided to tell him about my dream about David and his brother withering away in the empty room. His answer was the same mine had been to him in my sleep.

"That doesn't have to be us, Peanut, and to answer the question you first asked me... no, Ang, it's not in your DNA or mine. Whatever my brother had was in his heart, not his blood." He paused, unsure if I was ready to hear it or not, but since we had come this far, he continued. "And Willie, whatever makes him the way he is, just like my brother, it's in his heart, not his blood."

"I know, Grandpa." I sighed. "I'm trying to work it all out—the family, the baby, the loss, Willie, all of it. I need time."

"I've got plenty of time for you, Peanut. Just call."

There was more silence, but not the awkward or half-confused, angry kind we'd had before. It was just peaceful, like we'd resolved some small part of the issues we had locked away.

"I promise, Grandpa...night."

Then I heard the same empty dial tone that never failed to make me feel...empty.

A few seconds later the phone rang again, He was already talking midsentence. "Do you remember what I told you on your thirtieth birthday?" he asked, yawning.

"Yes," I replied. "This is only the millionth time you've reminded me."

"Well, let's make it a million and one," he said, preparing to repeat himself one more time. "I had sixty wonderful years with your grandmother and if I had chosen the wrong person back then, I can only imagine how much I would have regretted wasting my life with the wrong woman. You just be patient and wait for the right fella. He'll come along."

"I know, Grandpa," I was, trying to convince him as well as myself that I believed it. I felt the weights in my eyelids becoming heavier and began losing interest in the conversation since we had already covered this an hour ago. "I'll wait for just the right one and save myself the heartache," I assured him.

"Good girl," he replied. "I just remembered you saying that since I had Grandma I couldn't understand how you felt and I wanted you to know that every day since she's been gone I understand *exactly* how you feel."

My heart skipped a beat. "I'm sorry I said that, Grandpa. I was frustrated. I never thought of it that way."

"I just want you to know, Angie. I do care and I do understand." On that note, we hung up again and I dragged myself to bed. I didn't want to get my days and nights too mixed up so that I could definitely make it to church this weekend. Saturday would be gone before I knew it and Sunday morning was always here before I felt the weekend had even started. I decided long ago that I would know what kind of husband God wanted me to choose if I went to His house once in a while.

I was surprised to find myself awake in plenty of time to get ready and make it to church on Sunday without the help of my alarm, even after having stayed up late the night before. I walked in and took my usual seat. Just as before, Miss Claudia's blanket kept sneaking into my peripheral vision. After the service, I waited for the sanctuary to empty, which didn't take long as we were a small group. The preacher was still outside shaking hands when I walked over to the blanket. It hadn't been touched since the last time Miss Claudia had used it. I couldn't bear to see it draped there collecting dust anymore. I picked it up and folded it in half twice. I was just about to leave when Pastor Chapman came back in and walked up the aisle behind me.

"I was wondering when you'd take it," he said with a comforting smile as he began remembering how much Miss Claudia had meant to me. "I'll never forget trying to concentrate on my sermon while she sat there clicking those knitting needles together with her bible open on her lap and a ball of yarn beside her." We laughed together over our memories, almost forgetting the empty feeling we'd both gotten looking at her vacant spot on the pew.

"When I was older and had worked up the courage, I tried to tell her how rude that was," I assured him jokingly, attempting to stick up for myself.

"She was a sweet lady," by the look on his face, I could tell he was thinking of his own age, wondering when he might be going to join her. He didn't seem anxious about the possibility of his own passing, just nostalgic about his old friend.

"She loved you too, Pastor." I knew he already knew that but the smile on his face told me it was good to hear the words. I hugged him as I had done many Sundays since I was a kid, took the blanket, and left.

February 21, 1863

It is hard for me to write to you everyday, my little one. On occasion, you have begun to turn my stomach into quite a string of knots. I am sure that some of my uncertainty over your existence is also a factor in my physical health. I fear everyday that my father will discover your tiny presence and I will be forced to tell him the truth of your father. I also fear for the safety of my mother. He will undoubtedly blame her for my behavior. Never doubt for one second that I would ever erase you from my body or my life, for without hardship, there would be no true joy.

Before I continue telling you the circumstances under which your father and I came to be, I must first tell you of another man who became very important in both of our lives. I wish I could also tell him of my condition, but he too is gone. It comforts me to know he is with your father. When my father, your grandfather, sold Ruben, he was gone for three days. It was the same time I mentioned earlier, during which my mother hid Ophelia in the basement and cared for her wounds. As Mother knew he would, my father returned with a new male slave, a man both your father and I would come to love and respect.

The new slave became known as "Reverend." He had been owned by one man since he was a child. He had been taught by his master to read and write. He was the only slave his master had ever owned and was the only one by his side when he passed away. His name came from the fact that not only could he read the Bible, but he also owned one. It was given to him by his master's wife. They apparently had no children of their own and had purchased him when he was only twelve. Although he worked their small farm, they also raised him and cared for him for many years. Reverend was about thirty when he came to our plantation and had only heard stories of people like Master David. His experience of being born and raised in the South was quite different from many others who had the same dark skin. After being exposed for only a short while to the lives many of the others lived, he was indeed grateful for his early years of respite.

The first thing Master David did was strip Reverend of his Bible and threatened him with what would be a severe beating—quite possibly death—if he was caught teaching any of the others to read or write. Reverend was calm and quiet, not wanting to provoke Master David's wrath. He simply stood silent as the precious book was taken away. He told me once that even though he no longer had a Bible in his hands, no one could ever steal the one he carried in his heart. I was only about five when he said it, but the words have never left me. I want you to remember them, my precious. People in this life will treat you differently, often times they will be cruel, but just remember, they can take what you have in your hands, but never what is in your heart. I want you to carry my love inside you and know that despite his physical absence at this time, your father will also soon be with you. Nobody can ever take that away from you. You are different, but you are also special. You, your father, and I have a bond that can never be broken, not by the hands of others, distance, time, or this wretched war. Reverend taught me that and I only hope he will be as much a part of your life as he was your father's and mine.

Chapter 12
"Love is Born"

It was a beautiful Sunday, but after having lunch and a short nap, I decided to be selfish and spend my entire afternoon sitting on the porch swing wrapped in Miss Claudia's blanket and continue reading. I turned off the phones after having declined an invitation to go to a movie with friends. I just wanted to be alone and read as much as I could before the new week started. Keno and I sat all afternoon, enjoying the soft breeze on the front porch. I think he enjoyed smelling the dogwood and magnolia trees as much as I did as their scent drifted across the veranda. Over the top of the journal, I could see him raise his nose in the air every time a gentle breeze brought floral fragrances our way. I wondered if Emmaline and Annabeth had sat in this spot and enjoyed themselves in the same way we were.

March 3, 1863

It has been several days since I last wrote to you, my love. I have been ill. Mother is worried and thinks I need rest. I have been in bed while both she and Ophelia bring me broth and constantly wipe my face with a cool, damp cloth. Your presence is becoming more real to me everyday. I will tell Ophelia soon. I want to make sure I finish your story first. If my father discovers my secret and I am punished, I want everything to be said in case I am no longer able to say it. Have no fear, little one, I have no regrets. You are the only tie I have to the only other soul in this world I love as much as you—your father. I do have happy news. Ophelia received a letter from him this morning. He included one for me. I read it many times and now the words are burned inside me. I can close my eyes and see them. "I miss you and I love you" were the last words on the page. I hang onto them as I do my love for you, my precious child.

I wish I could keep the letter in my possession, but I am afraid my father might find it. It is safe in Ophelia's hands, just as safe as those I have sent to him through her. It is enough of a burden for me to hide my words to you without worrying over hiding your father's letters to me. Just as Reverend said, "Nobody can take what is in your heart." My love for you and your father's love for me are buried safely deep inside. I have gotten off track once again. I must finish telling you of how your grandmother's plan brought your father safely into her arms.

As soon as my mother discovered she was with child, she went to my father and asked if it might be appropriate for Ophelia to move into the main house to assist her while she was expecting. My father protested at first, saying it was enough that he'd moved her in from the fields and allowed her to work in the house during the day. My mother accepted his answer at first, but after she kept him from sleep for a few nights pretending to be ill, he moved Ophelia into the basement and said she could stay there until my mother's time to deliver arrived. The timing was perfect for Ophelia as she was nearly three months along. She was, as I am, beginning to worry her secret might soon begin to show itself.

The bigger Ophelia got, the sicker my mother pretended to be. By the end of her fifth month and my mother's second, my father allowed my mother to take up residence in the back bedroom and Ophelia was allowed to live in the room that adjoined it. It was as if they were children hiding secrets and sharing living quarters again. The less my father had to hear of his ailing wife and her maid, the happier he was. Ophelia felt guilty looking out the long window, watching the others work in the fields, but she knew she had to protect her unborn child, she would do it for Ruben. They had not yet decided what they would do after Ophelia gave birth and they both spent many days in prayer hoping some answer might come to them in time. Ophelia left my mother's side only to fetch food or water for both of them. All of her activities were done either in the early morning before anyone was awake or late at night after everyone was asleep. No one questioned it. Everyone, including the other slaves, assumed that my mother was having a difficult time carrying me and Ophelia was constantly occupied in her care. Occasionally, my father would come knocking on the door and my mother would hop into bed while

Ophelia would gather what she pretended was clothing or bed linen that needed washing and hold them in front of herself as if she were just about to leave the room with them.

As the months went by, my father's initial hesitation about having a child began to diminish. He became obsessed with the idea of having a son. As Ophelia became larger and her secret all but impossible to hide, she simply excused herself to the adjoining bedroom and hid behind the door when my father came to visit. My mother would play master and insist that Ophelia leave the room to give her and my father some time alone together. My father would go on and on about his Irish roots, hoping that his son would have yellow hair and blue eyes just as he did. Occasionally, my mother gently tried to remind him that their newborn might be a girl, but my father would laugh and simply dismiss the idea.

He desperately wanted a son and was determined that my mother was going to give him one. It was a cool night on March 1, 1847 when Ophelia came to my mother saying it was time. Everyone in the house was asleep and Ophelia knew that even the slightest sounds of the pain of childbirth would bring her secret to light. She laid in agony for hours until dawn, struggling to stifle any sound of her pain. It was early on the morning of March 2nd that your father, Isaiah, was born. My mother tells me that never in the history of *childbearing has a woman accomplished that task in near silence, her cries stifled by a blanket over her mouth. There was no sound in the house as it was dark and my father was sleeping. There was also no sound in Ophelia's room as she fought with all that was in her to bring her son into this world undetected. My mother's hands were the first to touch your father and later it was Ophelia's milk that nourished me.*

There was a large closet on the far side of Ophelia's room and she and my mother kept Isaiah quietly inside it for the first three months of his life. It was a difficult task, but their determination was stronger than their circumstances. They both loved the boy and vowed to protect him with their own lives, if necessary. My father, the only other resident in the large house, was usually working or often away. Mother and Ophelia came to know his schedule better than he did. They knew when he would rise, sleep, and even come and visit my mother and his unborn "son".

Nearly three months to the day after Ophelia gave birth, my mother was in labor with me. Just before the pains signaling my arrival began, she told Ophelia that she did not feel well and this time she was not pretending. She became weak with fever. My father sent for the doctor after Ophelia knocked on the door of his study and told him that his child was about to be born.

I arrived on June 1, 1847. My father was so pleased with my yellow curls and fair Irish skin that for a brief moment after my birth, he forgot that I was not the son he had hoped for.

My mother was very weak and sick after the labor and continued to run an uncontrolled fever. The doctor informed her that she must attempt to nourish me. My father became worried that I might die, as was the physician. I was very small and frail at birth and in desperate need of my mother's milk. The doctor believed that I had contracted the fever that was ravaging my mother. Unwilling to accept her weakness and illness, my father became enraged and tried to force her to attempt to feed me. He yelled at her to obey, caring less about her well-being than my own. I suppose because I was his blood, my life was more important to him than hers was. In her confused, feverish state, my mother whispered in my father's ear that he should take me to Ophelia.

Ophelia was sitting on the floor of the dark closet holding Isaiah when my father opened the door. She had been hiding in there with him since the doctor's arrival. He never allowed black hands to help him deliver any of his white babies, so he sent her into the other room as soon as he arrived. Ophelia wanted to take her son to the slave's quarters and hide him with the others, but there was no way for her to leave during my mother's labor without being seen by my father. She had never been so afraid in her life as she was when she looked up from the darkness and saw his angry face. She was shaking so hard that Isaiah began to cry. My father had discovered her secret. Ophelia covered her son with her own body, crying and begging my father to have mercy on him.

He stood there holding me in his arms and took the only course of action he could to save my life.
He told Ophelia that if she would feed and care for me, then he would allow her to keep her baby boy.

He handed me down to her and she immediately agreed. After discovering their deception, my father was furious with my mother and ordered the doctor to leave, content to let my mother suffer for what she had done. The physician put up a small protest, saying my mother could die without his care; however, my father insisted that he go and this time it was a demand. It was against his medical judgment, but the doctor respected my father's decision as head of the household. My mother laid there for two weeks, fighting for her life while Ophelia cared for her, her own son, and me. Much to my father's dismay, she survived.

I sat there swinging back and forth, picturing the bedrooms on the second story of my old house. The two back rooms were adjoined. The far room had a large closet on the back wall. I closed my eyes and pictured Ophelia standing in front of the window where Miss Claudia had seen her own father stand and where I had seen her pass many an hour. All three of them were seeing something very different. Ophelia looked down on acre after acre of cotton and witnessed the plight of the others with brown skin like hers. They were working themselves nearly to death under the watchful eye of Master David and his ever-present whip. Mr. Wainwright had stood in that same spot watching the trees he and his daughter had planted grow into the thick woods they are today. Miss Claudia stared out through the glass dreaming of her childhood and her family long since gone. In that moment, I felt so privileged that it was I who got to share in the lives of all three of them. I got to know what each one of those very different people saw while gazing out the same window, looking down on the same land. The original glass had been burned and broken and the landscape had changed dramatically, but the wishes and dreams of each one who stood there were the same, all had come from deep inside their hearts. All three desperately wanted to look out that long window and see a picture that eluded them. One wanted to see the face of freedom, one wanted only a peaceful forest, and Miss Claudia wanted to see the past and the simpler times to which she longed to return.

I sighed to myself, waking Keno from his afternoon nap. I was appalled at the way Ophelia was forced to hide her baby, sad for the way Jackson treated Emmaline, and afraid for what I would read next about the fate of Annabeth and her baby. It's like a scary movie—you want everything to be all right, but something deep inside tells you to look and turn away at the same time. I wrapped Miss Claudia's quilt around me and turned the page.

Chapter 13
"Andrew"

March 7, 1863

    I have just finished a letter to your father and returned from sneaking it down to the basement and giving it to Ophelia. She will hide it for me until she is able to send it in secret. I can tolerate his absence as long as I know he is safe. He is, as I was, unaware of your presence when he left. I wrote to him in great length about you and how I am also writing an account of our lives together so that you can someday read the love story that brought your wonderful life into my womb and into my heart.

    Ophelia continued to nurse your father, and me, even after my mother recovered because following her convalescence, her ability to feed me with her own milk had diminished and become an impossible task. Your father and I were bonded at birth. I was conceived to hide his presence within Ophelia and because of him, I was nourished and survived. Ophelia took great pains to ensure my well-being, although my viability was uncertain after I was born. Your father and I came into this life protecting and nourishing one another. Our beginnings were a prelude to how our childhood and our adolescence would unfold.

My father saw my mother's inability to care for me as weakness and reminded her of it daily. He had also had time to dwell on the fact that she had deceived him and that he still had no son. As soon as my mother was up and about, all traces of her illness gone, my father decided that there was only one way to save his pride and regain control of his home. It was kept a strict secret between them—he, my mother, and Ophelia—that they had tricked him. He would have been the laughing stock in his circle of friends if that tale were ever to be told. Until the day he died, it was made known that my mother was ill and Ophelia had cared for me because Emmaline was not able. The subject of Isaiah was avoided, if possible, but when asked, my father would joke and say that he had changed his way of thinking and decided to grow himself a free field hand. My mother was repulsed by him, but that did not sway his plans regarding how to remind her that it was he, not she, who was in command of their home, finances, and lives.

I was barely two months old when my father began to force himself on my mother night after night. He said that if she was going to lie and oblige him to care for Ophelia's son, and make him suffer the indignity that his only child was being nourished by black milk, then she would produce him a son of his own. He looked at it as repayment for his kindness in allowing Ophelia to keep her baby boy. He moved Ophelia and Isaiah into the basement while my mother and I shared the adjoining bedrooms. Ophelia was to feed me, but my father insisted that my mother meet all of my other needs. He told her again and again that she needed to prove herself as a woman, just as he would prove himself as a man. My mother was once again expecting by the time I was only four months old.

Mother had recovered from her illness, but her body had not yet regained all of its strength. The second pregnancy was very difficult for her, but my father would not allow Ophelia to move out of the basement to assist her. She struggled daily to care for me and still preserve her diminishing stamina. She treasured the moments when Ophelia came to feed me.

It was the only time my father allowed Mother to have company other than mine. Her pregnancy had become her punishment and her womb his prisoner.

It was a long, hard road, but my mother walked it with dignity. She did not allow my father to break her spirit. She forced herself to eat and keep herself well. She prayed daily that she would survive another birth because she wanted to see me grow up. As many times as my father told her I was a boy, she secretly prayed in her heart that I would be a girl. The only name she had chosen when I was born was mine, Annabeth. She had not even considered a boy's name. It is almost as if she knew I were a girl, just as I feel in my heart that you, my angel, are a boy.

During her second pregnancy, my father informed her that when his boy was born, his name would be Andrew, after his great-grandfather. It was almost as if he was telling her she had better figure out a way to make their unborn child a son.

Andrew was born two weeks early, just a few months after my first birthday. My father did not send for the doctor this time as my mother's prayers had been answered. She had gotten well over the months and seemed strong. Instead, he sent for Ophelia, then listened to the agonizing sounds of Mother's labor from his own bedroom down the hall. Hour after hour, he waited patiently to hear the sounds of a baby's cry.

When my brother made himself known, my father rushed into the bedroom and was overjoyed when Ophelia informed him he had a son. She dried the baby and handed him to his father for inspection.

My mother was tired, but happy and relieved when she heard Ophelia say the child was indeed male. It was her only chance to bring any sort of peace back to their household. She felt it was unfair to put that burden on an infant, but any hesitation diminished when she heard the cries of her newborn son. Despite how or why he was conceived, my mother already loved him. She hoped he would bring joy and perhaps instill a spirit of forgiveness in my father. It was only moments later when she realized the only spirits that ever lived in the man she had been forced to wed were anger, bitterness, and pride.

Her dreams for a better future for our family were literally ripped from her arms, leaving a hole in her heart that would quietly fill with a profound hatred and more disdain than she could have ever dreamed possible. It happened in an instant and festered for years afterwards.

Ophelia was the first to see the look of anger cross my father's face. That anger quickly turned to rage as he began to shout at my mother. She managed to push herself up to a sitting position and take the baby from his arms, fearing he was about to drop their son in his blind fury. He was hollering about how the boy had dark hair and skin that looked like he had been baked in the sun.

His voice almost rattled the windows as he continued to raise it to be heard over the crying of both my mother and his baby. He accused my mother of all manner of adultery while she begged him to listen. She shook with fear and clung to the infant as her hot tears fell from her face on to his. Jackson McGrath was out of control and frightened everyone in the room. He was stomping about, flailing his arms, spouting obscenities, and hurling wild accusations. My mother finally began screaming and through her tears, begging him to listen, when he turned suddenly and grabbed her face with both hands, bunching her hair into his clenched fists. His intense anger caused his entire body to quiver, but for an instant he stopped shouting. He held her face and hair so tightly that his palms and fingertips left marks on both of her cheeks. He silenced himself just long enough to hear what my mother had to say. She was unsure how long he would remain somewhat calm, so she hurriedly explained. Her voice was shaking and her face was burning from his grip as she told him that her grandmother was full-blooded Mohawk Indian and that she herself was one-quarter Mohawk. She quickly went on to say how her grandmother had married a man with red hair and very pale skin so very little of her Indian roots manifested in either her mother or herself. The seemingly dormant bloodline was a logical reason why the child was born with shiny black hair and lightly tanned skin. He relaxed his intense grip on her face with his right hand just long enough to slap her. He was outraged at the discovery that the woman his father had chosen for him was not of pure white descent. Everyone knew that Blacks and Indians were heathens and far less intelligent or industrious than Whites. Still recovering from the blow she had just received, my mother relaxed her grip on her son just long enough for my father to jerk him from her arms. He ran downstairs with the boy and practically threw him to his foreman, Master David, who was standing several feet away. Ophelia followed, leaving my mother alone, helpless, and screaming for her child. Father told David that he never wanted to see the mongrel breed baby again and that he was never to be spoken of under any circumstances.

Without question or hesitation, Master David took the child and headed towards the corral.

Boldly and courageously, Ophelia ran after him, grabbing the man who had previously beaten her so mercilessly. It was a feeble, yet fearless attempt to stop him from leaving with my brother, but she too was slapped down. Once she fell, my father stomped over to where she was and kicked her several times until she lay bleeding in the dirt. When he finally stopped, she struggled to her feet and returned to the house. She was filthy and covered in her own blood.

Father watched her stagger away. He held his ground, panting and salivating like a wild dog. Just as she reached the top of the steps, he barked after her.

"I could have done the same to your son, so you best keep your mouth shut. You have no place in this matter."

Ophelia felt faint. She used the column nearest the door to support herself as she turned to look at him, but her gaze went beyond him to the dust trail left by Master David as he rode away with Andrew, taking no more care with his tiny frame than with a parcel or bedroll.

Thereafter, even though he was Andrew's father, Jackson spoke of him easily, as though his son were only a lost calf or colt, matter-of-factly telling all those who knew my mother was expecting that their son had been stillborn.

Mother was forced to endure the calls of neighbor women who brought food and flowers to her bedside. They meant well, but it was torture for her to withhold the truth about her beautiful baby boy. No one was ever allowed to ask Master David what became of the baby. My mother told me years later that had it not been for her need to carry on for my sake, she would have mourned herself to death. It was another of life's hardships that she and Ophelia endured together.

Ophelia returned to my mother's side that day to comfort her, but there was no way, no words, that could have helped. Mother cried until she was physically ill. She was inconsolable. Returning to the room of his birth without him and recounting my father's actions to her friend nearly tore Ophelia to pieces. The truth she had to tell was far more painful than any beating she could have received at the hands of either of her masters.

They sat together on the bed nursing both their physical and emotional wounds. My mother was in complete shock, perhaps denial. She secretly prayed for weeks that my father would retrieve their son and return him to her, but she never again laid eyes on him. Thinking of her own son, Ophelia wisely kept silent.

Andrew was gone and all they could do now was accept it. That's why, my sweetheart, if you are a boy, I will name you Andrew. My mother was not ashamed of her lineage, or his, and you should never be ashamed of yours. It is about time a McGrath child, including me, was proud of their heritage. I suppose I am lucky. I was born with a coloring that was pleasing to my father, despite my Indian blood. Had I not been, perhaps I too would have met with whatever fate befell my brother.

Chapter 14
"Tiny Secrets"

I closed the book, unable to read another word. I tried to picture Emmaline's face, but somehow in my mind it kept crossing with my mother's expression the day Sissy never came home. It was dusk and the words were beginning to melt into the page in the fading sunlight. My heart was too full to read anymore anyway. There they were again, emotions running all over each other, mixing like vinegar and water, one strong and pungent...the other necessary for life. My heart and soul needed truth, starting with my own, but the process was painful. It was beginning to blur where I started and my past and the ghosts of this house began. Keno and I went inside and sank into the couch. I reached over to the end table and turned the phone back on. I was startled because as soon as I hit the ringer switch, the phone rang.

"Hello?" I answered, having nearly jumped out of my skin.

"Hey, Ang." It was Grandpa.

"Hi," There was a blue note in my voice that he could have seen had he been in the room. I didn't greet him further in return I just started talking. "It is amazing, isn't it..." I went on, my voice soft and forlorn, almost defeated sounding, "how one shade in tone darker or lighter can allow the rest of the world to define your character, to determine your station in life and map out a future based on something so out of your control—something that we, as individuals, have absolutely nothing to do with."

He was speechless, but I think silent because he knew I wasn't finished.

"It isn't Willie I'm mad at or afraid of, it isn't the drug addict mother or Dad and Sissy being gone. It's not about me being a racist, it's about the unfair randomness of it all. The *Whys* that I can't answer—why your brother, why my dad, why Emmaline's son, why my mother's daughter. I mean, what is the point if something as trivial as white, tan, olive, or dark brown, which are uncontrollable, can control everything? Why should it make any more sense that the drunk would be on the same road as my dad or the addicted babies I see be born to their mother and not another who would care for them? I can see it now, Grandpa. More importantly, I can try to start to separate it now. My resentment, my anger over things I can't control is nothing like what my uncle was or felt. It just is what it is and we either make it better or worse based on what you said—our hearts, not our blood."

Words failed him for a minute before he attempted an answer. "I've been wondering about all those things, Peanut—the randomness, the 'what makes one person act or think so differently than another since the day I left my brother in prison in Alabama. I don't have an answer except to say what we'd already decided we knew was right, 'Don't let it be you too.'

"It doesn't have to be as random as you think if we do our best to make it right...ask God to help us make it right within ourselves. That is the best I have figured to do in my eighty-five years. I know it's simple, but it works for me."

It helped a little to hear his thoughts. I did figure with years and wisdom he might have said something more profound, but that was unfair. Lots of years and plenty of wise people haven't figured it out before, so why should I expect him to have it all worked out now? Of course, maybe nobody has figured it out because they're looking too hard maybe it's that simple, just don't let it be you and control what you can. Let God do His work, huh, makes sense I guess.

"After what I've just read in this book and learned about our family, don't worry. It stopped with you after your brother and I won't allow anger like that to take root in me. I'm ashamed to say how resentment had started to take over my life, but no more, not me too, not in my blood, not in my heart."

He breathed a sigh of relief that I'd finally had a breakthrough and he knew it. We didn't even need to say it outloud.

"I don't mean to get off track here, but I need to know. Grandpa, where exactly in the basement did you find the crate?"

After what I'd just read, I had to have every detail. Something in me knew that the moment I finished the page. I had to find Annabeth's descendants. I had to do something so that whoever was connected to this book could know what I knew and feel what I felt. I was finding the best peace I could with my family and myself so maybe I could do the same for Andrew's kin. In one page, the need had turned from curiosity into a quest. I caught Grandpa up on the story and told him about my mission. He agreed it was the right thing to do.

"It was under the stairs, sort of pushed back into the wall," he answered, when I was finished giving him the scoop. I had almost forgotten I had asked him the question.

"Into the wall?" I asked. "What do you mean "into the wall'?"

"Well," he started slowly, jogging his eighty-five year old memory into action and taking a moment to think. I didn't know it at the time, but he was counting. "There were about eight or ten bricks missing from a small section of wall close to the bottom angle on the back side of the stairs. The crate was pushed into a hole of sorts, but not one big enough that it would fit in all the way. I only found it because I moved another box that was in front of it. I figure it must have been filled with some of Miss Claudia's family belongings because it was marked "Daddy's things" in black ink." He paused, remembering something else. "You saw the box that was sitting in front of the crate. It was one filled with the Wainwright family's old photographs and family stuff. Hannah mailed it back to New York."

"I don't remember," I started, thinking back, trying to recall the details of that day in my mind. "Why would someone try to hide a box in the wall?" I asked him, more confused than ever, wondering who that someone might have been.

"It could be those bricks just fell out over time and the boxes got pushed to the side," he was grasping, trying to come up with a logical explanation. He changed the subject.

"So, how do you intend to go about your little detective work and find the owner?"

I wasn't sure I had the stamina to tell him, but once I started talking, I couldn't stop. When I was through, he made me promise to be careful and keep him posted. We hung up a few hours later. Once again, my ear was sore, but I had one more call to make.

"Hello Kathy? May I speak to Phillip, please?"

"Sure," she answered after her usual "glad to hear from you and ya'll have to come over sometime" chitchat.

"Hello," Phillip answered in his typical all business, straight man voice, after he learned it was me.

"Hey Phil, I'm sorry to call you on a Sunday, but I'm still not feeling well and I won't be in to work tomorrow." It was the first time since we'd been working together that I needed to notify someone I wouldn't be coming in. I figured he was as good a person to tell as any. "Will you let everyone know they can call me at home if there's an emergency or anything?"

"Sure," he agreed to help anyway he could, a little less business-like, but nothing nearly as chatty and friendly as Kathy. "I thought you were calling to give me really bad news, it being Sunday and all. No problem, you just rest and feel better."

"It's nothing serious," I assured him. "Just sore ribs from driving too soon, I think." It wasn't exactly a lie. I reached over with my free hand and petted Keno who had been nudging me with his nose since we sat down.

"I'm sure I'll be back in no time," I promised, feeling bad that I'd misled him. "Besides, I'm sure you all won't mind skipping the part where the bruises on my face go from black to purple to green. I'm about to look like the Incredible Hulk."

He laughed. "Glad to see you haven't lost your sense of humor. Take your time, Angie, and let us know if you need anything."

"Thanks, Phil, I will," I promised just before we hung up. "Okay, Angie," I told myself, "now you have the time, what are you going to do with it?"

Keno understood and had an idea of his own. I needed to clear my head for a while anyway, so a stroll around the yard was just the thing for both of us.

After I ate dinner, I went downstairs into the basement. I looked under the stairs and sure enough, just as Grandpa said, there were about eight bricks missing from the wall. It was the sharp corner where the wall and the bottom of the stairs met on the backside. I could see how the crate would have been easily overlooked. It was a dark corner and there was no reason other than storage to stoop under the stairs. It was an excellent hiding place, especially with the old gray bricks missing. The wall behind was rock and clay had easily worn away to conceal most of the crate.

Chapter 15
"Memories"

March 17, 1863

Father caught me up late writing by the dim lantern light. I was writing another letter to your father. I quickly closed the book and covered it with a writing tablet. I lied and told him I was writing a letter to Aunt Joanie Anne, my mother's sister. It has taken me quite a few days to get up the courage to write to you again. Every day I fear that this book will be discovered and my father will know, I have deceived him, just as my mother and Ophelia did. I think I am about three months along and if my calculations are correct, you should be arriving sometime in mid to late August.

I have news to tell you before we go on with the story of your father and myself. I managed to get Ophelia alone a week ago and told her of my condition. She nearly cried, but she is strong and managed to hold her emotions inside. She was extremely glad to hear that she will soon be a grandmother, but is worried for my safety and yours. I was afraid to tell my mother. I am unsure if her knowing will put her in grave danger where my father is concerned. If she truly does not know, then perhaps she can convince him that she is also a victim, although I am sure in her heart she would not believe she was. Father would certainly beat the truth from her if he felt she was hiding something from him. Mother loves Isaiah. She delivered him into this world and cried in secret, just as I did, the day he left the plantation. My beloved, I know that she will love you just as much as I do.

When I explained my reason for not wanting to tell my mother, Ophelia assured me that nobody could keep a secret from Jackson better than Emmaline McGrath. She told me not to worry about him finding out that she knew and kept it from him. She assured me that my mother would rather know and risk the danger than be unaware she had a grandchild coming. I was still afraid, but agreed I would tell Mother soon.

Three nights ago, before I went to bed, I opened the door that separates my room from Mother's. She and Father have remained in separate quarters since the night Andrew was born and then taken away. I sat on the edge of her bed and whispered my secret in her ear by the moonlight that shone through the window. She was as silent as Ophelia had been the night your father was born. She put her arms around me and whispered into my hair that I was not alone. With the help of Ophelia, we would figure out a way to keep you from my father.

For the past two days, I have seen Ophelia and my mother sharing whispered conversation. It is almost as if they can communicate without talking if need be. At dinner last night, the only time my mother, my father, and I are together, Mother made a suggestion that nearly caused me to choke on my food. It is difficult enough for me to eat without her surprising me in such a fashion. She simply told Father that her sister Joanie Anne was all alone since her husband died. She said she had received a letter from her requesting a visit from me, her favorite niece. She felt it would be good for me to spend some time with her in Atlanta, because, after all, she spoke French and was very educated. Mother encouraged my father to say yes by telling him that being around such a cultured person would only serve to improve my chances of marrying an affluent man someday.

Father's interest in my going improved when he thought about the fact that I was getting older. It occurred to him that I would soon be of suitable age to marry someone he deemed worthy. He also knew that my mother's sister had been left an incredibly wealthy woman and moved in prosperous circles. No doubt she knew of many wealthy, eligible, would-be suitors. Father had not yet considered that having a daughter might in someway benefit him. It was one of the few times I can ever remember him smiling at me. I believe he was imagining me in a white gown marrying into the money he so hungrily sought on a daily basis.

He agreed and it was decided I would leave in two days.

I had no idea everything Mother had just said was a well thought out fable. She and Ophelia had invented the story to remove me from my father's sight while still keeping me in theirs. Two days later, Mother packed up my things, had Reverend load our carriage, and we headed out to what Father thought was my aunt's home. In fact, when we were out of sight, we turned the horses around and headed for the far border of our property. We were about five miles from the plantation house when I saw it—a small shanty protected from the wind by a natural slope in the landscape, and from plain view by the pine trees on the edge of the plantation. It was perfectly hidden on the unused land. My mother and Ophelia secretly had Reverend and a few of the others build it long ago so they could discreetly nurse slaves who had been whipped or otherwise punished for their so-called crimes. The men worked at night by lantern light to finish it and neither my father nor Master David was aware of its existence. I am still amazed they managed it without garnering any attention. It is very small, but warm and comfortable inside. I hope it will be as safe for me as my womb has become for you, my little one. Mother will stay here with me for a few days, returning to the plantation as if she had really made the long trip to see her sister.

Reverend is hiding in the woods nearby, as he was supposed to escort us on our trip. He does not know our secret, but would never question our motives for deceiving father, especially since he knows the shanty was built in secret to protect those who needed its shelter.

Chapter 15
"Memories"

I finally had a reason to smile, other than the fact that I was thrilled to find the old journal and read its long-kept secrets and history. The thought of Emmaline and Ophelia hiding Annabeth and moving her to safety literally made me breathe a sigh of relief. Their friendship was inspiring. It defied both the times they lived in and all those who knew them, but did not *really* know them. I suppose women in those days either had to be clever and cunning or submissive and silent when it came to abusive husbands. I wondered if purchasing Ophelia for Emmaline when she was so young was wise, but now I see that the Lagoys' desire to appear wealthy by showing that even their child owned a slave served a much higher purpose. Had they not done it, they would have deprived history of a great friendship and the birth of what is slowly becoming the "New South."

Babies like Annabeth's are literally changing our face. I had new hope for a happy ending—or maybe I had just hit a plateau before the next valley.

I once again settled into my soft sofa and started to read. I had my glass of tea on the coffee table and Miss Claudia's blanket over my legs. Now all I needed was to know the ending. I hoped it would be good. I realized if it were not, I was praying, as I had been over that past few days, that I could change the past. It was different from reading about the Civil War and slavery in some watered-down history book. The book I was holding *was* history. It had changed my way of thinking and inspired me in so many ways. It was almost painful to think Annabeth might not fare as well in her journey through these pages. I wondered if it felt the same to my grandpa watching me struggle and hoping for the best all these years.

March 20, 1863

There is little to do in my hiding place except think about your father and watch you grow. I am indeed beginning to see subtle changes in my body every day. We are lucky, most expectant mothers in my situation do not have a mother who is as understanding as mine. I have no doubt that if I were anyone else's daughter, I surely would have run away or been put to death by now.

I remember when Mother started teaching me to read and write. I was about six. Father insisted I be educated at home as he would not have his daughter associate with the lower class children who attended the rural school closest to our plantation. Most of the children who attend there are poor immigrants. Had Father's family not come to this country and found good fortune when they did, we would certainly be among them. Father called me into his study and I stood there looking up at him while holding a book Mother was using to teach me. He took it from my hands, sat down, and put me on his knee. He stroked my yellow curls and commented again how my dark eyes did not match my light hair and skin. I never understood until years later that he found them disturbing and unappealing. Apparently, they served to remind him of the son who not only had brown eyes, but also an unsuitably dark skin color.

Father opened the book and asked me to begin reading. I did so as best I could as I had only been practicing for a few months. He set me down on the floor and patted my head as if I were a dog who had just followed his command well enough to deserve his praise. He explained to me that reading and writing were very important and meant only for those smart enough and worthy enough to partake of it. Even at that very tender age, he made me understand that only white people fit the criteria and that I was never to teach any of the slaves or Isaiah to read and write or to learn their numbers. Having acquired the childish notion that Ophelia and Isaiah were my friends, his instructions confused me, but I also feared the backside of my father's hand, so I showed no emotion and agreed to comply with his orders. It was also around the age of six that I now realize I began to show signs of my mother's spirit and stubborn will. As soon as I left my father's study that day, I began to think of ways to hide the fact that I had already begun to teach Isaiah how to read and write the moment my mother began to teach me. I am convinced that Mother knew all along what I was doing and it was just the first of many things between your father and me that she and Ophelia hid from my Father. Perhaps that's why she wasn't surprised to learn that she and Ophelia will soon share a blood tie—perhaps they have considered themselves blood since the day they met.

Your father was a quick study and it was a lucky thing for him. As he grew older, our time together became increasingly shorter. As were all the slaves, he was required to begin working in the fields as soon as he was old enough to take any sort of direction from Master David. When your father was ten, he was moved out of the basement, away from Ophelia and me. He was forced to live in the slaves' quarters with the rest of the men. Father allowed Ophelia to continue to live in the house, but she was the only servant he permitted inside. I think that deep down in his heart he was still worried that someday the truth about Isaiah's birth might be discovered. If Ophelia was forced to move back into the slaves' quarters with our other female slaves, then she might tell the secret of how he had been duped. He could not afford to be undermined in such a manner and maintain the respect of Master David or any other man he considered his equal. Having control of her every word and movement provided him with the peace of mind he would have lost had he not been able to keep a close watch over her. He had also gotten used to having Ophelia wait on him in the evenings after all the other slaves were forced to return to their cramped quarters. If Father is up late working in his study, he often has Ophelia bring him coffee or a late dinner.

After your father was required to move out of the house, I cried for days. I missed him terribly. When we were little, after everyone had gone to bed for the night, I would sneak out of my room and down to the basement. It was then I would teach Isaiah everything I had learned that day. We would sit under the stairs hiding the lantern's light in the dark corner while we filled my slate and writing tablets with letters and numbers that over the years turned into addition, subtraction, and words. I believe I loved him even then. As a young child, he was my playmate and then later, my only schoolmate, but from birth, he was my soul's mate.

After Isaiah was made to leave the basement, I would slip outside in my nightdress to meet him behind the men's bunkhouse. Night after night, we would sit by the water's edge and continue our lessons. I reason now that Mother must have heard me leaving, just as Ophelia had when we began in the basement. They both pretended to be asleep, but as I look back, I am certain that they had to have known. Sometimes we would blow out the candle's flame that we used for light when we heard Master David making his nightly rounds. He would walk in a complete circle around both of the slave cabins to ensure no one was trying to escape. As the years of forced servitude went on, we would occasionally hear of one or two slaves who had managed to flee from beneath their master's watchful eye. Some were successful, but most were killed. When we began to get older and had to extinguish our candle's flame, another started burning. It was the kind that lights inside of you and only the person for whom it glows is able to see it clearly. Your father would cover my white nightdress with his own body as we lay in the bushes, sometimes only a few feet away from the bottom of Master David's boots. Once I felt his whip brush through my hair as it dangled from his waistband. The tall grass around the waters edge became our refuge. We were afraid to go farther away from the slaves housing because occasionally Master David would go inside and count them as they slept. Several times your father was nearly caught sneaking in through the window above his cot. Had we been across the field, he would never have made it inside in time to escape the cruel end of the foreman's whip. The last thing we wanted was for Master David to misunderstand our meetings and assume Isaiah was trying to escape, he would have surely become another story and statistic just like the other runaway slaves.

April 1, 1863

I have been ill for several days now. My belly is growing, but it is because of you, my little one, and certainly not because I am over-indulgent in my eating. Mother comes to see me whenever she is able. She tells me it is common, but my sickness and my solitude are beginning to feel like a prison. I feel the only comfort I will have is either the sight of your father's face or yours. Whatever the cost, my beloved, I will stay here and hide you, for now I am having a good day. I am able to continue the task at hand and focus my attention not on your father's current situation or mine, but on the circumstances that brought us together and created you.

When your father was twelve we received news that several slaves had been caught trying to escape from a neighboring plantation. The man who owned them was a friend of Father's. He came to our house one night for supper and recounted how four of his best field hands were returned to him after having run away. They traveled under the cover of darkness over a period of two weeks and had been able to progress nearly seventy-five miles from his home. He then informed my father that is why he advocated branding his slaves and encouraged Father to do likewise. He explained that in case any slave escaped, they could be easily identified as his property. The two men laughed together when the man spoke eloquently of his kindness—that instead of having the runaways hung, he simply had them whipped and saltwater poured into their wounds. His fat cheeks were red as he could hardly breathe and tell the story through his high-pitched, girlish giggles. He recounted in some detail how open wounds and saltwater make the slaves dance and scream. The account was all the prompting Master David needed. The next day, he and Father had what they thought was a private conversation in his study. They decided that all the slaves should be branded with the same mark as was given the cattle.

I had been crouched by the study door listening and immediately reported to my mother. She went to my father and insisted that because Ophelia was a house servant who lived in the basement and was rarely out of their sight, therefore unable to sneak away without detection that she should be exempt. Under great protest, Father relented for no other reason than to silence my mother whose tongue he had long ago grown tired of hearing. Just before noon, Father and his equally heartless foreman rang the dinner bell, calling all the slaves in from the fields or whatever other chore they had been assigned that day. The women left the wash laying wet across the wash boards and the men left half-filled buckets of water in the fields where most of them were irrigating the soil. They gathered together, awaiting whatever dreadful news usually came with an untimely ringing of the dinner bell. The fire was burning on the other side of the barn just out of their sight, but I could easily see it through a loose board I had moved aside from my position in the loft. I was shaking. I knew your father was about to be in pain and if all I could do was be near him and will some of my strength into his body, then that is what I intended to do. Master David used his ever-calloused words and hands to push each man around to the fire. All the others could do was stand at bay, held there by the end of Father's shotgun. They could hear the screaming coming from the other side of the barn, but there was nowhere to run, nowhere to hide. I covered my ears and cried every time a new victim rounded the corner of the barn and realized what was about to befall them. The women begged for mercy with tears running down their faces. The men tried to be strong, but the hot branding iron broke even the toughest of spirits. Your father was the fourth in line. When I saw his face as the flaming hot iron approached his skin, he looked away, focusing on the side of the barn, as if turning his face might somehow diminish the pain. It was at that moment I slid the board hiding my presence farther over to the side. Doing so turned my vantage point from a small opening between the boards to almost a window. Master David was concentrating on the task at hand and did not see me. Mother says to this day how lucky I am that my presence went undetected; however, your father saw me. We locked our eyes together and held our breath. There was something else deep in his dark eyes behind the fear when he looked into mine. I could read the thoughts so full of meaning in them as his expression was nearly screaming at me not to look, he didn't want me to see his pain, he of all things wanted to protect me. I did not look away; I could not leave him alone in the fear. I could feel the pain on his skin deep in my heart as he cried out, never turning his eyes from mine. Tears streamed down both our faces as Master David pushed the hot iron deep into the flesh of Isaiah's right arm. When he was finished, I quickly pushed the loose board back into place and turned my face away from the gruesome sight. I sat in that loft with my hands over my ears, sobbing until the last slave had endured their branding. When it was finished, all of them had a large "M" on their right forearm. Master David undoubtedly slept well that night knowing that all of my father's possessions were distinct. Now if they strayed, just like the cattle they could easily be returned; however, when the cows strayed away from the plantation, they were simply placed back with the herd. I knew the slaves would have no such luxury. It was made perfectly clear to them that any escape attempt would be severely punished. The criminal slave either would be hung or whipped.

Master David laughed at them standing there, nursing their wounds. He dared them to go ahead and try to flee, because their life, or death, would depend on his mood when they were returned.

I thank God everyday that I was born a girl because for most of my childhood, Father simply let me be. After he took my brother away from my mother, he assumed that she would never defy him again when it came to raising me. I learned to be what he wanted when I was in his sight and I was allowed to follow the convictions of my own heart when left under the supervision of either Mother or Ophelia. I will be forever grateful to my mother for instilling in me the knowledge that despite the times we live in or the circumstances in which I find myself, my heart, soul, feelings, and dreams are important. She once told me that her Indian grandmother passed on to her that every human being has value. She told me that even though she was very young when they left the North, she would never forget sitting on her grandmother's lap, encircled in her brown arms. It was then that she heard the words few women ever hear—a lesson she has since passed on to me—women are of great value and use in God's hands and no matter their station in life, each has a distinct and wonderful purpose in God's plan. This wise woman would have been my great-grandmother. I am grateful every day for the simple truth she taught my mother and even more grateful that my mother has tried to do the same for me. My sweet baby, I hope that despite the hardships you will likely endure, you will also hold *fast to that lesson. You are safe and will be saved because of it and my mother's courage in hanging on to it and passing it down.*

I was startled by my grandfather clock. It was ringing in the midnight hour, but I didn't care. I was tired, but knew I would never be able to sleep until I had seen Annabeth's journey to the end. I stood up, stretched, and went into the kitchen for a fresh glass of iced tea and a bowl of chocolate chip ice cream.

"That ought to be enough to wake me up," The spoon clinked against the empty bowl disturbing one of the twenty hours Keno managed to sleep out of his twenty-four hour day. Every time I look into his big brown eyes, I can't believe my luck at having found him at the pound. He had been abandoned, but was housebroken and gentle and most of all, he loved me right away. I like to think it's because he knows how much I love him and not just because I feed him everyday. I sat beside him and stroked his soft fur while he snored on.

After about a twenty-minute break and having gained my second wind, I couldn't stand it any longer. I went back to the couch and found my place. I was determined that even if I had to read all night, I would finish.

Chapter 16

"Young Love"

April 12, 1863

I rest most of the day. I never thought I would be so tired. I have received a response from your father to my last letter. He is now aware we are expecting a child and his reaction was just as I had hoped it would be. He is very excited. He says he dreams of us at night. He told me sometimes the thought of my face, and now yours, is enough for him to escape into his mind and away from the death and destruction that surrounds him on all sides. It is difficult for him to send word to me that he is well, but he sends his love and will write again soon. I have no way of knowing if the letters I write to him nearly everyday are reaching him. I pray so. I pray for his safety, I pray for our safety. When I am ill and unable to write, all I have strength enough to do is pray. When Ophelia visits, she reminds me that prayer is the strongest thing I have where both you and your father are concerned. As important as these written words are to me, the ones I say to God hold a great deal more weight. I hope that you will feel the same someday.

There was no denying the deep and growing feelings your father and I had for one another. We spent every moment we could together. Even when there were no lessons for the day, we would still meet behind the slave quarters and sit by the creek.

Our conversations were whispered for fear Master David would detect our presence. We dreamed of a time or place when we could display our love for each other in the light of day for the entire world to see. He would hold my hand and I would look at the contrast of my fingers intertwined with his. I wondered then and still do how so many people could be completely blinded by the darkness of someone's skin. Your father has a good heart and he always treated me infinitely better than my father ever treated my mother. He is kind and gentle and all my physical eyes could see was a picture overshadowed by my heart. We were young and in love. It seemed the entire world was against any such relationship, but we were determined to hide ours and keep it alive as long as we were able. Our mothers had told us the story of our births and how we had saved one another, even since the day of our conception. I could not deny it to myself, despite what Father or anyone else of his mindset thought, I was born to love Isaiah and he was born to love me.

When I tell Mother of the endless well of emotion Isaiah and I had discovered so young, I can see in her eyes that she wishes she could have had the same with Father. Maybe that's why she is protecting me so fiercely from him, even at the risk of a terribly high cost to herself. She has finally seen what true love looks like and just as her grandmother told her, true love is worth fighting for and protecting at any cost.

Your great-great-grandmother had to fight to marry outside of her tribe when she fell in love with a white man. My grandmother Lagoy and my mother were products of that love. Now you and I, my angel, will fight just as both sides of our family have done for years. My father's side, the McGraths, came to this country with nothing. It seems they have quickly forgotten what it is like to be different or an outcast based on circumstances that were beyond their control. My mother's side has hidden their Indian roots since their arrival on Southern soil, but no more. You will never be ashamed or hide from anyone. Together we will learn from the mistakes of those who came before and when your father is home, we will be a family. I will do my best, my angel. It is only a dream, but I will do my best to make it your truth.

Chapter 17
"Lofty Kisses"

May 1, 1863

I have watched the sunrise give way to the moonlight enough times to mark the passing of another month. Mother sneaks away from the house often and catches me sitting on my small wooden stool crouched in dim light over a makeshift table writing letter after letter to your father. I have received no further word from him since I informed him of your impending arrival. Mother stops my writing, both to him and in this journal, insisting that I rest. She says although my body is young, I will require all of my strength when you arrive. I have been complying with her request, but I am afraid that every day I do not write to you is one less day I will have to ensure that all is recorded.

Although your father and I are young, we are no longer children. Those days are not long gone, but nonetheless have passed. I miss the long stretches of summer when Father was away bargaining for the best prices for his crops and we were allowed to run and play freely. It was simply understood that when we were under his watchful eye, we were to pretend as if we had no relationship. We became almost as adept at non-

spoken conversation as our mothers had been when they were children. By the time I was thirteen, I knew that my feelings for your father were different from any other person in my life. He knew what I was thinking and could anticipate my every need, just as I could his. We had a special hiding place in the barn and when we were unable to talk to one another for several days, I could always go there and count on the fact that he would have left me some little note or gift. He loved to leave me flowers or wooden trinkets. He seemed to have inherited his father's ability to whittle. I would often leave him candies my father would give me when he returned from town. They were the only expression of affection I can ever remember receiving from him and I passed them on to Isaiah. It was a game when we were children, but as we grew older, the notes and gifts became more personal and meaningful. I can honestly say I have loved him all of my life, but it turned into something different, when as Mother said, 'I began to blossom.

It was late one night when I once again sneaked out of bed. Master David always kept a closer watch on the slaves during harvest time, so it was difficult for your father and me to meet by the creek. The cruel taskmaster increased his rounds at night and we were more afraid than ever that we would be caught. He thought if a slave were going to try to escape, he would do so during harvest, the busiest time of year. It never made sense to me because he seemed to work them just as hard during the other seasons, but very little the man did ever seemed to be reasonable.

I had written your father a note and folded it around a small pocketknife that I had taken from Father's desk. It was shiny and sharp. I knew Isaiah would use it far more than Father would. It was much better for woodcarving than your grandfather Ruben's old rusty one that Ophelia had kept. I had just buried the parcel under the hay in the corner when I turned around and nearly screamed. Your father was crouched right behind me. Neither one of us had seen the other in the darkness until we were face to face. It was that moment, after I caught my breath from the fright, I realized we had been close, but never that close before. Neither of us moved, uncertain of what to do. We could feel the emotion between us, but it was a new sensation, unfamiliar territory. After a few moments of being close enough to share the same breath, I knew in my heart that our relationship was about to turn a corner and head down a road we had been walking since birth. We each leaned foreword across the few inches that separated our lips. There, in the loft with the crickets chirping and the stars shining in through the crescent-shaped window, we shared our first kiss.

There were no words spoken before or after. He simply pulled himself away and hugged me close to him. I could feel his fingers combing through my hair again and again as if they were memorizing its texture. I am unsure how long we sat there before he reached into his pocket and handed me the gift he had come to leave. It was a beautiful wooden butterfly. I silently turned and reached back under the pile of hay and retrieved the note wrapped around the knife and placed it in the palm of his hand. He unwrapped it and tears welled in his dark brown eyes. He silently leaned over and kissed me again before descending the ladder and quietly making his way back to his cot. I waited a few moments until I knew he was safe before I sneaked back to my bed.

That's it, I thought to myself resting the journal open against my chest and taking a moment to picture in my mind the events I had just read. I knew in some time or place throughout the ages and the times of man, there had to be at least one perfect kiss in the world. "How did I get lucky enough to be the one to know about it?" I asked Keno who had woken and been sitting by the couch for the past half hour watching me wipe my misty eyes with a Kleenex.

Once I realized the topic, I read slowly and savored every word. Of course, Keno didn't answer me, he just made that grumbling noise he makes when he lays down and was about to fall back to sleep. "Typical man," I said to myself, "always sleeps through the beautiful parts of any book or movie." I reached down and patted his head before lifting the book back up and finding my place. I closed my eyes again to picture it before I read on and instead of the face I had conjured for Isaiah, my mind flashed on Willie. For one split second I was afraid and in the very next I felt pity. He hated me simply because of who I was and I had lumped him in with a heap of criminals I had defended because of the color of his skin and the repetitive nature of his crimes. I was sorry for what I'd done and tried to reconcile those feelings within myself; he, on the other hand, was likely in prison, becoming more bitter, more angry. Another why, another random for which I had no answer. The book was changing me and the determination to find its owner began to burn. I had to pass it on. It had to be shared. I had to know their kin and see if hearts and blood like Annabeth's and Isaiah's could survive all these years. For my own peace of mind, I prayed so.

Chapter 18
"Our Wedding"

May 15, 1863

I wait everyday for word from your father. Every time I see Ophelia approaching, I hope and pray she has a letter. Today it seems my prayers have been answered. Along with my dinner, she has brought me news of my beloved Isaiah. He is well, but says little about his circumstances. Knowing your father, he does so to keep me from worry. He only sends his love and encourages me to be strong for both of us—me and you, our unborn child. Ophelia takes the letter back to the basement with her and hides it for me with the few precious others. We fear that if Father were to stumble upon me here that his anger would be uncontrollable, but for the safety and wellbeing of both our mothers, it is best he does not find our correspondence. I hide this journal daily outside under a pile of rocks. On the face of it, the book appears innocent. Even if left in plain sight, it might not attract attention, but a letter surely would be noticed. Your grandmother rubs her hands over your hidden frame before she leaves, offering a prayer for your health and mine.

After our first kiss, I looked forward to many more in the future. That night when I slipped back into my bed, I dreamed of the day I could tell the world, 'I love Isaiah McGrath!' However, if I did reveal my feelings, they would surely be dismissed as something children cannot possibly understand. Little did they know that your father and I could not be more certain of anything else in our lives. Although we were only thirteen, we held a deep passion for each other. Circumstances forced us to keep our love secret, our passion smoldering untouched for two more years. For some time we had been discussing marriage. We decided that fifteen was old enough to make such a commitment. We'd been told stories about Ophelia's and Ruben's wedding, so we knew that a church and all the amenities would not be necessary. We confided in the only person we thought might be able to help us. Reverend graciously pretended to be surprised when we told him of our love and devotion, but he knew our secret. All of the slaves knew and had been keeping our undisclosed truth to themselves for several years.

December 20th, five days before Christmas was freezing cold. The midnight wind whipped around us, but we proceeded undaunted. Even though Reverend's Bible had been taken from him long ago, he remembered the words as if he were holding it right in front of him. He knew very well that if he was caught helping us, he would be killed by my father or Master David, but Reverend was a man of great courage. The other slaves looked up to him and he did his best to be a good example. He showed us all that it was possible to rise above your circumstances, because no man can cage another's' spirit. He used to say that slavery was holding down the bodies of all men of color, but it had not clipped their soul's wings. He helped the slaves' spirits to soar when he led them in song as they labored in the fields, secretly fostering their faith. Isaiah loved him and was more than proud that Reverend had become a father to him in the absence of his own.

I was wearing the same white nightdress that I always wore when I slipped out of the house. It billowed in the wind as I promised to be faithful and love Isaiah for the rest of my life. He held my hands in his stroking them, warming them, as he made the same promises to me. He placed a round wooden ring on my finger that he had no doubted spent hours smoothing and shaping. I'm not sure if Reverend took the ceremony seriously as we did, but he obliged us as if we were grown-ups and had made the decision with the blessings of our families. He may have seen us as half grown children, but respected us as individuals, as he did all the oppressed people living on the McGrath plantation.

Our wedding was as real to me as if I had gotten permission from my father and married in our church. I knew in my heart that it didn't *matter where or how I made my commitment to Isaiah, only that I meant it with all my heart. I know beyond any doubt that the vows we made that night came from deep within our souls and were just as true for him as they were for me. It's difficult to hide a love so big that it consumes your every thought and action, but hide it we did. The only true evidence, other than our solemn vows, is you, my sweet child. My growing figure is unable to hide you any longer. Your undeniable presence is the only tangible thing I have of our love, a love which transcends all time, color, and acceptance of those who consider themselves worthy to judge others. You, my child, are proof that love can endure any hardship.*

Chapter 18
"New Beginnings"

May 23, 1863

Whenever possible, your father and I met by the creek. Two days after Christmas, under a dark sky, you were conceived. Even before I slid back between my bedclothes, some small part of me knew that my life had profoundly changed. It was the first and only time your father and I had the opportunity to take full advantage of our marital vows. It was cold, but I didn't feel it. I was afraid of getting caught, but I did not consider the consequences. It was forbidden, but neither one of us concerned ourselves with the blind ignorance of others. Love is love and no matter what color it presents itself, it's always more powerful than any circumstance. That night there was no cold, there were no slaves or masters, there was no black or white, only passion and commitment deeper than any I have ever felt...that is, until the first time I felt you move within me.

Never doubt for a second, my sweet angel, if the feelings your father and I have for one another could have created you without our touching, you would have been made a hundred times, even if we had been hundreds of miles apart as we are now.

At first, I was unsure if my prayer should be that your skin be totally black or completely white. I know if you are only black, you will live in as much peace as our times allow. I also know that if you are born only white, Father will surely insist on knowing who your father is and your life will be labeled a mistake. He will consider you a bastard.

Now I pray that you will be a beautiful mix of everything that is good about your father and me. Whatever the shade of your countenance is, it is the shade of love.

On January 1, 1863, President Lincoln signed the Emancipation Proclamation. I was once again listening to Father and several of the other plantation owners. They were irate at the thought of losing their slaves. The Union had difficulty enforcing the presidential order, so Father simply decided to force the slaves to continue working as they always had until he was required to set them free. That day was not long in coming. In mid-January, a small battery of Union troops arrived on our plantation and at gunpoint Father was obliged to relinquish his slaves. They were seeking to turn slaves into soldiers. They were free, but many of them had nowhere to go, no means of supporting themselves, so they joined the ranks of the Yankee forces and became the first colored men of war. All of the slaves left except Ophelia.

Mother and I wept as we watched them go. Father stomped back into the house. He was angry, both at our reaction to their leaving and the fact that they were gone. Reverend promised Ophelia he would look after Isaiah. He was only fifteen when he became a soldier, just a few months away from his sixteenth birthday. In my heart, I couldn't help but think they had traded one condition of forced servitude for another. As I watched him walk away, I thought to myself, 'At least when the war is over, Isaiah will be free, as free as a society that was once his prison will allow him to be.' Either way, we would be together.

I will never forget the look he gave me as he followed the men on horseback, marching down the road and away from our house. He spoke a thousand goodbyes and I love yous in that look, but most importantly, he promised he would return to me. He knew I would wait forever, if necessary. It was not long after he was gone that my suspicions were confirmed. I was indeed with child, our child. You, my sweet love, are the only part of my dear Isaiah I have for now. We will wait for him together.

I climbed up to our favorite spot in the loft when he was out of sight. The plantation seemed so lonely after the slaves were gone. Mother and I missed them as friends, while Father saw his livelihood walking away. In that moment, the only thing certain to me was that a piece of my heart and soul had just disappeared down that road. I leaned against the same board I'd moved years before on the day Isaiah was branded and cried for hours. Mother and Ophelia kindly hid my absence from Father until dinner, allowing me time to grieve.

Just before I climbed down the ladder, I noticed the corner of a small, white piece of paper not completely covered by the hay. I reached for it and discovered that even though he had no idea he would be leaving the next day, Isaiah had left me a note and a gift. "I love you. Just as we were born to protect each other, I will spend the rest of my life keeping you safe in my heart." There was also a thin, smooth piece of wood in the shape of a fish. It had my name carved on one side and his on the other. The only possible thing that could have made me smile on that day was his note and that beautiful gift.

Chapter 20
"Keepsakes and Dreams"

June 1, 1863

I am trying to write to you as often as possible, my love. My belly is swelling daily as you grow and it is becoming harder to do even the simplest tasks. I have given up trying to sit at my makeshift table. I can no longer get the stool close enough to write comfortably. Now I spend my days either walking short distances around my little home or getting as comfortable as possible on my bed to continue your story. The queasy feeling in my stomach has subsided and I am feeling well. Mother told me that it often passes as the child grows. I can see by the tight seams around my waistline that you are definitely doing your part.

I had hoped that when the Union army came and forced Father to free the slaves that he would have also relieved us of Master David's presence, but Mother informed me that he has decided to keep him on. Apparently, the two of them are trying to figure out a way to keep the plantation profitable. Grandfather McGrath, your great-grandfather, has passed away and Father's brother is encouraging him to come north and start a new life. Mother is discouraging it, knowing that if he decides to leave, we will most certainly be discovered. She and Ophelia are once again manipulating the situation to their satisfaction without Father being any the wiser. Mother simply insists that a man of my father's talents and education can make this plantation a success with or without the use of slave labor. Not being one to pass up a compliment or a challenge, Father agreed. Yesterday he sent a letter to his brother, politely declining his offer.

I have been passing the hours today remembering each time I went to the secret hiding place in the barn and found a gift from your father. Each little carved creature has some special memory attached to it. All together, there are seven—a bird, a fish, a squirrel, a horse, a butterfly, a frog, and a ladybug. I remember finding each one and I have kept the notes that accompanied them. My favorite, of course, is my wedding ring. I can no longer wear it as my fingers have swollen along with the rest of my body. I will wear it again as soon as I am able after your birth. Even the wealthiest king could not offer a queen a ring as precious a treasure as this simple piece of wood has become to me. I can feel your father's hands carving it every time I hold it in my own. For now, it will stay in my tin box with the rest of the things that are most dear to me.

I dreamed of you in your father's arms last night. I could feel his joy as he smiled down upon your sweet face. He called you 'Andrew' and then gave you a second name I had not considered—Ruben. I had just assumed he would want to give you his own name, but just as he has spoken to me a thousand times without one word, I know without a doubt, he did so in my dream. I know in my heart that you are a boy and your name will be Andrew Ruben McGrath. I hope that someday you will think it a worthy name to pass on to your own son. It is just as much a part of your history as the words in this book. When you need a reason to be proud in your life, you have only to say your own name to yourself and know that it represents your heritage. Andrew, who showed your Indian blood in his face and skin; Ruben, who knew how to love without condition and passed that trait on to his son and now to you. Do not remember your surname with hatred or resentment. Remember it as having belonged not to your grandfather, but your grandmother and me. Change the fact that it is associated with intolerance and oppression and make it your own. The change started when my mother took it as hers and continued when I was born into it. You have the chance to carry on what the women of your family have begun so that when I am long gone, you can make the McGrath name synonymous with freedom and acceptance.

It is dusk and I am extinguishing the lantern for the night. I thought I heard Master David riding by on his horse last night. He is no doubt still trying to make himself useful by securing the property. I believe he misses dominating the slaves infinitely more than he misses the success of the plantation. Mother tells me to be careful burning the lamp inasmuch as on a clear night she has seen it from her window, flickering in the distance. I wonder if Father ever misses me or asks Mother if I am well at Aunt Joanie Anne's. I am sure while I dream of you and Isaiah,

Father dreams of all the suitors he thinks I am attracting and how wealthy he hopes they will be. Please know, my love, I would rather live in this shack with your father than a glorious mansion with anyone else. I have no regrets for the life I have chosen. I only hope you feel the same as you endure what I am sure will be some measure of hardship on your path.

I stopped to think for a moment about how worried Annabeth must have been for the wellbeing of her baby, not just in hiding him until and after birth. I considered the hardships of bi-racial children today and could not even begin to imagine how hard it would have been to live in those times and circumstances with skin color that was both too light and too dark. Annabeth must have truly believed that the love she and Isaiah could give their child would be enough to see it through the rough times ahead— either that or she was blinded by her youth. She had seen the slaves beaten and tortured. She must have been terrified at the thought that something like that could happen to her own baby. She always seemed so optimistic and thought that love would be enough. I hoped that she was right, but just as before, deep in my heart, I doubted it.

The clock chimed four a.m. For a split second, I was alarmed thinking I had to get up in three hours and then I remembered my conversation with Phillip. I had to finish. I rubbed my tired eyes and turned the page.

Chapter 21
"Father's Plan"

June 16, 1863

I hardly know what day it is anymore. I just wrote another letter to your father and did not realize until I went to date it that I had no idea what to write. Mother came with my dinner and caught me up. There is news on the plantation that is worrisome to us. Both of your grandmothers spend much of their day in silent prayer for our safety. Your arrival should be soon, my precious, but the days ahead seem to stretch into an eternity when I think of them. Our hiding place may be in jeopardy, but for now, we do as we have been doing, we wait.

Father is considering selling some of the land due to the small crop we will have this year. He says we will need the money to hire men to harvest it in the fall. Unfortunately, the piece of land he feels is least valuable to him is the one where we have been hiding, the woods need clearing and Father has never used it for planting. Mother says he is bargaining with the man who owns the fields adjacent to the one that has become our home. The decision will be made soon. I fear the worst, but hope for the best. There is still no new word from your father, so I continue to do for him what I do for this land, fear the worst and hope for the best. Mother assures me that men have been at war since the beginning of time and like all the others, this one will end. I pray that when it does, your father will march back up that road just as he did when he left. If I close my eyes, I can almost see him in his uniform, so handsome and proud. My heart and my arms ache for him. When I hold you in my arms, I know I will finally be touching part of him. You are my sanity and my hope. I will gladly risk my life for you because without you, my heart will be dead. It almost seems as if the sun has just come up and yet it is already near dark. I am blowing out the lamp's flame and as I have done night after night, I will lie upon this bed and feel you move and grow inside me as I dream of my husband, the other greatest love of my life.

July 15, 1863

Over the past month, I have re-read all of the pages of this account of my life with your father. I believe I have recorded everything of importance. I am giving this journal to Ophelia for her protection along with the things your father made for me, the notes he wrote to me, and the letters I have received from him since he has been gone. Today is an important day. Father has sold the land and we are forced to move. Tonight, under the cover of darkness, Mother and Ophelia have decided that the best place for me to hide is the old slave quarters once occupied by the women. Although it is closer to the house, if I am quiet and stay inside, hopefully Father will not discover our presence. There are only two windows and we must stay out of sight of both of them. If I must sit in darkened silence forever, I will do so to keep you safe; however, Mother feels that we will be seeing you within the coming weeks. I hope and pray that she is right. We have not yet decided what we will do after you are born. Just as before, Mother and Ophelia will wait and see what each day brings and face it as it comes. I will see you soon, my love. The next time I write to you, it will be to tell you of your birth and how beautiful you are. I love you, my angel. I would not change one thing written in these pages because these are the events that have brought us together.

Chapter 21
"Lost Children"

It is August 20, 1863. My name is Emmaline McGrath and I am your grandmother. Annabeth was my daughter. You are as she said you would be, a boy. Ophelia and I have named you just as she wished, Andrew Ruben McGrath. It is about ten o'clock in the morning. You have been with us now for about seven hours. There is a sad reason why your mother is not the one telling you of your birth. It falls to me to explain it to you in this book, just as she would have wanted to do herself.

Her pain began yesterday afternoon. Luckily, your grandfather, Jackson, and David, his foreman, were away for the day. Your mother labored with great joy in anticipation of seeing your face. Despite her pain, she was smiling and happy that the time of your birth had finally arrived. When Jackson did not come home early last evening, Ophelia and I were grateful. We thought perhaps he would miss the entire birth, but it was not to be. They arrived just a few hours after sundown.

Your mother did all she could to remain silent as the hours slipped by into the early morning. Ophelia and I had no choice but to leave her alone until after Jackson and David had been fed and retired for the evening. It was nearly midnight before we were able to sneak out and attend to her again. She was in tremendous pain and very frightened. I feel her youth played an enormous part in her fear and her inability to remain calm and somewhat silent. She was brave and did the best she could to stay quiet, but it was a harder labor than either Ophelia or I had endured or seen before.

At three in the morning, your mother finally screamed out in anguish. It was the last sound she made before you were born. Your grandfather and David burst in through the door just as you emerged from your mother's body. The look of sheer elation on her face quickly changed to one of terror when she saw their shadows fall on the floor in the lamp light. My Annabeth was pulled into the angry eyes of her father and screamed once again, this time in terror.

Ophelia was unable to sever the cord that still bound you to your mother because Jackson forced his way past me and yanked her away from the bed. He ripped the flesh that connected you to your mother from deep within her body and she began to bleed profusely. He threw his own daughter on the floor and told David to whip her until all of her blood was spilled, then to do the same to me. My Annabeth was right about him being blind with anger at my knowing and hiding her secret from him.

David grabbed Annabeth and dragged her outside, leaving a trail of blood behind them. Her last thoughts were of you. She screamed for Ophelia to protect you from them. Before either of the men were able to catch me, I ran to the house and found Jackson's shotgun. He had stolen my son from me and I did not intend to allow him to harm my only child or my grandchild. By the time I returned, David was whipping Annabeth with all of his might. Without a second thought, I took aim and shot him. He had used his whip on my little girl and I made sure that it would be the last time he ever held it in his cruel hands. Without an ounce of remorse about what I'd done, I pointed the shotgun straight ahead and walked toward the sounds of Ophelia screaming and Jackson shouting. He was in the slave's shack trying to take you from Ophelia. She was crouched in the corner, covering you with her own body while he beat her with his fists. She would have protected you until she had used her last ounce of strength or taken her last breath. I had Jackson in my sights. There was only one shot left in the gun, but I ensured my accuracy as I fearlessly narrowed the distance between us. With the memory of my own son and now my daughter's lifeless body fresh in my mind, I had no trouble pulling the trigger. Jackson had stolen both of my children and any feelings I had for him died with them. He toppled over onto the bed from which he had just torn his own child. There was a hole in his chest as big as the one he left in my heart. I ran outside, frantic to hold my Annabeth one last time. Summoning all of my strength, I rolled David's vile body off your pure and precious mother, inasmuch as my first shot had caused him to fall on top of her. Some might say I am also a murderer and no better than either David or my husband. I say Jackson absolved me of any guilt when he mercilessly took my children from me. I still have life, but without them, the best part of me is dead.

My efforts to save her came too late. My sweet daughter, my Annabeth, was lying in a river of her own blood. It was soaking into the earth with the tears of both Ophelia and me. She had just become a mother and I knew my days as hers were over. My heart broke into tiny pieces as Ophelia and I buried her in the field behind the house. Ophelia took four of the bricks from the wall in the basement and marked the head, foot, and sides of the grave, then covered them with dirt.

We had to hide the fact that Annabeth had been killed so that the next part of our plan would not fall under suspicion. I, for a while, allowed myself to become numb and to buried my grief with my child I had to cover my emotion with the illusion of my innocence. We left the blood and bodies as they were. I retrieved another shotgun from the house, laid it next to David, and placed the other next to Jackson. The next morning, I informed the Sheriff that we had found Jackson and David just after sunrise. I told him that I had heard them having a dispute over some missing money the night before, but decided it was not my business and kept silent. Seeing how distraught I was, the Sheriff simply took my word as an upstanding citizen and Southern woman of fine breeding. He took the bodies and had them buried behind the church as we had no family plot on the land. Ophelia stayed with you and I have just returned from "mourning" their loss. You will stay with Ophelia and me now, and I will spread word that your mother has decided to live in Atlanta with my sister permanently. We will continue to wait for your father to return home. This house has been full of secrets for too many years. Your father will be the only other soul besides you to know them all. We will hide this book well until you are someday old enough to understand. We are fortunate that Ophelia was able to save your life, she wrapped her apron string around your torn cord to stop your bleeding when you were ripped away from your mother. I have placed Annabeth's silver rattle next to you as you sleep. Your angelic face is peaceful, having no idea what has just transpired. Her initials, which are also yours, A.M., are engraved in the silver handle of the toy. One day you will understand how much she loved you and how great her sacrifice truly was. You are, as she said you would be, a beautiful, perfect mix of both your parents.

October 11, 1863

I don't rite so good as my boy do. Miss Emmaline teached me some when I were young but I learnt mostly from Isaiah after Annabeth teached him. Miss Emmaline say I shood rite in here for Andrew. She say I need to tell him just like Annabeth wood want me to. Reverend brung my boy home to me from war today. I seen them on they way up the road. Isaiah was leant over the horse and I knowed he was gone befow Reverend told me. He also say that Isaiah done met his daddy in the war. He say they met Ruben and he were pleased he had a son. My Ruben knowd what it were like to be free and he met his boy. I's glad bout that. Reverend say they died a frew days apart. He say Ruben wood wanted to come back to me after the war were over but he were buried on a battle field two day befow our boy were killed. Reverend say Ruben maked

177

him promise to bring our boy home to his mama if he don't make it. Reverend say he wood and he did. He say Isaiah were a good soldyer and I otta be proud. I love my boy and was proud anyhow no mater anythin. Miss Emmaline she help me bury him next to yor ma. I took fow mow briks out the wall and put them round the grave. Isaiah done keeped all the letters Annabeth done wrote him while he were gone in his pocket. I put them in the tin box with all them things Annabeth done saved that he give to her and bury it betwen them. They togeder now by all those things they love. He were only sixteen year old but he knowed true love by me and by Annabeth. I tooked off my ring Miss Emmaline done give me when I marry Ruben my Isaiahs daddy. I put it also in the box wif the rest of they things. Now my boy have somthin to remimber his mama and his daddy. Reverend he say a frew nice words over them. Miss Emmaline done saved his bible all them years and gived it back to him. He tooked it and left after the buryin. He free now jus like he knowed he wood be. Me and Miss Emmaline all we gots lef is this house and our grandboy to remimber our babys. We gonna rase him up good for our Annabeth and Isaiah.

Chapter 23
"Confessions"

I closed the book and had myself a good cry. It was 6:00 a.m. and I was sad, exhausted, and angry. I sat there holding the journal and Miss Claudia's blanket until my eyes forced me to sleep. I woke up around 10:00, still on the couch. My first thoughts were of Annabeth. She was in my dreams and had followed my thoughts into my conscious mind the moment I opened my eyes. I had to know more—what happened to Andrew, where were Annabeth and Isaiah buried. There were a few empty pages, but they were blank. There were no more answers. I forced myself to get up, knowing I would never fall to back asleep.

"Let's go outside," I called to Keno as I put on my slippers. I thought a walk around the yard and to the mailbox might do me some good.

The fresh air did clear my head a little as I remembered there were a few other books in the crate. Hoping for more answers, I took off running towards the house. I was out of breath when Keno and I reached the front porch. I had to pause and let the throbbing in my ribs subside. I realized then that the dissipating pain and faint bruising were the only reminders I had that anyone with dark skin had ever hurt me. I took what little breath I had and made a promise out loud so my heart would hear it.

"I will find you, Andrew, or whoever your family may be. I will do this for my sake and for...for Willie's. Maybe someday this peace will come full circle to him. This may not be his kin, but it could have been.

I felt relief, peace and contentment with all my circumstances for the first time in a long time when I made that promise. I tried to think when the last time was that I'd felt that way. It was the day my dad hugged me goodbye and Sissy smiled at me from her car seat. I had done it. I had finally made it back to a place of peace. I knew to stay there I had to help Annabeth and Isaiah find their peace as well. I went upstairs to my bedroom where I'd put the crate in the back of my closet.

It turns out the other books were school tablets with Annabeth's and Isaiah's childish handwriting and the pictures they'd drawn. There were also a few pages that appeared to be in Isaiah's and Ophelia's writing. It must have been from when he was teaching her what he had learned. Leafing through the tablets made me smile. It was a reminder that there were some happy times shared between the three of them. The big book on the bottom looked more recent. It was about antebellum homes and had been copyrighted in the Sixties. I picked it up and started to thumb through it, figuring it must have belonged to Miss Claudia. I gasped when I came to a page that was marked and found an envelope with my name on it, written in Miss Claudia's handwriting.

Dear Angie,

I left you this house knowing that someday you would find this letter. If you are reading this, then I assume you have also read the journal. I never told you about it for the same reason my father never told my mother. He found the box and the missing bricks when he bought the house when I was a child. I stumbled upon it one day when I was about sixteen. He did not think my mother would have been too keen on the idea of living in a house where there were people buried in the back yard and a history of violence, slavery, and murder. He confessed to me that was the reason why we planted all those trees just after we moved in. He wanted to turn the field into something beautiful, to cover up its past and the graves that lay beneath its surface. We never did tell my mother the truth. Every time we walked in those woods together, we would remember what really happened here. It is true we did enjoy the wildlife and shade the trees eventually provided, but make no mistake, those trees exist today to cover the secrets and sins of the land. I hope you are not angry with me for not telling you before I was gone. I wanted you to take the journey for yourself, to discover the people who used to live here before you made any decisions about keeping the house. I knew if I told you the story, I could never have done it justice. If you recall, I have told you partial truths about the land over the years. Remember all those summer days when you were a teenager and we sat on the porch swing together? If you think back, I'm sure you will see some of the story you now know in the tales I told you back then. We never found *the graves or the box buried between them. I have often thought of finding Andrew's kin and giving them the journal. I told Paul Hammond that you would appreciate and care for the house and that's why I didn't leave it to Hannah. Now you can understand why. We are kindred spirits, you and I. I knew then and still do now that you will love this house and live in it for years to come, gazing out that window just as Daddy and I did. I don't know if you knew it while I was alive, but you are the daughter I always wanted, Angie, and I love you very much. Thank you for letting me adopt you into my heart and now into my home.*

Love,

Miss Claudia

I cried again, seeing Miss Claudia's distinctive handwriting. The page she had marked was a picture of the original house that stood over the basement on this spot. I suppose I could understand her reasons for not telling me and letting me get to know Annabeth and Isaiah before she told me they were buried under the trees somewhere in the back yard. I assumed according to the picture of where the slaves' quarters used to be that Emmaline shot Jackson and David somewhere close to where the shed now sits. I had to get out for a while and think.

I jumped in the shower and then threw on some sweats and a ball cap. I put the top down on my little convertible and put Keno in the passenger seat. We rode all afternoon with the wind in our hair and the sun on our faces. I thought and thought all day as we drove the back roads. We drove from Roberta to Reynolds and Macon on the unbeaten paths instead of the interstate. Looking at the old houses and fields, the thought occurred to me that my land was likely no different from much of the other wooded areas. The only real distinctive quality between my property and any other is that I happened to know the history behind it. There were probably dozens of stories just like the one I'd read that in this day and age we would never be aware of. The revelation was comforting, but I knew of one more thing that would make me feel even better. When we got back to Fort Valley, Keno and I swung by the Dairy Queen and each got a vanilla cone.

On my way back through town, I noticed Paul Hammond standing just outside his office waving me down. "I saw you go by the first time," he was breathless, as if he had just leaped from his desk to run outside and catch me. "I never got a chance to tell you something about Miss Claudia's will."

I rolled my eyes and sighed. "Mr. Hammond, I really can't take any more surprises," I was, hoping he'd just let the matter go for a while. I also know that like Phill, Paul is a consummate professional and doesn't feel his job is done until every "t" is crossed.

"It's not a big deal, really," he said, trying to minimize his mistake. "It just happened so quickly that day and Hannah just left in such a huff that I didn't get a chance to tell you about the crate."

"Crate?" I asked, hoping there might be another one and some more clues as to what happened to Andrew.

"Yes, it seems Miss Claudia left all of the contents of her home to Hannah except one. Had I read just two more sentences before Hannah left, I would have remembered to tell you. I'm afraid it's all my fault." He stepped down off the curb and closer to my car door. "You see, we were leaving the next day, the wife and I, for our second honeymoon." He smiled remembering it. "I took her on a cruise to Alaska."

From the wide smile the memory brought, I could tell they had seen very little of the scenery. It was a bit of a scandal in town when he married a woman half his age who looked like she had just stepped off the pages of a glossy fashion magazine. I suppose the fact that he was the richest lawyer in town made up for his age and occasional lack of social skills. It must have for him to have a trophy wife like her.

"Anyway," he went on, drawing me from the mental picture I had conjured of the two of them on their trip—an image I was glad to shake from my mind. "Miss Claudia did leave you a crate. She said it was stored under the steps in the basement. She said you can't miss it. It's old and rickety-looking and Hannah would never want it."

I smiled, remembering how easily she had parted with it. "I already found it, Mr. Hammond. Don't worry, I was the one who kept it. Hannah didn't want it, so as luck would have it, Miss Claudia got her wish."

He breathed a sigh of relief, feeling he hadn't failed her after all. I bid him good day as I finished what was left of my melting ice cream and watched him walk back into his office.

I was exhausted from my lack of sleep the night before, but I knew there was one more thing I wanted to do before I went to bed early to catch up on my rest. I put the journal in a large Ziplock storage bag to protect its old, precious pages. I knew it was time to share it with someone who would not only appreciate it as much as I did, but be happy to finally have the scoop. I smiled, knowing what joy having the answer to my odd behavior of late would bring her. I hoped I would sleep well and that morning would come quickly. I was excited to pass on my sleepless nights to someone else.

Chapter 24
"Janice's Turn"

I walked into work Tuesday morning only to find things exactly as I had left them. It's funny how you can have a life-changing experience and the rest of the world simply keeps on turning, totally untouched by it. Janice looked up at me, pulling her bifocals down and peering over the top of them as usual.

"Morning, you're looking better." She was right this morning when I got up my face looked almost healed, I thought to myself again amazing what 24 hours can do. When all I did was thank her for the compliment she gave me the look it takes mothers years to perfect, but she didn't say anything else. I could tell she was forcing herself to stay casual and not threaten my life if I didn't stop and fill her in. I knew I wasn't going to make it past that desk until she knew once and for all what was going on, so I stopped and opened my briefcase on her desktop. She sat on her squeaky chair, waiting for the answer she felt she'd been entitled to since last week.

I took out the plastic bag with the journal inside and gently slid it over to her. I smiled and then passed her the extra orange juice and donut I had purchased. "This should answer all of your questions and then some," I felt a little bad, knowing what was in store for her, but she was the one who wanted to know everything. "When you're done, maybe you can help me figure out what we should do about it," I waved my hand over the journal as if I were a model on a game show... she looked confused

She started to open the bag, but I caught her hand and stopped her. "Trust me, you'll want to wait 'til you get home before you do that."

Every time I passed her desk for the rest of the day, she was sitting there either staring at the unopened journal or the clock.

* * *

At five minutes after five when I went downstairs to go home, she was already gone. I smiled to myself. Poor Janice was about to get everything she asked for. I slept like a baby that night knowing I would no longer be harboring the secrets alone; however, I'd put a note in the front cover of the journal that read "FOR YOUR EYES ONLY."

I was not exactly thrilled about the entire town knowing because there would be a constant parade of people in my backyard looking for those graves and wondering about the contents of that box. "No, thank you," was all I had to say to the prospect of everyone in town on my doorstep. Knowing Miss Claudia the way I did, I'm sure she'd also factored in the small town rumor mill when she decided to keep the secrets of her land and home.

It seemed like forever since Janice had her gall bladder out. It was the only time on record she'd ever missed work. After I gave her the journal on Tuesday morning, I didn't see her again until Friday night. I passed her empty desk three mornings in a row. I could just picture her sleep-deprived face and her empty box of Kleenex. A small part of me hated doing it to her, but she's the one who wanted to know everything and now I'm sure she was finding out in spades. The satisfaction of seeing her empty chair warmed my heart. I wasn't alone anymore.

* * *

187

It was nine o'clock on Friday night. I had just made some popcorn and was about to settle in and watch my favorite movie when the chimes of my doorbell began to play. I prayed all the way to the door that it wasn't some surprise visit from one of the many former dates I was trying to avoid. I was relieved to open it and see Janice standing there holding the journal and a large pizza.

"We should find them," she said, more of a declaration than a suggestion, she walked straight past me into my kitchen and maked herself right at home. She rifled through my cabinets looking for plates, all the while never taking a breath. "I mean, this is someone's history, someone's family, and they're buried in your back yard," she wildly pointed the spatula in her hand toward the woods behind my house. I just stood there, leaning up against a column that led into the kitchen, watching her work herself up into a frenzy of emotion and advice. "We can't just pretend they don't exist. I suppose Miss Claudia left it to you to do the right thing," she was still not coming up for air or giving me a chance to respond.

She had been through nearly every drawer and cabinet when I walked over and opened the one with the plates and cups in it. "I have some ideas about how we can do it," she, automatically included herself. "I have keys to the offices in the courthouse. We can start tomorrow." She walked over to my refrigerator, poured us both a glass of grape soda, and handed me a plate with a few slices of pizza on it. "We need to talk about this," she knew she was invited to sit down as always, just like in my office and, headed towards the living room.

Having not yet said a word, I followed her to see exactly what her plan was. Since I had already decided to find Andrew's family, I let her go on and on for a few more

188

minutes before I agreed. I decided to keep it between me, my grandpa, and God exactly why I needed to find them. For Janice, it was about the adventure. For me, it was all about the healing and "Dr. Janice" knew exactly where to start.

Chapter 25
"The Search"

"Tomorrow morning," she said, taking another bite of pizza. "We'll go to the office. I have keys to the file room. Surely there must be some clues in there. Fort Valley was founded in 1825 and there must be some record of the original house and land boundaries. If we can find them, maybe it'll be a clue as to what happened to the people who lived here. I mean, there must be some ledger of births and deaths kept by the early churches." She finally took a breath and looked at me for my input.

"Yes, but Emmaline hid the fact that Annabeth was dead and I'm sure very few records were kept on slaves."

A look of disappointment crossed Janice's face, but she was undaunted. "We're just going to have to go through everything we can find from that era," she started mentally, looking back into her memories of childhood. "I'm so glad that my mother grew up here and had me late in her life. Most everything I know about this town came firsthand from her and not some story she learned that got changed during the re-telling over the generations. I know for a fact that the story I told you about this house is true. Having that information about when the original house burned and the name 'McGrath' as the person who rebuilt it should get us started."

I agreed and finished my pizza while she rambled on about how excited she would be to meet a descendent of Emmaline, Annabeth, and Ophelia.

* * *

The next morning we met in front of the courthouse at 9:00 a.m. sharp. Last night after Janice left, I'd been thinking that I too would be interested to know how the bloodline of three such extraordinary women turned out. The only way we'd ever know is if there was some trace of evidence in that courthouse. The only place we knew that they ever existed was in the journal.

We went straight to the file room and began digging through the archives. After about half an hour I was sure the only thing we'd find that was as old as the journal was the dust all over everything. "Don't they clean in here," Janice wondered rolling her eyes. My answer did not make her feel any better. "Please, I think we're the first people in here since they put in the door and shut it."

We were both wiping our hands and waving the dust away, hoping this wouldn't take long. I could feel Grandpa's treasure-finding luck all over me like the spider webs hanging from the ceiling. We went through record after record, even found some old maps of the area from the right period, but nothing that brought us any closer to the truth seemed to jump out at us. Finally, after hours of searching and nearly choking to death a couple of times on the two inches of dirt on the filing cabinet it was in, I found one morsel of good news. It was an old death certificate with Emmaline Lagoy McGrath's name written on it.

"Look what I found!" In my excitement, I shouted it a little too loud.

I startled Janice who was crouched on the floor going through a disorganized stack of papers. She jumped up and hit her head on the open drawer above her when I shrieked.

"Sorry," I apologized the whole way while I was, rushing over to make sure she wasn't hurt. Not seeing any blood on her short, tight curls, I assumed she was alright.

"What?" she was, rubbing the top of her head, her irritation covered by her curiosity.

"It's Emmaline's death certificate." I handed it to her. "It says here she died in January 1897, which would have made her sixty-nine."

Before I even finished my sentence, I saw the light flashing in Janice's eyes. Her dizziness and bump on the head temporarily forgotten, she jumped to her feet. Seeing that she was unsteady, I grabbed her arm to keep her from falling.

"I guess that thump on the head shook my brain a little," she was again, rubbing the lump that was developing as she headed toward the table where she'd left a stack of old maps. She thumbed through them until she found the one she'd discovered and discarded hours ago. "Look here," she was obviously getting excited, pointing to the date on the bottom corner.

"1900," I read aloud.

"I saw something earlier, but didn't put it together until now." She adjusted her bifocals and leaned over to get a better look at the lines and landmarks. "Right here," she pointed. "It's the only cemetery I've seen on any of these." She gestured to the stack of maps made several years earlier. "It only makes sense that Emmaline would be buried here. I think I may know the area. When I was a kid, we lived behind where the bus factory is now. There's an old cemetery there. We used to dare each other to walk through it on Halloween."

I'd never been happier than I was at that moment that I was blessed with the gift of appreciating people older than myself.

"There are some new houses out there now and I'm sure most of the markers are in disrepair. I mean, it was old when I was a kid and that was when dinosaurs roamed the earth," she laughed, enjoying her own joke about her age.

"Janice, I don't care what was roaming the earth, I'm just glad you were there to see it," I drug her toward the parking lot not wanting her to get dizzy again and fall, but not wanting her to hold me up either. I was so excited about our find I could hardly wait to get in the car and drive out there.

* * *

The road that led out behind the bus company was unpaved and bumpy. We also had to cross the old wooden bridge that everybody in town was afraid of ever since a couple of kids almost went over the side a few years ago. Just as we rumbled across the lumber to the other side, Janice told me to stop. "It's over there." She was pointing to the empty, overgrown field that sat just on the edge of a small wooded area. On the other side of the trees is where the houses began.

"I suppose the city kept the factory from building here. The idea of living next to dead people kept anyone from wanting to put their house on this side of the trees." She went on to explain how the factory and neighborhoods had been built when she was in her early twenties. "I suppose over time as the relatives of the dead passed on themselves, folks just forgot about the graves. I mean, who would want to be buried out behind a bus company when they could be resting in the shade of some old magnolias over in the new cemetery?"

"Not me," I replied, tripping over a root as we headed towards the crumbling headstones.

Some of the markers were so overgrown with weeds and tall grass that we had to clear a path from one to the next. Some of them were also just inside the line of trees that had taken over the far boundary of the field. However, we did discover that all of the graves belonged to people who very easily could have lived on this land at the same time Emmaline did. My first discovery was not exactly what I was looking for, but at least it confirmed we had not wasted our day in the file room.

"Janice, come look at this," I wanted to be sure of what I was seeing so I, leaned down to clear away the debris from years of neglect.

Janice gasped when she read the words on the grave marker. The edges had crumbled away long ago, but the words were still intact. "David Kincaid," she read aloud. "Wow! That's the last person that even crossed my mind." She was remembering, as was I, how he had treated the slaves and taken the life of Annabeth.

"I almost want to kick over what's left of the marker," being this close I suddenly found myself very angry at him. Then silently remembering my promise to my grandfather... "Not me, I didn't want any of his hate in my blood or my heart."

"Me too," Janice agreed, putting her arm around me. "Well, at least we know we're in the right spot. I think I found part of the foundation of the church that used to be here," she started walking back over to where she had been standing.

We each stood on what we thought were the corners of the old building and sure enough, it made sense. It was a nearly a perfect square. We walked the field all day without any luck before we noticed the sun had begun to fade.

"I have a flashlight in the car," I remembered, heading back over to where I had parked. I kept waiting for Janice to suggest that we start again in the morning, but she never did. She was as determined as I was to find Emmaline.

It was about eight-thirty when we finally struck gold. After walking around in the open field all day, I decided to check some of the old stones near the edge of the woods. There were two headstones just beyond the second row of trees. They'd been protected a little better than the others due to their location. I directed the beam of my extra-large Coleman flashlight on the names. The one on the left read "Emmaline Lagoy McGrath" and the one on the right read "Jackson McGrath." The date of death on Jackson's grave was the same listed in the journal as the day Andrew was born. We spent at least an hour with only the street lamp and a flashlight to guide our hands in the dark, but by the time we were done, we had pulled every weed and root covering Emmaline's final resting place. We decided to leave Jackson's as it was, as we had about the same respect for him as we did for David Kincaid. It wasn't about carrying the same kind of animosity my uncle had, it was more about honoring Emmaline's memory, respecting her wishes—at least that's what I told myself.

Around ten, I took Janice back to the courthouse so she could pick up her car. "Want to get together after church tomorrow and go over the journal again?" she asked. "Maybe there's something we missed or haven't considered." There was a glimmer of renewed hope in her voice. Her enthusiasm was contagious and I agreed.

"I'll meet you at your house about one-thirty," she promised. Just as I was about to drive away, she rolled down her window and yelled, "How about Chinese?"

"Sounds great," I hollered back as I turned my car around and headed toward home.

All the way there, I kept thinking about how this must be an adventure for Janice, but it was more personal for me. Her excitement over the graves we'd found made the people in the journal real to her. Not only had they been real to me from the start, they had become a part of my life. After all, they once lived in my home, and on my land. They'd brought me an understanding of my own family and feelings that I never would have found without them. I had to resolve it now. It was the only way I could ever begin to repay Annabeth for all she'd taught me, the only way I could show Andrew that the world was capable of change.

I remembered the letter Miss Claudia had left for me to find and thought about all the stories she had told me over the years. She was right, each one did have a little bit of Annabeth and Isaiah in it. I hurried home so I could call my grandfather and catch him up on the day's events. It was not until I saw Keno and realized that I'd been gone all day that the call would have to wait until my buddy took care of some business of his own.

Chapter 25
"The Search"

I was so glad to talk to him. Nobody would ever understand why this was so important to me like he would, but leave it to Grandpa to point out the obvious. He immediately found something I'd missed.

After I told him all about the death certificate and the graves, he asked me the simple question I never thought to ask myself. "Didn't the journal say that Annabeth hoped her son would carry on his name throughout the generations to follow?"

Remembering that was a particularly touching moment for me, I recalled reading it as if I had just done so that moment. "Yes, she did," I answered, unsure where he was trying to lead me. I expounded on the point, hoping I'd answer his question thoroughly. "She said she wanted him to take the name and pass it on so that he could carry on the work of turning the McGrath heritage into something he could be proud of. It had something to do with the tradition that she, her mother, and Ophelia had started." I loved that part because it had come to mean to me what my grandpa had done with our name and what I was learning to do to make my father proud. Living without all that bitterness was getting easier and so was leaving the whys and the randomness behind.

"Well," he gently suggested, "Why don't you start there? Start with the biggest clue you have. It has been my experience in historical research that if you have a name, you have nearly everything you need. The South is very proud of its tradition and lineage. If Andrew ever read his mother's journal, I have no doubt that after what she did for him, he would carry on the name that obviously meant so much to her. I mean, she died protecting him, so why wouldn't a son carry out the request of a mother who clearly loved him so much?"

I sat and thought for a minute, wondering why I hadn't just called him the moment I decided to track down Annabeth's kin. I was glad we had found the graves, but it sure would have saved Janice and me a lot of guessing as to what to do next.

"Grandpa, I don't know what I'd do if I wasn't related to the smartest man I know."

He laughed and agreed. "Me neither," He wished me good luck and sweet dreams.

* * *

Janice showed up right on time with Chinese food as promised. "I have no idea what the sermon was about this morning," she admitted, but the guilt didn't curb her appetite as she once again helping herself to my kitchen. "All I could think about was what we should do next."

I took the plates from her hand and smiled, knowing I had the answer. "I, on the other hand, heard every word," I took the rare opportunity to, mock her and brag a little. "Would you like me to tell you about it?"

She gave me a dirty look and grabbed two bottled waters out of my 'fridge. "No, Miss Smarty Pants, I want to stand here in the dark all day." "I guess since your brain was not preoccupied, you must have some plan I'm not yet privy to." She waited for me to answer as she took her first bite of a large egg roll.

"Why yes, I do. I spoke with my grandfather last night and he pointed out a very important fact that we managed to miss, even though it was right in front of our faces."

Janice stopped chewing and swallowed hard. "What?" she asked, too excited to continue eating. I decided to make her work for it the way my grandfather had done to me.   "What   did Annabeth name her son?" I asked.

She rolled her eyes, knowing I already knew the answer. "Just tell me the plan," she was getting a little demanding and looking more than a little irritated, out of character for someone who has spent years in training waiting for the best scoop. She sat down on one of the bar stools next to the counter pouting a little.

I laughed, watching her pull her short frame onto the seat. "Just tell me," I repeated, unrelenting in my desire for her to discover our new course of action for herself. I knew she would appreciate it so much more once I made my point if she was actually able to figure it out on her own.

"Andrew Ruben McGrath," she repeated the journal quote, once again rolling her eyes and munching on her food.

"And what did Annabeth ask her son to do in regard to his name?" I asked, pretending to pull on an invisible rope to drag the answer from her.

Janice thought for a second, remembering the touching moment as I had the night before. "She asked him to pass it on," she answered. It was as if a million light bulbs started going off in her eyes and expression as she recounted the words, what she suggested next was not at all what I expected to hear.

"You need to call Rusty," jumped off the stool and handed me the phone.

"Rusty?" not a chance I immediately reached to, put the handset back in its base. "No way! Why in the world would I want to do that? I haven't even seen him since...well, that night and I don't have any idea what I'd say. Talk about your awkward, "Oh hey, Rusty, remember me? You know, the blonde bleeding all over the floor, whose door you broke down after our terrible date." I said it casually with big gestures so Janice would understand just how stupid I'd look trying to have that conversation.

Janice picked up the phone and handed it to me again. "Because he's a cop and cops have access to computers that have every driver's license and address in the state listed in them. Now suck it up and do it!"

I'd never heard her talk like that—and it was definitely an order. I paused before taking the receiver. "How important do you think this is?" she asked, dangling the phone from the cord around her finger. I thought about that for a second knowing how different our reasons were. I huffed at her and grabbed the handset.

I closed my eyes knowing she was right. "If he asks me out again, you're going to make up some excuse for me every time he comes through those courthouse doors." I am grateful, yes, but still he just ain't the one, Janice." Emphasis on my poor English *aint.*

"No problem," she promised, reaching out and shaking my hand to seal the deal. I sighed and dialed the number.

* * *

Within the hour, we were sitting in a small room huddled around Rusty and a computer screen. It was his day off, so of course he was dressed to kill in his after church Sunday best. This time it was sandals and socks that he'd matched to his red tank top. The ensemble was completed with shiny blue nylon gym shorts. I couldn't help but think that Rusty must be color blind. I mean, nobody dressed like that on purpose, did they? The only thing that did match was the red plaster cast on his right hand that went up to his elbow. He noticed me staring at it and got self-conscious. He moved it out of my view as if it were possible to hide such a thing. Janice saw the look on my face and went behind his back and made the same motion he must have made to break in my door and immediately I felt ashamed. How could I still think of him in any sort of unkind way when he'd done so much for me? For all he knew, Willie was armed and he was risking his life. It never occurred to me that he'd been hurt. 'Selfish' was the only word to describe how I felt, and it burned a little in my chest.

"Don't go spreading this around," he was basically, in his nice guy way, making us promise to keep his help a secret. "I could get into trouble for this."

"We promise," Janice held up her scouts honor symbol before starting to, rub his shoulders as if he were a boxer about to enter the ring. He typed in the name. I held my breath hoping something would come up. I felt like grandpa striking rare stamp gold when I heard him say the words.

"Here it is," Rust had a big Cheshire cat grin on his face. He was so proud he could help. "Andrew Ruben McGrath. There are four of them in Atlanta." There were at least ten Andrew McGraths listed, six with a different middle initial. I could just picture myself having to track down all of them. "Lucky for you, you have a full name or this could have taken a lot longer." He pointed to the screen and showed us listings for the four Andrew Ruben McGraths who might actually be our man.

"Can we have the address for all of them?" I asked, trying to act all sweet and charming. Janice saw right through me and gave me a look that said so. She didn't know I meant it. She also didn't know that I'd found a soft spot in myself for a lot of things lately. Seeing that cast on his arm and really thinking about what he did put Rusty right in the middle of it right now. On the other hand, Rusty was oblivious. He printed out the information and handed it to me with a smile. I took the paper and thanked him again.

Thinking she was doing me a favor, Janice acted like we had to leave quickly. She turned and stared at me when she realized she was at the door alone. "I'll be right behind you," I nodded, giving her the green light to keep going.

Deborah Robillard

Rusty may not be the one for me or even close to the man of my dreams, but he was the one for someone and the least I could do was not leave him scarred and feeling rejected when she found him. I reached out and sort of held his good hand. "Thank you for everything." That part came out soft and serious and then my sense of humor kicked in—the one that comes out when I can't face things. "You know the date...the dinner..." I cleared my throat, almost unable to say it. "Saving my life." I managed to sound as serious as I felt for that last part. If it were possible, he turned redder. For a second I saw past his clothes and his awkward demeanor and into his blue-green eyes.

"You're welcome, Ang, just doing my job." Knowing he was unarmed and off duty, I called him on it. "No, you weren't. You were looking out for a friend and I want you to know I appreciate it. If you hadn't been there..." I couldn't finish. We both knew the end of the thought anyway.

He leaned in and hugged my sore ribs with his good arm. "You're welcome, anytime, only let's hope never again" he smiled at me. I could see the acceptance of the word 'friend' in his eyes as he pulled away and escorted me to the door. I didn't see it through his uniform or his weird flowered shirt, but Rusty was made of something most people let alone most men aren't. He has a good heart. Lucky girl who would find him, I wanted to tell him so but I think he could tell by my gesture of friendship he know exactly what I felt. Another breakthrough.

* * *

Janice and I rushed back to my house and were immediately ready to start calling the numbers before it dawned on me that I had no idea what to say. "I can't do this over the phone," I said, realizing that this was pretty much a face to face issue. "I mean, this is going to change someone's life. I can't just say, 'Hey, is there an Annabeth McGrath in your family?' because then I'd have to follow up with, 'I think she's buried in my back

202

yard.' Janice agreed and we sat in silence, each coming up with our own solution. Before she could "gently" insist I do things her way, I spoke first.

"I have plenty of vacation time coming to me and I'm going to use some of it. I'm going to Atlanta tomorrow to visit the most likely candidates and see if one of them knows anything about this book. Who knows? Maybe if I find him he'll know where the graves are, but has no idea where the house is. He could have a map of my yard, but no idea where it's located. Maybe Ophelia and Emmaline showed Andrew where his parents were buried and it's been passed down in their family for years. You know how bits and pieces of the story get lost or exaggerated over time, maybe this Andrew Ruben McGrath knows more than we do."

Janice looked doubtful and protested a bit about my going off to Atlanta to meet some strange man by myself, but in the end, I won out. I believe that's the first time that has ever happened in our entire relationship.

* * *

The next morning I went into work without my briefcase and breakfast. I went straight up the stairs and had a long talk with Philllip. He was a little bit upset that I wasn't giving him any notice, but I pointed out that in all my years of service, I had never taken any of my vacation time. It didn't hurt that I held my side a little, favoring my ribs. My face had healed, but it felt like my ribs would be sore forever. He agreed and said he'd see me in two weeks. I walked out, waved at Janice, and headed to Atlanta.

"Call me," she insisted, as I swung open the heavy door. I think it was in part a comment of concern for my safety and part of her "thirst for knowledge" talking.

* * *

By the time I made it to Atlanta, it was 5:30. I cursed myself for leaving town so late and getting into the city at the peak of rush hour traffic. I had to run home after I left the courthouse and let Keno out and then ask my neighbor to watch him for a couple of days. I found reasonably priced lodging in what I thought was a decent area that might be close to one of the addresses I had. I went to the nearest gas station to get a map and hopefully some directions. It turned out I was in luck, had to be grandmas, she was always the best treasure hunter. The first Andrew on the list lived only a few minutes from my hotel. The cashier was able to draw me a map and I was on my way.

He lived in one of those high-rise buildings with a door attendant and valet parking. There was a reception desk in the lobby and they called to let Mr. McGrath know he had a visitor. I hoped he was not expecting someone else because without even asking who it was, he gave his permission for me to come up.

I stepped off the elevator and was standing in front of a rather large wooden door. For a moment, I felt like I was about eight years old. I had that same sick feeling in my stomach as I did the summer I had to go door-to-door selling Girl Scout cookies. I used to get so nervous after I rang the bell that I wanted to run away. This time, instead of cookies I was standing there clutching the journal, praying I had the right person. I was certain if I didn't, this Andrew McGrath would think I was some whacko off the street who'd managed to weasel my way upstairs. I mean this was a swanky place. I couldn't believe he just agreed to let me come up.

I checked my outfit, put on some lipstick, grateful that my makeup had covered any shadow of the light bruising still left on my cheeks. I took a deep breath, summoned my courage, and rang the bell. Before he opened the door, it occurred to me that if this was the wrong man, I'd have to do this again tomorrow. I prayed that just this once I would be able to hold onto grandmas luck and side step my grandfathers.

The Crickets Dance

A tall, attractive, clean-cut man answered the door. He was on the telephone and still wearing an expensive suit, silk shirt and tie. He was obviously a professional and had just returned from work. The thing that really struck me, which I had not considered until this very second, was that he was black. Standing still and across from him for not even a split second, I saw Willie's face. In the rest of that second, I thought, *I won't be that—not my heart, not my blood.* I couldn't believe how stupid I'd been to assume he was white. I just pictured him that way because Annabeth was white and I assumed the McGrath who had rebuilt the house had to be kin to Jackson, a nephew or something. *Did that make me a racist?* I'd been down this road and untangled this web already. Willie was gone for good. It did catch me off guard though. I knew Isaiah was black, so I wondered why I'd just assumed this man was not.

"Can I help you?" he asked, hanging up the phone and politely gesturing for me to step inside. He looked a little confused because he didn't recognize me, making me think again he'd been expecting someone else—either that or he was incredibly trusting.

I stepped inside beyond the threshold and my heart started racing. Maybe I was the one who was too trusting. Black or white, nice place or not, I was in a strange man's apartment. We stood in awkward silence for a moment before he sensed I had something to say and he must have seen how nervous I was. He stepped away from me, probably to show he meant me no harm. He saw the book in my hand and showed me into his living room. He followed at a more than proper distance, but I think I saw curiosity on his face before I turned to walk in the direction he had indicated. I tried to shake off the Girl Scout cookies feeling and the Willie fear that kept creeping up on me and think about the task at hand. I was doing this for Annabeth's peace...and for mine.

I was surprised that when I thanked him, my voice was shaking. I sat down and then he seated himself across from me. I put the journal on the table between us and reached across trying to steady my hand so I could shake his.

"My name is Angie Lawrence," It came out in a more formal tone than I had intended. "I'm a lawyer in a little town south of here." My brain was telling me this was coming out all wrong and I had only spoken two sentences. Now he probably thought that I was here on some sort of official business.

He must have thought I was nuts when I just sat there holding his hand because I stopped speaking. Now that I was afraid I had started wrong, I couldn't think of how to continue. Out of the blue, I had that flushed, embarrassed butterfly feeling. I took a second to take a second look at him. He was distinguished and very handsome and all flashes of Willie's harsh eyes and angry face seemed to disappear in this mans gentle expression.

I started looking around his clean, well-organized apartment. I had one hand on the journal and one hand in his and was about to explain myself when I not only forgot what I wanted to say, but totally lost the ability to speak at all because of what I saw sitting on a pillar of glass shelves behind him. It was polished to a high shine—a silver rattle with the initials "A.M." engraved in the handle.

Chapter 26
"Lost and Found"

I abruptly dropped his hand, stood up and walked over to the shelf. Next to the rattle was a black and white picture of a man standing on my front porch in almost the exact same spot where Miss Claudia was standing in the photo her father had taken of her when she was a child. I'm still not sure why I'd put that photo in my purse when I went home earlier to make arrangements for Keno, but I was really glad I had.

Andrew stood behind me, looking confused. I'm sure he was on the brink of asking me to leave. "I'm sorry, Miss, can I help you with something?"

It seemed to make him anxious that I was reaching up to touch the rattle, but he remained soft spoken and stayed at a non-frightening distance. I was in such a state of shock that I'd managed to find him so easily that I had no idea where to begin. It seemed just this once when I needed it the most I had my grandmothers luck... totally out of character for me. I silently walked over to my purse, took out the picture of Miss Claudia, and showed it to him. I hoped he knew I wasn't being rude, I simply had no words. My emotion must have been on my face, he didn't question. He gently took it from my hand, walked over to his and held them side by side. Except for the person standing on the porch, the photos were nearly identical.

He looked at me, confused and astonished. "Who are you?"

I answered his question with a question as I reached over and carefully touched the rattle that Emmaline, Annabeth, and her son Andrew had all held. "Where did you get this?"

"It belonged to my great-great-grandfather, the man in this picture," he was, turning it around so I could once again see the face of the man standing in front of my house. "Who is this child?" he asked, showing me my own picture. He moved gently and slowly closing the gap between us, more curious than ever as to my identity and the purpose of my visit. Yet also mindful that he was a stranger to me and didn't want to frighten me, although knowing I was in the right place, I had visibly calmed down.

I went back over to where I had been sitting and picked up the journal. He followed me, this time sitting next to me on the sofa, loosening his tie. I wasn't in the slightest uncomfortable being in such close proximity to him—same skin, same dark eyes, different man, and no traces of Willie.

"Her name was Claudia Wainwright. She left me the house in the picture when she died a few weeks ago."

"I've had this picture of my great-great-grandfather all my life and I've never known where this house is or when or if he lived there. My father died in Vietnam when I was very small. He and my mother hardly knew one another, so all I have is this picture. I have a few photos of my father, but no family tree or history." He leaned forward, almost hungry for my words. "Can you tell me about him?" he asked, once again holding up the black and white image. "What about the rattle? Do you know anything about that?"

He went on and on with question after question, but all I could do was sit and stare at his picture of Annabeth's son. He was the man who rebuilt my house to such perfection because he had grown up there as a child. He likely knew the story of the accident in which it burned. Looking at his face, it all made sense to me now. He came back and rebuilt his childhood home, so he must have known his parents were buried on the land. Why else would he have cared so much about it? Knowing how he had been forced to grow up without his mother and how he had lost his father in the war brought tears to my eyes, despite how I felt about crying in front of people. Putting a face with the pain and plight made the journal truly come alive in a way I had yet not experienced. The face of the man in front of me, the face in the picture. It made the flesh that had been torn and the blood that had been spilled even more real to me. The deep need I had to give Annabeth peace was burning in me. I knew it would not stop until this Andrew knew the story he had been obviously starved for his whole life. He saw my eyes welling up and handed me the handkerchief from his suit pocket. He was patient, waiting for answers, but searching my face, hoping to find just one clue in case it would be even another minute before I was able to continue talking to him.

"Mr. McGrath," I sighed and took a deep breat searching for just the right words. "I came here today hoping that you might have some answers for me, but I see now it is the other way around. I debated about whether or not to try to find you, but seeing you now and holding this picture, I am sure I have done the right thing. The man in this photo is Andrew Ruben McGrath. He is the son of a young, white girl named Annabeth and a slave boy turned soldier named Isaiah. This belongs to you," I hated to part with it, but handed him the journal. I would miss the people inside, but felt privileged to truly bring them home. "I think almost all of your questions will be answered when you're finished reading it."

He took the book, unsure of what to say. He had obviously been searching for his roots for some time without success. He was still speechless over just the few facts that I had given him. He had looked for his family everywhere and I could tell the last place he expected to find them was in the hands of a white woman standing at his own front door.

"I was an only child, raised by a single mother, who was also an only child. She had no family to speak of," he went on, almost sadly reminiscing about his youth. "I have always wanted to know more about my family. He paused and took a weighted breath "Well, my fathers part of my family really...and all I have are a few old pictures and this rattle. Before my mother died, she gave them to me and told me that all she knew about my father's past was that he insisted that my name be his own and that I be given this rattle." He held it up and shook the beads inside as if he had been listening to them for years, waiting for them to tell him the story of his past.

He hesitated and then asked. "Am I related to the little girl in this picture?" His desperate need for answers and thirst for the truth almost brought tears to my eyes again.

"No," I felt so bad to deny him anything it was difficult to look him in the eyes and say the word. All I wanted was to ease the long suffering on his face so I quickly, tried to clarify his misunderstanding. "Her family purchased the house after this man died," I, referred to his picture. "You should read this," I, pointed to the journal again. "However, I need to warn you, it's not an easy pill to swallow in some parts. I'm staying at a hotel not too far from here. If you have any questions or I can help you in any way, please call." I handed him the card the desk clerk had given me and wrote my room number on the back. It didn't even cross my mind in his gentle presence that I should be afraid to do so. "I wasn't expecting to find you so easily, so I'm paid up until day after tomorrow."

Around midnight the next day, the hotel operator put a call through to my room. I was restless thinking of the journey Andrew was taking and unable to sleep. Thankfully there was an all night marathon of "The Honeymooners." My father and I used to watch it together when I was a little girl. I muted the volume and answered the phone. To my surprise, I could hear the dialogue to the pictures I was watching in the background over the line.

"Hello?" I answered sounding board as if I were about to have the same conversation for the tenth time, I was thinking it was Janice calling me again. She was so excited when I told her about Andrew she could hardly stand it.

The words came in a soft almost whispering tone, possibly carrying a tear. "I'm sorry to bother you so late," not waiting for my response he continued, not in a rude intrusive fashion more like if he didn't say the words quickly he might choke on them a bit. "I finished the journal about an hour ago and I was wondering if we could talk." He sounded so softhearted and humble. I wondered if it was because he was sad over what he had just discovered or if that was just his demeanor. I flashed for a split second on how Annabeth had described Ruben and wondered if Andrew had that same docile yet masculine spirit. Regardless, he obviously had a sense of humor, as we were watching the same comedy show on TV. He took my moment of silence to mean that he had intruded on me and hastily apologized. "I'll call you tomorrow at a more reasonable time," he quickly offered, there was no mistaking the embarrassment in his voice.

"No, no," I answered, hoping he heard me before he hung up. "I can't sleep either."

"There's a coffee shop just around the corner from your hotel," he asked if I would meet him before he assumed anything and, then gave me directions to it.

"I'll be there in half an hour," I assured him, wondering why I suddenly had butterflies in my stomach. I had just sorted out so many of my feelings and now I felt like maybe I might be knotting a few of them back up again. Despite his tone, I was worried about how he would feel about the journal. Maybe he was angry about what happened to his family. He would have every right to be. I realized my subconscious was hoping he would not be upset with the messenger. If anybody understood random, unfair loss and pain, it was me.

I pulled up to the coffee shop. Andrew was waiting outside. "Cool car," he said, admiring my little MG. I was used to that response from men, and glad we had started the conversation light. No animosity to the bearer of the bad news, a good sign.

"It was my gift to myself when I graduated from law school," I explained, patting the hood. "None of my girlfriends like it much—you know, too small, convertible top messes up their hair. My dad had one when I was a kid. I suppose it just brings back memories for me." He opened the door and after the waitress pointed us to our table, he pulled out my chair. I knew this was no date, but he could have taught good manners to a few of the men I'd been out with lately. I figured all this light banter and casual conversation was leading to his real feelings and the butterflies I had were turning to bats. His reaction was bound to come crashing out any second and for about that long I was worried again, but then he spoke and just like the other day it was soft...manly, but soft.

"I started reading after you left and didn't stop until about an hour ago. I took about a two-hour nap this afternoon. I felt bad calling my secretary and telling her to cancel my appointments for the next two days. I told her it was urgent family business, so I guess it was kind of true," he, laughed at himself. I joined him, remembering my call to Philllip leading him to believe I was sick, but I don't suppose he knew I meant heartsick.

"That book has caused quite a few days of lost wages," I agreed, explaining my own sabbatical to him. "What kind of work do you do?" I asked, picking up my glass of water and taking a sip. Knowing he was finished reading, yet still composed and curious without rage put me at ease. I hoped he hadn't noticed my taking in his physical stature, despite his size and muscular frame, everything about him put me at ease. It was one of those "first impression in three seconds" things. There was no Willie or David Kincaid in him. I was proud of myself in that instant for including David— To my surprise I wasn't seeing Andrew as a black man or a white man, just what seemed to be a good man, who pulls our chairs and speaks soft and gentle like my father, but strong like a confident manly man would. The blame and outrage never came.

"I'm a lawyer," he said, smiling, knowing I was too. "I have a private practice downtown."

The waitress came and took our order. We both ordered breakfast. The conversation flowed easily. We talked about every part of the journal, Miss Claudia, and the graves. He was disappointed when I told him that neither Miss Claudia, her father, nor I had ever found them.

"I hate to impose, but could I see the house sometime?" he seemed almost embarrassed to ask. "I just want to stand where they stood and walk where they walked." There was a sense of urgency in him that only someone like my grandfather, who had such an enormous respect for history and family, could possibly understand. Well, I guess I was selling myself short because now I got it too. Knowing about my family—the pure and the ugly— had made me more sensitive to the need to know. The burn I had to help him, to help Annabeth, was undeniable.

"Sure, anytime, if anyone has a right to know them it's you." I smiled to assure him he was welcome. "I'm checking out tomorrow, but I still have quite a few days off left. I took two weeks of vacation time to find you and as it turns out, I only needed two days."

We talked some more over our pancakes. I gave him my address and phone number before we parted company. Again, not one bell or whistle telling me I should or shouldn't be afraid. As I drove away, I wondered how long it would be before I heard from him again. I guess I was just curious about how long he would be able to hold out before he had to come and meet his past.

Chapter 27
"Sin and Redemption"

It physically hurt to open my eyes at seven a.m. on Saturday morning when the chimes of my doorbell began to play. I had been in such a deep sleep that for a moment I thought I'd only dreamed I heard the bells. I would have rolled over and fallen back to sleep had Keno not also raised his head and looked at me with his squinted, tired eyes. He'd stayed up and watched the late, late show with me. He looked at me as if he were begging me to make the noise stop so he could resume his slumber.

"If that person doesn't have a life-or-death emergency," I was unreasonably snapping at him, "they will when I get down there."

I flung back my covers, threw on my robe, and headed towards the top of the stairs. Before my feet hit the first one, the bell rang again. I caught a glimpse of myself in the foyer mirror. I was still waiting on the custom stained glass I had ordered for the door, so the plywood kept me from seeing who the blasted early riser was. I knew that if my irritated tone didn't deter whoever it was, my appearance certainly would. My hair must have been flying in a million directions, still half-pulled up on top of my head, half-bed tossed, and scattered everywhere. I couldn't find the belt to my robe, so my threadbare t-shirt and my Betty Boop sleeping pants were partially visible. Whoever it was would certainly be able to tell they had not only woke me up, but also forced me out of bed. Keno followed me downstairs, more out of curiosity and the sudden need for a trip outside than for my protection.

The bell chimed for the third time just as I was putting my hands on the dead bolt, about to unlock the door. "Give me two seconds," I griped loudly, hoping the person would catch my frustrated drift through the closed door. After a few aggravating moments trying to focus my tired eyes on the lock, I was able to open it on about the third try. I flung the door open with slightly more force than necessary. Keno bounded around me across the porch and down the steps, almost knocking over Andrew McGrath.

It had been three days since we'd last seen each other and I was suddenly very aware that I probably had my homeless person look going on. On the other hand, he was quite nicely put together. For some reason, whenever a man is standing on my doorstep, the first thing I do is check out his outfit. Andrew was wearing a pair of nicely fitted blue jeans and a burgundy button down collared shirt. He looked like a guy who actually knew how to tuck in that shirt and put on a belt, all at the same time. I was speechless at the sight of him the fact that his dark brown leather belt matched his Timberland boots did not help me find my tongue any faster. When I got a gentle whiff of his cologne all at once, I became a babbling idiot. He was definitely not the typical male I usually found standing under my missing porch light. He noticed the door, but didn't ask. I'm sure he was curious since it was sort of his house—genetically speaking.

"I'm sorry," he humbly apologized, regaining his balance after nearly being knocked off his feet by my overzealous dog who quite obviously put his need to be in the front yard over our guest. It was then I noticed he was reciprocating and taking in the sight of me, just as I had him seconds before. I wasn't sure by his expression if he wanted to laugh or leave. I just stood there staring at him as if I had never before had company and had no idea what to do or say. He kindly recognized my surprise at his presence and continued to explain himself and apologize.

"I've read the journal again since we last spoke," he was explaining hastily. "I was hoping to find some small clue that I might have missed as to where Annabeth and Isaiah are buried. I wanted to call you, but I lost your number somewhere in the massive pile of junk on my desk, so I just headed this way and hoped for the best." He kept talking and seemed to be increasingly more nervous the longer I kept silent.

"You know, everyone in town knows you and this house. I had no trouble finding the place at all. About four people in the gas station all started giving me directions at once, all of them curious as to why I needed to come here, but polite enough to only stare and not ask outright." He chuckled a bit mentioning the colorful people who hang out at our local gas station at this hour. I felt like he kept talking because he knew in about two seconds it was going to happen, and he was right. The huge awkward pause. He took a breath and then he just stood there waiting for me to say something...anything. 'Go away' or 'Come in' — anything at all would have sufficed to ease the tension.

I finally found my words and this time they had lost the rude tone I'm sure he heard before I opened the door. "Please, come in," I offered an apology in my inflection, gesturing towards my living room. He must have accepted the implied "I'm sorry" as he graciously acknowledged the invite and stepped inside. I silently thanked God that I had cleaned up around 4:00 a.m. when I finally finished my all-night popcorn and candy pig fest. "Keno and I stayed up and watched too many movies last night," I said, inviting him to sit down. I could tell as he was listening to me that he was also taking in the atmosphere and, quite possibly, picturing his great-great-grandfather running from room to room when he was a child. "We started with *Paper Moon*," I said, trying to fill the silence. "I would have gone to bed after that, but it was a double feature. *To Kill a Mocking Bird* was next."

"I'm sorry," he apologized again. "I just couldn't wait any longer to see the house. As soon as I finished reading the journal again early this morning, I got in my car and started driving. I didn't really think about it, I just felt like I really needed to be here and see it for myself. If this is a bad time for you, I completely understand. I can come back another day."

"Nonsense," I, waved away his concern with my hand, not realizing that only served to open my robe and expose my mismatched sleepwear and very worn t shirt, I should have been paying better attention, it would have saved me near death by humiliation in about ten seconds. "I'm on vacation, remember? I have all the time in the world. Besides, I'd hate for you to have driven all that way for nothing."

It was at that moment I managed to pry my eyes away from his and I noticed my robe was open and I quickly pulled it closed. Now came the mortification and the deep deep red blush. He was a gentleman and pretended not to notice, sensed my discomfort and immediately thought of an excuse to leave and give me some time to get dressed. Any other man I knew would have just sat there like a big dope and taken the opportunity to stare at me, making the situation worse. He made me nervous, but oddly not in a creepy way.

"I saw a fast food place in town," he started reaching in his front pocket for his keys. "Why don't I go and get us some breakfast and give you a chance to wake up a little and change? What can I get you?" It was amazing he wasn't a blithering idiot not knowing how to handle the awkward moment he simply moved passed it with grace and let me recover my dignity.

Never having actually seen a true gentleman in action, it took me a minute to collect my thoughts. "Anything but coffee, I can't stand coffee," I admitted, as I walked around him and made my way to the stairs backwards. I was curiously unable to stop looking at this almost total stranger for whom I was having sudden and strange feelings. I supposed at the time that it was because I was so unaccustomed to a man being able to not only see my discomfort, but act on it in an appropriate manner. It wasn't lust or anything like that more like meeting a celebrity and not knowing how to compose yourself. I think a part of it was knowing he was related to Annabeth, someone I had more than a little respect for.

He returned about an hour later. I had showered, changed, and taken more than great care to make sure my appearance had drastically improved. We ate breakfast and then took a tour of the house. He spent quite a while in the basement. I think I saw his eyes get a little misty. "I can't imagine what it must be like for you," I was, trying to understand his emotion and perhaps comfort him a little. As much as Annabeth had changed me, she wasn't my kin. He had to be feeling their blood pumping through his veins to an almost painful degree.

"I've been looking for my family all of my life," he said, squatting down and tracing the outline of the missing bricks with his fingers. "Your bringing them to me is a miracle as far as I'm concerned. Knowing what fine people they were and that my roots run so deep here is just an added bonus."

"I know what you mean about roots," I said, explaining to him how Miss Claudia had always told me that I'd gotten mine late in life too.

After we'd gone over every inch of the house, I showed him the writing tablets I'd also found in the crate. We sat in the living room and read them for at least two hours. "You should keep those too," I offered, handing him the old box after we'd placed them back inside.

"I can't," he said modestly. "Miss Claudia left them to you."

"Yes," I agreed, sliding the old container in front of him, "but she also entrusted me to do what I thought was best. This is your family in these pages and you should have them to show to your children someday."

He became a little flushed and despite his best attempt to do so, he was unable to hide it. "Trust me, as much as I work, most of the women I meet are in orange jumpsuits and handcuffs." He laughed at himself. "I doubt I'll have children to show this to any time soon."

"I believe it," I commiserated, reaching over and patting his hand. "You're not rowing that boat by yourself." I thought about explaining the door and how the plywood related to those orange jumpsuits, but I couldn't. Bringing up anything that pointed about our differences would ruin what we had in common. There was no way around telling him about Willie without pointing out the pink—or should I say black and white—elephant in the room. It felt like taking a Band-aid off too soon. The journal and the people who lived here had already put the race topic right on the top of the list and we had somehow managed to avoid it.

"Thank you for allowing me to see all this," he said, gesturing to my house.

"There's one more place I think you might like to visit," Then I thought I should warn him, "but it might be kind of tough on you—at least it was for me." I recalled how I felt when I first saw the grave markers only a few days ago.

"What!?" he was, obviously excited that his adventure was not yet over.

"Feel like going for a drive?" I tried to give him a smile with a hint of mystery.

He sat thoughtfully for a minute before he answered. "Only if you don't think me too forward if I ask, can I drive your cool car?"

I walked into the kitchen, grabbed my keys off the hook, and tossed them to him from across the living room. "If you can handle the top down, then I can handle you driving," I said, leading the way out the door. He surprised me when he took the trouble to figure out which key locked the house before he trotted down the steps and opened the passenger door for me. It left me wondering, *If he can do it, why can't all men?*

When we arrived at the old cemetery, he looked over at me confused. "I thought Annabeth and Isaiah were somewhere in your woods," he was not considering, the way I hadn't, the others mentioned in the journal.

"They are," I agreed, leading the way, but still not telling him who we'd found. I decided to take him to see Emmaline and Jackson first.

We walked over to the line of trees and he noticed immediately that Emmaline's grave was clean and well-kept, while Jackson's remained overgrown and nearly in ruin. "Who did this?" he was very surprised and what seemed a little upset at the difference in their care.

"Janice and I found them just before I found you," I felt like I should be more in tune to the reason behind his annoyance but for a second not yet having deep insight into his character I was confused. I just started explaining myself.. "We searched through nearly every old record in the courthouse before we found Emmaline's death certificate and a map of the cemetery. There used to be an old church over there somewhere." I motioned to the open field and pointed to where Janice and I had found the cornerstones. When I turned again to look at him, Andrew was on his hands and knees clearing away the brush and weeds that had taken over Jackson's grave and nearly toppled his marker. I felt incredibly unobservant, now realizing the source of his emotion. I was sure now he had Rubens heart.

"What are you doing?" I asked before I could stop myself, knowing I was the one who was still mad at Jackson. I was seeing him more clearly, but still a little shocked that he would care if anyone ever found Jackson at all. He was such a horrible man that even the woman who lay next to him hadn't mourned his passing.

"He was my family too," he said softly, looking up at me this time with unmistakable tears in his eyes. He quickly blinked and got his emotions under control, integrating his tender heart with his masculinity again. "I deal with young black men all the time in my practice," he said, all the while continuing to pull weeds and clear debris. "Some of them are gang members or drug dealers and nearly all of them grew up without a father, listening to everyone tell them about their raw deal." I knelt down and began to help, sensing this was an issue about which he felt passionate, even if I didn't agree I wanted him to keep talking so I could hear what was in his heart. Maybe he could change mine.

His tone changed and he took a deep breath as if he was about to make a speech he had been writing all his life, I knew it wasn't possible, but maybe he had some of Reverend in him too. "How are we as a nation, black or white, supposed to move past this if we spend our lives allowing our youth to remain shackled by slavery? Maybe the chains are gone, but we're still bound by them. How can we make a better future for ourselves if we keep hanging onto the injustice of the past? I'm not saying we should ever forget our history, but can we have any kind of future if we live in the past? You don't know what it's like seeing one young black man after another locked up for life because somewhere it has been engrained in him that his life has already been mapped out and all the streets on it are on the wrong side of the tracks. I don't want to spend one ounce of my life or energy hating this man. He beat Ophelia and abused Emmaline, but somewhere inside me, I have a few drops of his blood. He stopped for a second and looked at the veins running up his arm. "I wish I could make all the young kids I try so hard to mentor see that we're all a little part of each other. I can't tell them to respect *all* life if I don't respect it myself. If I can forgive Jackson, then a little more of the hate in this world goes away." Suddenly I understood Willie...and so much more. The pity I'd once felt for him suddenly turned to compassion. I gave him a minute, even though my heart wasn't really in it, but listening and Andrew softened my anger, maybe if I gave him more than sixty seconds I might understand like he does...someday.

I felt so guilty I stopped helping him and rocked back on my heels. It was my turn to be honest and break down a few walls. He sensed I had something to say, that was just as important to me as his feelings were to him, and put his task aside. I could tell by his soft eyes he could see it all over my face and he remained just as calm as I had imagined Ruben had the day he allowed Master David to tie him to that pole. It seemed a shame, we were developing a friendship and I didn't want to ruin that, but I couldn't go on and not tell him.

I told him all about the plywood on the door, my great-uncle dying in prison and the hatred that flowed through his veins that caused him to shed innocent blood in Alabama so many years ago. The story gushed like a wild river, I was afraid my character was changing in his eyes with every turn of the tale, but the softness in their deep brown never wavered. But, there was one last thing that I had to admit, that I was sure would make him hate me. "For a split second I was afraid of you when you answered your door. For one second I saw Willie, felt the fear of the beating and so many other emotions that I don't think I even have a name for yet. I owe your family a lot. Annabeth taught me so much. I'd never considered myself a racist or anything of the sort, but it made me take a harder look at myself and how I look at others."

I hesitated for one beat, then kept going despite the confused look on his face. "I expected you to be white." I knew if I didn't say it now that I'd never have the nerve to say it later. "I just kept thinking of you as Annabeth's descendent. I knew Isaiah was a slave, but I just kept thinking of the child Annabeth had as hers. I don't know why I never even considered the possibility that you would be black. I've wondered for days if that makes me a racist."

I hung my head in shame, only to raise it back up again to the sound of his laughter and the smile on his face. My fears were unfounded; he didn't hate me and was appauled when I admitted that I thought he might. He leaned across the grave and took my hand. He inhaled like the air was as weighted to him as his next words would be. "You're not a racist, Angie, you're just human. We all are." He pointed to himself. Remember how you said you pictured Willie as a black man before you saw him. Every time I get a call about a deadbeat mom or a prostitute, I see the same white woman I defended right out of law school. We're lucky," he, paused seeming to want to get his words just right. "We have had some really good teachers." He looked over at the graves. "We have a chance to get it right."

Relief flooded through me. Until now, nobody has ever understood me like my grandpa, but Andrew did. He got what was in my heart and maybe a little piece of it too. Even though we were talking about really serious things, I noticed that my heart fluttered a little when he said my name. *Weird* ,especially since our relationship spanned days not weeks and certainly not years. "Angie, if you tell a three-year old black child about Santa Claus who has never seen society's picture of him, what color do you think he imagines Santa is?"

I thought for a second and began to see his point. "I suppose he'd imagine someone who looked like himself," I reasoned.

"There's nothing wrong with seeing things through your own point of view or through the eyes of your own culture. It's when you see that the truth is different from your imagination and still refuse to admit you were wrong is when trouble starts. When I read a book, I imagine all the characters as black unless the author tells me they're not because I relate to life and circumstances as a black man, the same as you do as a white woman. What I try to make my clients and the kids at the youth center where I volunteer see is that we have to stop looking at people on the outside. Are the bones in this grave any different from mine?" he asked, holding the palms of our hands together to demonstrate his point. "We're all guilty. It's what we do about the truth once we discover it that makes us better people." I took the opportunity to interlace my fingers with his when he put our hands together, the way Annabeth and Isaiah had done on the creek bank. It was more to show the contrast in our skin than emotion, but I wondered to myself how I had been able to do it so easily, after all I had recently been through at hands that looked like his. He smiled at my gesture. "If you can teach a child that lesson while they're young, it will save them and society a lot of trouble later...not to mention my poor crippled fingers filling out stacks of paperwork putting people in jail," he added with what I now saw was his sarcastic sense of humor.

"Amen to that," I agreed. Yes, it was genetically impossible, but I believed I had just met Reverend.

We finished clearing the grave in silence and moved on to David Kincaid's when we were finished.

Chapter 28
"Bright Lights and Brighter Ideas"

It was a little after two in the afternoon when we made it back to my house. Andrew studied the picture of the original house and layout of the land in the book Miss Claudia had left me. About thirty minutes later, we were standing on the banks of the dry creek bed, now full of trees and kudzu. It was where the slaves used to bathe and where Annabeth and Isaiah broke every rule of society in their day.

"I can't believe Annabeth and Isaiah used to sit right here, near this spot," I was so excited that he had managed to find it.

"I want to find them," it was as serious a tone as I had heard from him. "They deserve to have proper headstones and to be remembered as brave young people, not hidden away as if they should be ashamed."

I agreed, unsure of how any of this might be accomplished. "I don't mean to be negative, but how? Miss Claudia and her father planted this field when it was bare and never found them. How can we do it now with all these trees and foliage?" I asked, picking up a handful of kudzu leaves.

"I suppose we'll just have to think of something," he was clearly determined, as he turned to walk back towards the house. He looked back suddenly and called Keno to follow. He'd been doing little things like that all day. I wondered if he was really that thoughtful or just trying to be nice. "I'd hate for him to get lost out here," "I heard on the car radio this morning that it's supposed to rain tonight."

By the time we made it back up to the house, it was evident that both of our sleepless nights were starting to catch up with us.

"I'd better head back." He, yawned and stretched before he reached in his pocket for his keys.

I'm not quite sure where my next words came from, but they seemed to roll off my tongue before my brain could take over the driver's seat of my mouth. "Why don't you stay and have a nap before you get on the road? You look as tired as I feel and besides, if it's supposed to rain, I'd hate for you to be out driving in it." After everything we had shared that morning, it just felt natural. He had become like an old friend through his family that I cared so much about and after our talk this afternoon, I was genuinely starting to like him. He looked as uncomfortable as I had felt that morning. "I have a guest room," I assured him, reading his face. "Get him, Keno," I commanded with little authority as Keno usually made up his own mind whether or not to obey. Keno lazily got up from his sunny spot on the back porch and herded Andrew into the house. "He lived on a sheep farm before I adopted him, can't begin to guess why he was abandoned at the pound." I explained. "He herds me all over the yard all the time." Keno followed Andrew inside, pacing back and forth behind him, forcing him to walk in a straight line.

We both slept longer than we had intended. When I opened my eyes, it was dark outside and the clock numbers glowed 9:30. Andrew must have heard me get up and creak across the floor because he met me at the top of the stairs. "I think I could have slept all night," he said, noting the time as he looked at his watch.

"Me too," I agreed, yawning. "I'm starving." It had just occurred to me that I hadn't eaten since breakfast. "You like Chinese?" I asked, not giving him a chance to answer. "This isn't Atlanta. If you're hungry after nine, it's either Chinese or fast food."

He thought about it for a minute. "I could eat an egg roll or two."

"Just give me a minute to fix my hair and I'll be right down."

When I was finished getting ready, I stopped at the top of the stairs and watched him for a minute. He was sitting on the end of the couch, petting Keno. Every time he'd stop, Keno would get insistent and nudge Andrew with his nose until he resumed stroking his ears.

"That's the only other thing he does," I said, making my entrance into the room. I could tell by the look on his face he was a little impressed. I was not exactly Miss Georgia, but I'd been told I clean up better than average. We took his car this time. Once again, he opened the door for me. *I could get used to this*, I thought to myself, but then my next thought was, *Could everyone else*? I could hear it now, "Angie's crazy. She gets attacked by a black man and still doesn't learn her lesson." Or... "Well, you know how Yankees can be about that sort of thing." I could live here a hundred more years and some of the people in this town would still call me a Yankee, especially since I would never tell Grandpas truth. I tried to focus on what he would say. "Let all that other stuff in the past go, Ang, and go for what's real." On the way to dinner, I decided that Grandpa was right. I walked into the restaurant as I always did, with my head up.

We talked over dinner about everything under the sun. I was surprised we had so much in common, more than just Annabeth and Isaiah. I told him all about Miss Claudia and my grandpa and the stamps, and how he was the reason I'd come to have the crate. He talked about his law practice and how he was a volunteer youth counselor for at-risk kids after school and every third weekend.

At 11:00, they started cleaning up around us, so we reluctantly ended our conversation and got up to leave. When I opened my purse, he rolled his eyes and shook his head. "What kind of guys do you go out with?" He reached down and picked up the check before I could even see the amount.

"I didn't know this was a date.?" I was half asking with a coy smile.

"Well, maybe it is and maybe it isn't, but if my momma were alive and found out I let a lady pay for dinner, she would skin me right here and now." He reached into his wallet, left a generous tip, and then proceeded to the cash register. I just stood there in awe, thinking he did have Ruben's gentle spirit and he was a good tipper. This guy was just too good to be true.

I nearly had myself convinced it was all an act and he was just trying to make a good impression until we pulled up in front of my house. I noticed it immediately. There it was, shining like a star in the distance. I could see it from the moment we pulled onto the end of the driveway. "I noticed you forgot to put a bulb in the porch light when I was waiting for you to answer the door this morning," he was, almost apologetic, as if I would mind he had taken the liberty. "You shouldn't be out here on this dark road going into a dark house—it isn't safe, so I picked up a bulb when I went out to get our breakfast." He shot a glance over to my broken door, but didn't bring up Willie's name. I almost cried. It was as if he could see exactly what I wanted or needed and anticipated it before I was even able to ask. All I could say was "Thank you."

As I got out of the car to go in, he caught my hand to stop me. "I'm going to think of a way to find them," he spoke with such determination and conviction that despite the failure of others I believed him.

"Are you sure you have to go?" I asked, inviting him in to talk about possible solutions.

"There are thirty kids counting on me to referee a basketball game tomorrow afternoon," he replied, smiling at the thought of them. "I'll call you later tomorrow evening," he promised, shifting his car into reverse, avoiding the awakward front porch moment that I used to dread counting on the darkened lamp to save me. It was so nice to have light above my head and a tiny ray of hope in my heart.

"I'll be here," I said aloud to myself as I watched him go. I knew I was moving this along way to fast in my mind, but my heart seemed pleased with the prospect. Maybe I had seen enough wrong to immediately identify right.

He stopped after he had backed up about ten feet. "Will you go inside already?" he yelled out the window, playfully annoyed. "Just because you have light now doesn't mean you need to stand outside."

He sat and waited for me to unlock the door and go in. I flashed my new bulb at him so he would know I was safe. I hoped to dream of him tonight and wondered to myself if the feelings I was having were simply my imagination or if I'd actually found something that might be real. The last thing I wanted was feelings based on the love I had fallen in love with in the journal or more of just missing the family that Grandpa helped me see I'd been trying desperately to replace. One thing I knew for sure, if it was real, everyone in this small town was going to have an opinion. I only hoped his coming around wouldn't give away the secret buried in my woods—at least not until I was ready for it. "When we find them, then I will tell," I told myself.

It was late, but I knew I needed to talk to Grandpa. Of course, he was up and ready to hang on my every word. Before he hung up, he reminded me that he had told me so. "Unwind all your feelings and see yourself for what you are, Ang, and the right time and the right place will find you a lot sooner. I don't care what color he is, Peanut, if he's that good to you, he's good enough for me." He paused, as if wondering if it would be okay to mention. "It would be okay with your dad too, Ang. It really would." I didn't realize until he said it how bad I needed to hear it—not just his approval of the color of our skins, but letting go of my need to find his replica and moving on to something real.

My phone rang Sunday night, just as Andrew said it would. "How was your day?" he asked, chipper and genuinely interested in the answer.

"I went to church, went to the grocery store, and now I'm a big lazy lump sitting on my couch, exercising my remote control thumb. I would say my day was not bad at all. How about yours?" I slowed my channel changing to pay attention and only flipped one more time not caring what show it landed on.

"I, too, went to church and then spent the rest of the afternoon running up and down a basketball court blowing my official whistle and wearing my official black and white striped shirt. They try to entice people to volunteer by giving them a uniform and a little bit of power. I do it just because I need an extra shirt."

Yes, we definitely have the same sense of humor.

"You're just being modest," I teased and accused him a little knowing he could take it. "I know you really do it for the whistle-blowing power." We made light of the situation, but he was actually being very humble. I knew he really did it to try to help those kids, especially the ones who need to see that even the kid with a bad jump shot, as he put it, is still the same as a pro on the inside.

"I just wanted you to know that I've figured out the answer to our mystery," he, exaggerated the length of his pause to allow me to be sufficiently impressed and excited.

"What?" I asked, too eager for his answer to hide my enthusiasm.

"It came to me today while I was blowing my whistle. We've been looking for the bricks and the graves," he was, stating the obvious and piquing my curiosity. "What we should be looking for is the box."

"The box? How are we supposed to find the box if we can't find the graves?"

He patiently explained something I had not yet considered. "The journal says the box is made of tin and it also has Ophelia's silver ring inside. What we need is a metal detector. We find the box, we find the graves." He was so proud of himself he could hardly stand it. Even Grandpa had not come up with that solution. "How many more days do you have off work?" I could hear him flipping through his own calendar.

"Seven," I answered.

"I'm due a vacation myself. I called my secretary and my partner this afternoon and I'm taking next week off. We're going to find that box. Is there a hotel around there?" In knew in his gentlemanly way he was, preparing to stay for the entire week, but would never even consider the alternative to a hotel.

"Don't be silly, you can stay right here in my guest room. I have plenty of room and I won't take no for an answer. Besides, we can get started earlier if you're here in the morning."

He sighed and thought for a minute. "Angie, this could get complicated... for you. I mean, you don't live in a big city where folks could care less about what you do every day. I grew up in a small town. I know how people talk. I don't want to cause you any trouble." The fact that he had even considered my feelings or was worried about my reputation made me want him to stay all the more.

"You're staying here and that's all there is to it. Now, where do we get a metal detector?" I had already dismissed his concerns and moved on with our new plan.

"You just let me worry about that," he had an air of confidence that made me think he had already addressed the problem. "I'll see you and Keno tomorrow." My heart skipped a beat when he included my buddy, Keno. I could definitely respect a man who cared about my dog. "Get some sleep tonight," he was teasing and chastised me for staying up all night the night before. "We literally have a lot of ground to cover."

"I promise," I said, and wished him goodnight before I hung up the phone.

Chapter 29
"Hide and Seek"

Andrew arrived Monday afternoon with a medium-sized duffle bag of clothes and a metal detector. We started searching right away. Keno trailed behind us as we started in the corner of the woods and worked our way inward, one row of trees at a time. Andrew studied the old drawing of the original layout of the property and decided it made the most sense to start on the right side of the woods behind the shed. That seemed to be the closest place to where the slave cabins would have been, and Emmaline found her justice with Jackson and David.

"I don't imagine Emmaline and Ophelia would have carried Annabeth far from where she died." "She was bleeding and they were trying to conceal her death, so I think they would have been careful about leaving a trail." I just stared at him as he gently swung the machine over the dirt and brush. He had more than read the journal, he had studied its every detail. I supposed that if they were my family and it was part of my blood spilled on this field, I would have done the same.

Three days passed and nothing – nothing, that is, except nosy neighbors wondering whose car was parked in my driveway and why I wasn't going to work. It seems word was spreading around town that I had a visitor. Everyone knew I was single and I think there must be a running pool on when I would finally get married because everyone was suddenly very interested in my life. Had they really known anything about him, I'm sure there would have been people camped out on my neighbor's land with binoculars. They were looking for answers as hard as Andrew and I were looking for the box.

The only two people who knew the truth were Grandpa and Janice, inasmuch as I had been keeping her up-to-date on the situation or I know she would have done so for herself. If everyone knew, anyone else with a metal detector would have been inviting themselves over to "help." The only thing everyone did know was that Janice certainly would have all the information they "needed." She loved having the scoop and playing innocent. When the news finally breaks, I will give her my permission to plug in the grapevine and shift it into high gear. For now, I wanted Andrew to be the first to visit the site and I wanted to be the only one to be there with him.

On Thursday morning, the sense that we were running out of time finally started to hit me. Part of the day was what I called "wasted" when the stained glass arrived and Andrew insisted on sending the carpenter away and replacing it in the front door himself. He said he wanted to contribute something of himself to the house his family loved. I think part of it was he also just needed a break we were both starting to feel more than a little disappointed. I waited patiently knowing I had to return to work in three days. We started again around eleven and by lunchtime we heard the first beeps the detector had made since we'd started. Andrew was holding it and I quickly put on Miss Claudia's gardening gloves and pulled the spade from my oversized overall pockets. He stood watching as I began to dig.

I pointed the spade downward and pushed it into the ground. It was about two-thirds of the way in when I hit something hard. Andrew knelt to help me. Both of our hearts were beating rapidly in unison in the hopes that our search had ended and Annabeth and Isaiah would finally have proper graves. He began to clear away some of the dirt next to where I was digging and suddenly stopped. It was about that moment that I retrieved the object I had hit with the spade. It was a pair of rusty shackles with two links of heavy chain holding them together in the middle and two large bolts clamping the circles closed on either end. Andrew had tears in his eyes, and a look of horror on his face as I held them up for his inspection, he realized where we were on the map much faster than I did. He was paying less attention to my find than he was to his own.

"It's the whipping post," he choked out horrified, clearing the rest of the dirt away so I could see the top of the wooden pole. It was about one foot in diameter and had obviously been cut down, but a few feet of it remained planted in the ground. Over the years, the end of it had been covered by the dirt and kudzu. The shackles had likely been discarded and left on the ground after one of the slaves had been beaten and released.

Andrew turned his face away and I knew he was crying, not as before when I could simply see deep emoting misting in his eyes, but tears that flowed from his soul. I dropped the heavy irons on the ground. They clanked together and made a loud thud when they hit the dirt. I walked around him so I could see his face, but he kept his head down. Even his unshakeable faith in our ability to overcome the past seemed washed away by the cries coming from his heart and over flowing down his cheeks. He seemed ashamed and was obviously not used to showing such vulnerability, I was touched he was comfortable enough to show it to me. Or maybe he was simply overcome and wished I was not witnessing what I knew he perceived as a private occurrence. Although he wasn't audibly sobbing the moment could not have been more intense or real for either of us.

"Look at me," I put my hand on his shoulder kneeling in front of him. He gave no response, only raised his head. "Remember what you said about never forgetting, but choosing not to re-live the past?" I wiped his silent tears with the cuff of my sleeve, leaned in closer, and put my arms around him. "Annabeth and Isaiah managed to find love in the midst of all this," I whispered in his ear. "There was a lot of hate, but we are so lucky to know that there was also some love here," I was so hoping to ease his pain. I knew there was no way I could possibly tap into what he was feeling. "I know I will never understand the way you do, but Annabeth tried and so will I." Those words seemed to mean more to him than anything else I could have said. He pulled me closer and hugged me softly to himself. For the first time ever, I felt like I actually belonged in someone's arms. It was a bit of a struggle not to move in closer and hug him tight. I managed to keep my feelings to myself as I was not sure if the gesture was only one of thanks. After all, feeling like I knew him through the journal and just having met him were two concepts I was trying very hard to balance.

The rest of the week went by as did the first few days—empty and without a single trace of Annabeth or Isaiah. On Sunday morning, I got up to go to church and readied myself as quietly as possible, hoping not to wake Andrew. I would say we'd become a bit closer since finding the whipping post, but I still wasn't sure if he thought of me or dreamed of me both awake and asleep, as I seemed to be unable to stop myself from doing about him.

"Don't be stupid, Angie," I said, looking at myself in the mirror one more time before I went downstairs. "Remember, all the good ones are taken. He probably has some amazing girlfriend who is also very compassionate and understanding." I sat down to put on my shoes while continuing to talk aloud, this time directing my conversation to Keno. "I mean, whoever the unbelievably lucky girl is that he's already interested in is probably some saint who gave him her blessing to come here and stay with me for a week to search for his long lost relatives. He's probably been calling her from his cell phone every night after he closes his door."

I continued to give every reason in the book to my dog as to why this handsome, intelligent man with all his own teeth, a good sense of humor, and a kind heart would not be interested in me. "Besides that," I went on, he probably isn't attracted to pale white girls." I looked at my dog that was both black and white. "Why can't we all be like you, Keno? You're black *and* white and everybody just thinks you're pretty." I reached down to pat him before I left the room. As I turned to go, I realized I'd left my bedroom door cracked open. I nervously reassured myself that Andrew was asleep and hadn't heard me as I headed down the stairs.

I almost lost my balance and fell down the last seven or eight steps when I saw him sitting on the couch wearing a suit and tie. He looked really good and I was betting smelled even better. *That's it, if he smells good too, I'll know God has a sense of humor.*

"You look nice," he was obviously admiring my dress. I was glad I had decided to wear it. It was my "I-feel-skinny-and-good-about-myself-today-dress." Miss Claudia always pointed out I could stop traffic in it whenever we crossed the street to go to the Dairy Queen. It's navy blue, which brings out my eyes and kind of short, which shows off my legs.

I walked over to Andrew to adjust his tie and repay the compliment and then I did what I always do when I'm standing next to a man. *I can't believe he passed the height test too. I'm wearing heels and yup, he smells great.* I prayed in my head, listing this man's good qualities, ones that I might add are difficult to find all in one person. *Okay, God, could I please just this once have some good luck?* I no sooner sent the words up than He sent the answer back down right out of Andrew's mouth.

"Funny thing about these old houses," he said, looking up at the high ceiling, "sound sure does echo and travel well."

"Really?" I half asked half agreed, sitting down on my couch in response to his gesture for me to do so. My throat went dry and I felt a little sick, hoping I wasn't turning green or worse, bright red with embarrassment.

"First of all, I would like to say that I was telling you the truth when I told you in the restaurant that I'm not currently involved with anyone." I felt my face turn red hot. Dang, now I really did wish I were any color other than white, I must have looked like a siren. He'd heard every word I'd said upstairs, meant only for Keno's ears.

"Second, it's true you are white and blonde, but you're really not all that pale. I'm sure if we could get you out of the office and into the sun, you would tan quite nicely." He smiled, comparing our skin as he took my hand. "Now, are you going to stop hiding me in this house and take me to church or not? I mean, I really love to meet new people and show off the fact that I have all my own teeth." He sat quietly, satisfied with himself for catching me off guard.

"I guess we have been spending a lot of time around here," I conceded, agreeing with him that we had been either in the woods or in the house for the past six days. It was difficult to talk given my mouth had really gone drier than the cotton that used to grow here. Mortified was not even close to the word. He took the keys from me and locked the front door. He held my hand as we walked out to the car and then drove us to church. I felt so lucky to know such a man. He didn't even tease me for being so insecure or having a deep meaningful conversation with the dog.

Thank you, Lord, I whispered quietly, remembering that my prayer had been answered. Maybe the man who had been hiding himself from me for so long was finally sitting right next to me. Not even once did I compare him to my superhero, my dad. I knew I'd finally let go— and not just of my mixed up feelings about work and race, but of the bitterness I hadn't even realized I felt all these years about losing the only man I ever loved...that is, the only one until now. I'd tried to slow my feelings down, but they were galloping like a racehorse let loose to run. I'd told myself a hundred times this week, 'Go slow, Angie, go slow,' but I couldn't anymore. I was at peace with myself and my heart was more than ready. The question was how did he feel about me. Yes, he admitted he wasn't involved with anyone, but he never said he was ready for me to be the one to fill that role in his life. Agreeing to go to church and agreeing to take the next step in a relationship were two very different things. My other worry that was more than just a nagging feeling, but more like anvil waiting to fall on my heart, was how people in this town would react. *Nobody is ready for this,* I thought, looking down at the contrast of our hands so close to one another on the arm rests of our seats.

We got a few stares in church but people were casual and polite. I was sure it's just because they thought he was an old college friend who'd come to visit. Andrew was very careful not to be too familiar with me in front of everyone, considering the repercussions I would have to live with, or maybe he didn't want to lead me on knowing how I was beginning to feel about him. My heart told me, and I hoped it was right, that he was thinking as long as people thought he was leaving or just a friend, I would be fine to face them alone if I had to. As he said, if things got "complicated" between us things could get difficult for me, I just could not figure out how much he cared for me, and how much he was just being a gentleman and trying to protect me. I was hoping at least the people who had gone to my church and known me all of my life would be supportive and leave the ignorance to the rest.

Chapter 29
"The Crickets Dance"

The workweek flew by and I could hardly wait until Saturday. I was a bit disappointed because it was Andrew's weekend to coach the kids, so we were only going to have one day together. He arrived late Friday night and we got an early start on Saturday morning. He usually left between nine and ten after we'd eaten dinner and had some time to talk and make plans for the next weekend. I knew he had to go, but it was hard to cut our time together short. I was sitting across the dinner table from him, watching him eat what I had explained to him was my grandfather's famous spaghetti when I began to miss him. He was right in front of me and I already felt an entire week's worth of his absence.

"What?" he asked self consciously, feeling me staring at him.

"I was just wishing we had more time to look this weekend is all." He smiled across the table and I knew by the look in his eyes he could see right through me.

"Me too," he agreed, not letting on that he not only wanted more time to search the woods, but more time with me. Neither of us said it out loud, but we both knew what the other was thinking. Knowing he was too much of a gentleman to say it made me want him all the more. I was just hoping and praying that he was developing feelings for me just as I had been for him since we had breakfast at the diner in Atlanta. I was however doubting myself, after so much bad it was very hard to trust the good, and even harder to feel like you deserved it.

He left, promising to keep thinking about the map and likely locations. It was just idle chitchat really, skirting the issue that was on both of our minds. I promised to do the same as I closed the door behind him and climbed the stairs to bed. The house suddenly felt very empty and I was more than a little sad.

I awoke early, my mind wandering, but Andrew was my first thought. I wondered what time he'd gotten home last night, if he'd thought about me on the way, and would I cross his mind today? I looked over at my clock. It was only seven-thirty. I started thinking about his day and his schedule before I even considered my own. I knew he only went to Sunday school on the days he had to officiate and the game started at eleven.

"You know, Keno, if I leave now I might be able to catch the game." My subconscious said it aloud before the part of my brain that was only half-awake had a chance to really think about it. "No, that's a stupid idea," I argued with myself. "You can't just show up unannounced. I mean, if he does like me even a little bit the way I'm starting to like him, I'm going to ruin everything. I used the words "starting to" because I still hadn't allowed myself to use the "L" word out loud because even I knew it was too soon and I didn't want to jinx it. He'll think I am a crazed stalker or something."

Keno perked up his ears and cocked his head as if he were trying to figure out if I had finally lost my mind. I laid there debating until eight o'clock. Something inside me just had to see him, so I did the only thing I could do, I picked up the phone on my bedside table and called Janice.

The phone rang several times. I was hoping she wasn't in the shower this early and getting ready for church. When the answering machine picked up, I started talking loud, hoping to "accidentally" wake her or get her out of the bathroom.

"Janice, are you there? Janice, pick up if you can hear me." She suddenly answered and scared me as much as I imagine I had startled her.

"The whole neighborhood can hear you,"

"What, did you win the lottery or something?"

"Maybe just as good," I answered, knowing that what I was about to do was either a big leap of faith in our relationship, or a bigger mistake. "I'm going to be gone today. Can you come get Keno after church and watch him 'til tomorrow? Oh, and cover for me in the morning until about ten or so? I may be late. You know, just answer my phone, but don't necessarily tell people I'm not there."

There was silence on the other end of the line for a few seconds. I thought she was about to ask me why, but instead I got, "You don't even like basketball."

"Janice, how do you know everything?"

She laughed. "Well, I don't, but after watching your dog and covering your tracks for you tomorrow, I better."

"I promise," I said, as I hung up the phone and ran to the shower.

I packed my overnight bag, just kind of throwing things in, expecting that after we ate dinner I would stay at the same hotel I had used before. After all, it was the closest one to his house, and I didn't think he had an extra bedroom like I do. "If I leave by six tomorrow morning, I can easily be to work by ten," I was, scurrying around the room getting my outfit ready for the next day. Keno sat in one place watching me run back and forth. I'm pretty sure he no longer wondered if I'd lost my mind, he was convinced.

I was out the door and on the road by nine. It would give me just enough time to make it to the game and hopefully see Andrew for a minute to let him know I was there. I had no idea what his reaction would be. Until I was half way to Atlanta, it never even crossed my mind that maybe he had other plans for the rest of his afternoon. I nearly turned around and went home half a dozen times, but something inside me just kept my foot on the gas and the car headed north.

I got lost on my way to the youth center and was thirty minutes late for the game. When I walked in the door, all I could hear were yelling kids, blowing whistles, and the sound of what must have been a million tennis shoes stomping on the hardwood floor.

"Great," I mumbled to myself, "I'll never find him in this crowd." I found a seat about three rows up on the bleachers and tried to spot him. I was really hoping he'd know I was there before the game started. I began to get a little paranoid. *What if I can't find him after the game? What if he leaves and never even knows I was here? Maybe that would be best. Maybe if he never knew I was here, he wouldn't know what an idiot I am right now.* I was suddenly so embarrassed I wanted to dig a hole and bury myself. Here I was, uninvited, unannounced, and late. "I should just go and forget the whole thing," I said aloud, causing the stranger sitting next to me to look at me as if I were an escaped mental patient. I smiled politely and made my way back down the crowded bleachers toward the doors.

I'm not sure if it was my standing up or my looking out of place in a crowd of yelling kids that caught his eye, but as soon as I heard him yell my name, I wanted to disappear.

"Angie! Angie!" It was so loud the entire section of people around me stopped to see why the official was no longer involved in the play. He blew his whistle and called time out. Now, not only did I want to die, I was thinking of ways to do it before he could jog across the floor and ask me what in the world I was doing there. A loud *Ahhh* sound came from the crowd because apparently the game was getting good when he stopped it.

He signaled to the coaches he'd be back in a second and they too seemed annoyed. I felt like the entire room was watching me. When I finally got up the nerve to turn around and face them, I could see I was right. Realizing what he'd done without thinking, Andrew tossed his whistle to the other guy wearing a black and white shirt. The crowd started to cheer when his replacement ran out onto the court. Never in my whole life have I ever been so relieved to see that many heads turn back around.

He just stood there looking at me. I must have felt like he did the day he woke me up and I just let him stand there on the porch. "Hey! I wasn't expecting to see you today." I could tell he was really surprised.

"Um, well, I wasn't expecting to be late, interrupt your game, and embarrass myself to death, so I think that's enough for one day and I'll just go now. I would really appreciate it if tomorrow you might remember this as a dream—or not at all."

There it was—that smile and that look in his eye—the one where he knew exactly what I was thinking and what I needed him to say. "Are you crazy?"

"I think I just might be," I answered, having no idea what he would say next.

"I needed a fishing partner today and now I have one." He leaned in and hugged me. "I'm thrilled! Now I have someone to cook the fish."

He turned around and trotted back out onto the court. He stopped the game again to the sound of two hundred kids booing. He whispered something to the other referee and the man nodded, looking over at me with a smile.

"Let's go," he grabbed my hand half pulling half escorting me out. "Day's a wastin'."

* * *

Once we were outside in the sunlight and the quiet, I was mortified. He had just left the game and put his responsibility onto someone else for me. "Andrew," I half grabbed his hand stopping him as he ushered me to the parking lot; I lowered my eyes truly ashamed. "I'm so sorry. I never meant for you to leave the game. I know how much the kids depend on you. I feel so selfish now. I just wanted to see you today and I didn't even think of your plans."

There, I'd admitted it. He knew I just had to see him and that I wanted to be with him. I braced myself for the rejection and his 'I'll see you next weekend and we should just be friends' speech. Instead, he put his arms around me, right in front of the whole world and whispered, "I wanted see you this morning before I even got out of bed." A million weights lifted off my heart and soul and I felt lighter than air, we had finally said it. He didn't wait for me to respond, he just grabbed my hand and led me away from the building towards the cars. "Besides, I've covered for the other guys a million times on way shorter notice."

We walked over to a red Chevy pickup truck. "This is my cabin truck and it's kind of beat up because I use it to go to my hideaway and I haul lumber in it all the time. Now you can see my woods. They're not quite as interesting as yours, but they're my quiet place." He drove across the parking lot to my car so I could get my bag and then we were off.

We drove for about forty-five minutes away from the city. The landscape turned from one of big buildings and suburbs to farmland, red barns, and fields of cows. "It's about another thirty minutes out," he said. "It isn't much, just a small cabin on a pond, but I come here most weekends to get away from the city—that is, until recently when I found something better to do with my Saturdays." He reached across the seat and took my hand. I couldn't hide my blush or my smile, another small step forward.

"I thought I'd die when all those kids started booing. I never thought I'd draw the attention of the whole place to myself. I guess I kind of blew my surprise and my quiet entrance. It never would have happened if I were even remotely any good at reading a map."

He laughed. "Well, if it makes you feel any better, the kids boo at me all the time when I make a call they don't like. I've even had a few things thrown at me before. Just kids, I guess, they don't mean anything by it."

* * *

We turned off the pavement and onto a dirt road that wound around and seemed to be going nowhere. If I hadn't already seen a glimpse of his gentle spirit and kind heart, and now his fondness for me I might have been a little nervous. He must have sensed that I was wondering where he was taking me or maybe he thought I was remembering Willie. Surely he knew by now that was well in the past and not even a factor in my feelings towards him. I hoped so. He reassured me after about ten minutes of driving through the woods that we were getting close. We rounded the last dusty bend and there it was, a quaint little log cabin nestled in the trees on the edge of a big, beautiful pond.

"You fish?" he asked me through the thin layer of dirt on the windshield as he strolled around to my side of the truck to open the door.

"Well, I don't bait the hook and I don't take the fish off the hook, but I'm an excellent pole holder."

"Good enough," he laughed that musical good natured sound that made my heart flutter before helping me down off the high bench seat and grabbing both my bag and a cooler from the back.

The inside of the cabin was beautiful. It was one bedroom with a small den, a kitchenette, and a big bathroom with a whirlpool tub. You could see every room from the center of the den. "Took me three years of Saturdays to build it. I love it here."

"You built this yourself?" Given Rubens DNA I shouldn't have been surprised at his vision and talent. I thought maybe he might be past some of the pain of their plight so I cautiously brought it up. "You must have inherited Ruben's and Isaiah's woodworking skills."

He stopped and thought a minute as he went into the bedroom to put my bag on the bed. "You know, I never knew where that came from. Funny how knowing your kin explains where you've been and want to go. I almost feel like a piece of me that's been missing for a long time has finally been found. Little things you wonder about yourself like 'Why do I love working with my hands?' or 'Why was I so driven to finish law school?'— they're all traits I see in Ruben and Ophelia, and even Annabeth." I smiled to myself, he was reaching a place where remembering didn't hurt, he returned my smile,

He knew I was gaining insight into his heart and his face said it all. He didn't mind a bit.

He insisted I put on some sunscreen. "I'm sure we can tan you up a bit, but I'd hate to burn that pretty skin of yours," he, handed me the bottle. I had no idea what to say, so I just complied. I felt like a princess as he helped me into the little boat and then waded into the water nearly up to his waist to push us off the bank. It occurred to me just before he hoped in that he likely didn't need the lotion to protect him from the sun as much as I did. I wondered why he even had any handy. I didn't know how to ask so when he was sitting across from me I took a gamble. "Don't you want any?"I half extened my arm with the lotion in my hand. He rolled his eyes and pulled his ball cap lower to shade his face. "As long as the rays don't blind me I am good." He smiled at his own sarcasm. "Then why do you have this here?" I ventured my voice shyer than I intended. "It was more of an impulse buy." He admitted sort of hiding his eyes in the shade of the brim of his hat. "I remembered the other day while I was at the grocery store that you had put some on before we started hunting in the back yard, I thought maybe just in case....." He didn't finish his answer, but I could guess the ending, "just in case I ever came here." It didn't escape my attention that he was thinking of me while doing something as random as picking up a few groceries. I blushed bright red as if I really had been burned and waited as he straightened the oars and began to pull us through the tiny ripples the ducks nearby were making.

He rowed us out to the center of the pond and dropped our lines in the water. We sat and drifted for hours without one bite, but it didn't matter, we were so lost in our own conversation that we hardly noticed the sun dipping below the horizon. We talked about everything from our favorite books and movies to our strangest cases. He was so easy to talk to and he was stealing my heart one beat at a time. But as easily as the conversation flowed, I was still unsure if his feelings for me were developing at the lightning speed mine seemed to be for him. Maybe I was just thinking this was too good to be true. I mean, things like this never happen to me. I knew he cared for me, but as far as being on the same page, I felt like I was on the last chapter while he was still reading the cover.

"We'd best be heading back into shore," he, looked up at the dim sky and started to row. Just as he began to move the boat, my pole tugged for the first time all day.

"Andrew, look!" I screeched, trying to move as far away from the flailing fish as possible. I was sure it was about to jump into the seat next to me. He was laughing so hard at my reaction he could hardly grab the pole. I nearly rocked the boat to the point of tipping it over.

"It's not the Loch Ness monster," he joked, still laughing at me and starting to reel in the line. Once he began to pull the fish on board, he realized that maybe he was wrong. "Look, Sweetie! Look what you caught!"

At that point, I could have cared less if I *had* caught the Loch Ness monster, he'd called me "Sweetie!" *He called me Sweetie!* I shouted it again and again to myself in my mind. Had he been concentrating on my face and not the fish, I'm sure he would have seen my reaction.

"Well, there's dinner—and I mean fit for a king." He held up what he later told me was the biggest catfish he'd ever seen. I'm not sure if he was just saying that, but what did I care about a slimy smelly fish, he'd called me Sweetie!

I took a swim in his large whirlpool tub while he cleaned and grilled the fish. We had fresh garden vegetables he had grown and canned himself and the best catfish supper I think I'd ever had.

"I'm not sure if this is so good because I caught it or you cooked it," I said, finishing my last bite.

"It has to be my cooking," he smiled, proud of himself. "I would say, technically, we both caught it. I mean it was your pole, but I actually brought him in."

"You trying to take credit for my fish, mister?" I was trying to sound annoyed, playfully threatening him with my fork.

"I'm just saying that as luck would have it, he happened to hit your line first, that's all, and I, being the man and great hunter, brought him on home."

I picked up the dishes and bumped his chair with my hip on my way by. "It was my pole, so it was my fish. Face it, I bring home the bacon and you fry it up in the pan." I laughed all the way to the sink. I was completely caught off guard when he came up behind me and put his arms around my waist as I started doing the dishes.

"Well, since I've already done my share of *woman's* work today, I guess you get to do all the cleaning."

"Whatever saves your pride," I teased, which caused him to start tickling me. It was unfair because he knew I was helpless with soapy hands trying to hold a slippery plate. Finally he let me finish my "womans work" and announced the mighty hunter was in need of a restful bath.

By the time he was out of the tub, I realized my dilemma. Earlier, I had packed my bags so fast that I'd forgotten my pajamas. I'd found the extra sheets and blankets and had made up the couch for myself. I was about to just lie down in my blue jean cut-offs and light pink summer sweater when he came out of the bathroom wearing his own sleeping attire. It was red and blue plaid boxers and a blue t-shirt. I was surprised. I'd never seen him so casual before. It made me feel good to think he was comfortable enough with me to be so relaxed.

"You're not sleeping in that are you?" Before I could answer, he went on. "And you're certainly not sleeping on the couch, missy. You just march yourself right into that bedroom this minute." I laughed at his attempt to sound serious.

"You're going to make an excellent father someday because for a second there, I almost felt some authority behind that tone."

"Authority? You want to see authority?" He leaned down, scooped me up off the couch, and carried me into the bedroom, dropping me on the mattress. "That about do it for you?" he asked, knowing I could never overpower him.

I sat up cross-legged in the middle of the bed and saluted. "Yes sir, that about does." I went back to his original question and told him that I had forgotten to pack my pajamas.

"No problem, I think I have something in here that will do." He reached in his chest of drawers and pulled out an extra large softball jersey. "It's from the company league I played with a few years ago, before I went out on my own." I took it gratefully and he excused himself to let me change. "I suppose I should let you get some sleep," he started slowly, backing out the door. "We have to get up early in the morning to go get your car."

I agreed, put the shirt on the bed, and walked over to where he stood. "Thank you for today. It was perfect."

He gently kissed me on the cheek. "You're welcome at my cabin any time." With that, he left and closed the door. I flopped backwards on the bed my head spinning and my heart racing. I didn't get any better when I realized the jersey smelled like his cologne.

* * *

About 1 a.m., I was awakened by a squeaking sound. Unsure what it was, I crept out into the den. The covers were turned down on the couch, but Andrew wasn't inside. I looked out the window above the sink and discovered where the noise was coming from. I felt a little self-conscious, but I followed the sound anyway. I gently slid open the glass door and stepped outside onto the porch in my socks and my jersey that said "McGrath" across the back. The large shirt fit me like one of Hannah's short skirts. He was sitting there rocking back and forth by the light of a citronella candle.

"I heard the rocker on the porch and came to see what it was. Sorry, I didn't mean to interrupt your thoughts."

He rose from his seat and came over to me. "How could you interrupt thoughts that were of you?" I started to answer him, but he put his finger over my lips. "Listen, they're playing our song." There was no radio and I was confused.

"They?" I whispered.

"Listen," was all he said as he took me in his arms and we started to slow dance across the porch.

After a few minutes, I realized what he meant. We were moving to the rhythmic sound of thousands of crickets. It was the most perfect song I'd ever heard. We stood there slowly swaying, not speaking for what seemed like a lifetime. He began running his fingers through my hair, memorizing it, just as Isaiah had done to Annabeth so many years ago.

I should have been exhausted the next morning, but I couldn't remember ever having slept so well, peaceful dreams of dancing, dancing in my head. No nightmares this night. Andrew knocked on my door at around six. "We had better

253

get a move on if we want to get your car and get you to work on time." I was dressed and ready in no time.

* * *

The ride that seemed to take forever to the cabin flew by on the way back to the city. He took my keys, opened my car door, and kissed me on the cheek. "Call you later, but I'll definitely see you next weekend."

"Promise?" I asked, putting on my seatbelt. I couldn't hide the lighthearted feeling behind what I know was my huge smile.

"Promise," he answered.

He stood in the parking lot and watched me drive away. I know, because I was watching him just as closely in my rearview mirror.

* * *

Janice was starry-eyed when I finished telling her about my weekend. "I don't care what color he is, girl, you better hang on to that man."

She was even more excited on Wednesday when she brought a special delivery package into my office. It had Andrew's return address on it. She helped me rip the paper off and cut the heavy tape with scissors. Inside was a little machine that played sounds of the outdoors – ocean waves, chirping birds, and about five others. He had it set it to crickets. The note simply read, "So you can hear our song any time." Both Janice and I were so weak in the knees we had to sit down.

Chapter 31
"Mixed Emotions"

Everyone was nice to us in church. Even though we'd missed the previous Sunday, people remembered Andrew's name and greeted us politely, but I could feel that we were getting more than a few stares and I knew Andrew felt it too. The whole visiting friend façade had worn off and people were catching on to feelings we had for each other that we hadn't really spoken aloud ourselves. I'm not sure if it was because these people who had known me for years weren't used to seeing me with a man, let alone a black man. Either way, I didn't care. Andrew made my heart at peace and unbroken, and I'd never had that happen before, not with anyone. I knew that if they loved me, then it was only a matter of time before they would also love him; however, I wasn't naïve enough to think everyone would feel that way.

We had lunch with Janice at the Dairy Queen after the service. It was kind of like sitting down with every member of your family and letting them embarrass you one by one, only Janice did it all by herself. She must have told Andrew every funny or embarrassing story about me she could think of. She ended by saying, "This is our special girl, so you better be good to her." She was acting like we were engaged or something. Andrew just took it all in stride.

Mr. Baxter, my mailman, also happened to be dining after church and, as usual, he became the instant busybody. He had known my family and me all my life, but today chose to act as if he knew nothing about me. He stopped at our table, resting his tray on the edge of it and interrupted our conversation. Initially, I was glad for the break, that feeling quickly faded when I noted the change in his stance and demeanor. Janice was talking about the first time I entered a courtroom and how I'd tripped and nearly fallen in front of everyone. I would have happily had her continue than face what I instinctively knew was coming.

"Well hello, Angie. Haven't seen you since the funeral. His tone was harsh and sarcastic even the look on his face was a far departure from the harmless gossip who delivered my mail and I knew whatever was about to come was not going to be pretty. The men at the table he had been sitting with were all staring, cruel smirks on their faces. He focused the unmistakable hate in his eyes on Andrew. "This must be one of the felons you're so good at getting off the hook," he said, laughing and looking down at him and then to me. He was obviously trying to guess what crime this undesirable black man had committed. I thought he knew me well enough to know I didn't usually work on Sunday, much less have lunch with Janice and a criminal. I was extremely angry, but Andrew just smiled and looked down at his plate. I had seconds to decide, *Am I Annabeth and Emmaline or am I a coward?* There was no question, I was no coward. It wasn't in my blood.

"No, Mr. Baxter, this is Andrew McGrath, my dear friend," I defiantly, took his hand. "He's also a lawyer. I had no idea you thought of me as the one around here who gets felons off the hook."

"Well," he went on, without an ounce of remorse for obviously hurting my feelings or embarrassment for doing it in front of a crowd, "people talk, you know, especially since you seemed to be so fond of that Willie character before well....you learned the hard way. I mean we all know the only reason he was loose was because you convinced Phillip he should be. Maybe you should be more careful who you have lunch with and people won't assume the worst. I mean, you do defend some unsavory characters and most of them are African like your...um *friend* here." I think you misunderstand, Mr. Baxter. Andrew is from Atlanta. He also speaks perfect English and totally understands that you're being an ass."

I started to get up and really let him have a piece of my mind when Andrew squeezed my hand and stopped me. "Mr. um...Baxter, is it?" he asked as calm as could be, not waiting on an answer. "Speaking on behalf of all my people, the *Africans,* as you say, I'd like to thank you for diligently paying your tax dollars so Miss Lawrence here can provide us with the best defense possible. Like she said, I was born and raised here, as I am sure you were, but we appreciate the support all the same. I mean, some folks around here might consider paying a fine lawyer like Angie to defend the less desirables in this town as a bit liberal. You know, there are still a few racists left among us. Glad to see you're not one of them."

I was speechless as I sat there holding his hand. Janice had to cover her face with her napkin to keep from laughing. The next thing I knew, Andrew had risen from his seat to shake my mailman's hand as if he meant every word he had just said. I'd never seen Mr. Baxter without words before, but today was my lucky day. He turned to go gritting his teeth and shaking his head as he went.

Janice lowered her napkin. "I have to say...if anybody can stand up to what folks think, you two can, you make a pretty good team." She high-fived us both.

When we got into the car, he looked at me and finally commented on the encounter. "I grew up in a small town too, remember? Don't worry, when you meet my family and friends, I'll get the same treatment. I'm sure someone I know will have something to say about your..." he looked me up and down searching for the right words, "...lack of pigment."

My brain heard every word that came from his lips, but all my heart heard was "*when* you meet my family and friends." I couldn't believe he'd already thought about what my meeting the people in his world would be like. With every little step in our relationship I was starting to trust my own judgment as to where it might be headed, I had been wrong so many times before.

I started to apologize, but he stopped me. "Don't you be sorry for one ignorant old goat. You just keep defending all those 'Africans' — that's the best way to show him." We laughed all the way home, but in my heart I couldn't believe someone I thought was my friend had treated me that way. I couldn't deny to myself that it hurt and I knew deep inside that despite his wit and charm, Andrew felt it too.

We searched the yard for a few more hours and when the sun started to go down, I knew Andrew would have to leave soon. We had both exhausted our vacation time and despite not wanting to go, he knew Monday would start with or without him. He went upstairs and packed his things while I made him a sandwich for the road.

"I'd hate for you to have to stop after dark," I, handed him the brown paper bag as he closed the trunk lid. He smiled and graciously accepted it.

He looked as nervous as a twelve-year old at his first school dance when he finally asked, "Can I keep coming back every Friday to look until we find them?"

"I just expected that you would," I wanted to skip the chit chat and move on to more important things, anxious to see what kind of goodbye gesture he had in mind.

He took a few small steps towards me knowing I couldn't back away because I was between him and the car. "'Til next Friday then," he said taking my hand and kissing my cheek. He set my heart all aflutter, although I was wondering when he might show all the emotions I was feeling. "I'll call you during the week," he promised as he drove away.

* * *

I'm sure that somewhere between here and Atlanta when he opened the brown bag and took out his sandwich, he'd be surprised at the note he'd find in the sack. I debated about writing it, but decided for once in my life to be brave and take a chance. It said, "See you next weekend. Call me. Here's another copy of my number." I couldn't believe I'd written everything we had discussed at the car before we'd even spoken our goodbyes. I knew he'd get it too. I was so glad I'd decided to take the risk of embarrassing myself and happy that I'd gone to the game and seen a small piece of his world. I knew that if my phone rang that night, then he was definitely as smitten as I was and about 11:30, it did. He wanted to thank me for the note and the sandwich. I'm sure he heard me listening to our song in the background. I felt relief. I didn't have to wonder anymore—my heart was singing louder than the crickets.

All Janice could talk about was how cute and smart he was and what a gentleman he seemed to be. Every morning at our breakfast talk, Andrew was the topic of the day. I told her everything about him, even most of what we talked about when he called me every night at 8:30.

"You know, Ang, those of us who love you don't care, but I've heard more talk around town about his being black and what your poor momma would do if she were here."

"I'll tell you what my poor momma would do," I almost spit the words, angry that I felt I had to defend our racial difference. "She would wish me well and all the happiness in the world. The reason I can have feelings for Andrew is because she raised me to believe that all God's children are equally important and loved in His eyes. If we're truly striving to be like Him, then we should feel the same." If you don't believe my momma, read the journal again and ask Annabeth.

Janice raised her juice glass and toasted with me on the sentiment. Nothing further was ever said about it between us, but I'm sure she was put in a position to stand up for me on more than one occasion around town. Mr. Baxter never spoke to me again and I learned to avoid going outside when I knew the mail was coming.

On Friday, I was trying to get home early and have dinner cooking, but no such luck. I didn't leave my office until 7:45. Andrew was sitting patiently in my driveway when I pulled up. I must have looked as exhausted as I felt because he immediately took my briefcase from my hands.

"Long day?" he asked, escorting me to the couch and taking off my shoes.

"The longest," I answered, telling him about the rape case I had been dragged into earlier that afternoon.

"You just go take one of those baths I know you love so much," he, insisted I do as he instructed as he shooed me up the stairs. I sat there in the bubbles for a few minutes before it dawned on me just how much he had been paying attention over the past week. I think I had only mentioned my grandpas word the "mulligrubs" and their cure to him once and that had been a few days ago. I felt at ease enough to go downstairs without makeup and in my pajamas. After all, he'd seen me in them the first morning he'd appeared on my doorstep. I rounded the corner of the kitchen just in time to see him setting the table.

"Nothing fancy," he said, almost apologizing for his efforts. "I decided on something simple, so it's just burgers and fries." I stood there and watched him cut up the extra meat patty he had made and feed it to Keno.

"I love burgers and fries," I took my seat feeling more at home in my own house now that he was standing in it.

* * *

The next several weeks went by just like that. Every weekend our emotions would fluctuate between joy at seeing one another, disappointment at not finding the graves, sadness at goodbye, and excitement over the anticipation of our next meeting. My kiss on the cheek turned into a peck on the lips about week number three and by week five, it took us nearly forever to say goodbye. It quickly became tradition that I would pack him a snack for the road, but he confessed to me that the first thing he reached for was the note. He looked forward to the note about as much as I did the feel of his hands in my hair and his soft lips on mine. I had to stand there a minute in his arms to get my legs back under me to make it back up the driveway and into the house.

Every week the people in church began to treat him more and more like a member and eventually just expected to see him. I could not have been happier that the people I thought loved me were proving me right. Eventually the separations seemed too long no matter how brief and Andrew would even come down on the weekends he volunteered at the youth center. He joked and said it saved me the embarrassment of stopping the game. It was hard getting to spend only one day with him, but I knew the kids were important to him and respected him even more for never disappointing them.

As I expected, just as some of my friends were happy for me, others began to shun me. The gossip and rumor mill were turning at lightning speed with my name fueling their engines. I'm sure most of the idle chatter came from people who lived on Mr. Baxter's route. I was positive he was as curious to see their reactions as he had been mine the morning Miss Claudia died. Janice kept encouraging me to follow my heart and I frequently thought about Annabeth and Isaiah. If they could make it during the worst time in history to be involved in a mixed relationship, then surely I could withstand a few whispers and the gossip of a few bored people. Andrew asked me about it, knowing I must have been getting some grief. I simply told him it was nothing I couldn't handle and certainly not worth losing the best guy I'd ever met over.

He knew me too well. "If that sarcasm and sense of humor start to fail you, you let me know first," he said. "I don't intend for my girlfriend to fight our battle alone." I knew the moment he used the word "girlfriend" that we were definitely in a solid relationship and I was happier than I could ever remember being.

Andrew had been using the map and the location of the whipping post as a guide. We had searched every inch of the right side of the forest behind the shed all the way to the property line. We decided to start at the back and work our way forward when we searched the second half. I loved the time we spent together searching and I was excited about finding the graves and the treasure, but didn't want our conversations and laughter to ever end. All we did was talk and talk about our lives, our jobs, and our families. I believe we knew just about everything there was to know about one another by the end of the tenth weekend we had spent together. I even told him about my dad and Sissy, and all the feelings of resentment and loss, how I had struggled after Willie and during my reading of the journal. I was embarrassed to admit everything to him, especially how the bitterness of being single related to my dad and started to color my feelings at work, but his compassion was boundless. It was a twisted mess of emotion to explain, but he was so patient. He got it, just like Grandpa. He saw me for me and I loved that he knew and accepted me, even after he really knew me.

I could hardly believe we had been searching for just over two months when the sound I thought we would never hear again finally snatched us from our conversation and brought both of our eyes to the ground in front of us. Without even realizing it, we had made our way nearly back to the house when the beeping started again. I looked down at the machine and then up to get my bearings. When I did so, I saw that we were standing about thirty yards from the house, directly in the line of sight of the tall window that Ophelia, Miss Claudia, and her father had all spent hours gazing out. They had been right in front of us for so long and nobody knew it.

In that moment, we knew we'd found them. In his excitement, Andrew carelessly dropped the metal detector and began to dig. I estimated by the location of the box where the bricks marking the graves might be and dropped to my knees. Sharing in his excitement, I began to dig. I had no gloves to protect my hands, but without regard for my manicure, I feverishly moved the earth with my bare hands.

Within twenty minutes, I had uncovered all eight markers. They were buried about six inches under the surface. It took Andrew a little longer to reach the box. In his elation and unbridled excitement, he ran to the shed to get a shovel. We had to contain ourselves and use the detector to pinpoint the exact spot to dig. In our frenzy to unearth the box, we had to remember to use caution as we didn't want to inadvertently disturb the graves. He dug carefully only where the metal detector had sounded its alarm.

I had a chance to think about it while I watched him dig and prayed with all my heart that the time we had spent together had ignited enough of a fire to keep our relationship going. I didn't want the end of our quest and common bond to be the end or our bonding altogether. I had no idea at the time, but there was more than a spark burning in his heart, it was more like an inferno.

As soon as Andrew handed me the box, I left him with a bewildered look on his face as I ran to the house with its precious contents. I immediately picked up the phone and called Grandpa. I described in great detail the stamps left behind on the letters that Ophelia had sent between Annabeth and Isaiah. He was breathless with excitement at the possibility that his poor luck had finally changed. The crate he had purchased so many weeks ago and generously given to me because he knew how much I would love the journal, might actually have led him to the biggest find in his stamp collecting career. Having no real idea of their value, I promised to send the letters to him right away. In a whirlwind of excitement for both his joy and my own, I blurted out my news.

Chapter 32
"Dear Annabeth"

I have decided to fill the last three pages of this journal myself. It is, after all, someday going to be yours. I think its original author, the brave woman for whom you were named, would give her blessing. The day your father and I found her grave, he was filthy and on his knees from digging up the box about which you will undoubtedly hear many stories. He opened the burlap sack Ophelia had placed it in years ago and took out the tin enclosure.

The first thing he did was gently move its precious contents around until he found it. He was looking for the silver ring Emmaline had given Ophelia. He remained on his knees and slipped it on my finger as he asked the question, the answer to which both he and I knew would be 'yes.' We were married four days later.

He has taken the wooden animals Isaiah carved for his beloved Annabeth, painted them with bright colors and hung them over your crib. As soon as we learned you were on the way, he started making the beautiful mobile. The ring Isaiah carved remains in its original condition and hangs in the center of the collection of animals. As soon as I laid you under it for the first time, it seemed to capture your attention. The silver rattle that bears your initials is waiting for your tiny hands to be big enough to shake it. For now, it sits on a shelf with two black and white photographs of two people who also grew up in this house. I have no doubt they both would have loved you very much.

It is difficult for me to believe that you are here and already three days old. Unlike Annabeth, I never struggled with what color I wanted your skin to be. I decided the moment I discovered you were inside me that I wanted you to be a perfect blend of both your father and me. My prayers have been answered. You are the most beautiful little girl I have ever seen.

Your father has taken over my job because I have found the one I was born to do—that is be your mother. My once big empty house is now full of everything I ever wanted most in this life. Your great-grandfather Lawrence also got his wish when we opened the box. I sent him the letters Annabeth and Isaiah had sent to one another. He called me immediately after he received the package and revealed to me its great value. He found what he had been looking for the day he bought the old crate from Hannah. It seems as though when his luck changed, it did so in a very profitable way. There was a pigeon blood red three cent Washington stamp with a running chicken cancellation on the very first letter he examined. I know that is a mouthful to say, but it made your great-grandfather very happy. They were printed and cancelled in that fashion for a short period of time and in a limited location. Had it not been for his love of history and his hobby, your father and I would have likely never met. The stamp was in near-perfect condition as it had been buried and protected in the box for so many years. He says it's a miracle that even back then Isaiah would have come into possession of such a rare stamp.

I have only seen Grandpa smile like that one other time and that was yesterday as he stood looking down into your crib. He told me he couldn't wait to tell you all about the stamp God used to mail you to our lives. It's a rather interesting way to look at it, but it is true, his seeking it did bring us all together. He is writing his own account of that stamp and his many others so that you will always have a piece of his spirit and passion within you. Now that he lives with us, he spends many hours, just as Miss Claudia, her father, and Ophelia did, looking out that tall glass window.

I hope for you, just as Annabeth did for her own child, that you will come to love and appreciate your heritage and hang on to it as you grow older. Your father has done as she requested and kept the McGrath name moving towards freedom and acceptance. You, my lovely Annabeth, are the face of the New South and the face of a new nation. It is up to you to carry on the tradition set before you long ago by those who risked their lives to preserve the blood that runs through your tiny veins. Your father and I are determined to help you do so.

Although we both lost our own parents young and doubted we would have much of a family tree or history to pass on to our own children, God has blessed us otherwise. He has not only provided us with roots, but also ensured they were written down in these pages in black and white. He has gone to great trouble to make you exactly who you are. His wisdom never ceases to amaze me.

Never let the color of your skin determine the scope of your possibilities. You will never be too light or too dark; you will always be beautiful, strong, and loved. God says in His word, "Love suffers long and is kind; love does not envy; love does not parade itself, is not puffed up; Does not behave rudely, does not seek its own, is not provoked, thinks no evil; Does not rejoice in iniquity, but rejoices in the truth; Bears all things, believes all things, hopes all things, endures all things." That is what we put on the tombstone where we inscribed both Annabeth's and Isaiah's names and it is what I want you to remember all your life. God has given us His characteristics of love and none of them includes its color. I love you, my sweet little Annabeth.

Love, Your Momma
Angie Lawrence McGrath

22929059R00168